Acts of

Assumption

D0817219

Twisted Road Publications LLC

Cover Photo by Getty Images

www.twistedroadpublications.com

For Mama Belen—who taught me about the BVM

And for Aunt Lucy—who believed

Acts of Assumption

A Novel

S. W. Leicher

CONTENTS

Definition of Assumption:

1. *The act of believing something or taking it for granted without actual proof.*

2. *The act of taking up a new position, possession, or burden.*

3. *The act of rising straight up into heaven.*

Merriam-Webster's Dictionary

PROLOGUE: AN UNUSUAL SHIVA

"Magnified and sanctified and blessed and praised and glorified and raised and exalted and honored and uplifted and lauded be the Name of the Holy One."

Mourner's Kaddish

The first day of the Gottesman shiva was unfolding exactly as planned. And how could it be any different, given who was in charge? When Serach's mother, Gittel Gottesman, takes control, things go just the way she wants.

The little Spanish cleaning girl that Bertha Weinstein had recommended had arrived before eight o'clock that morning, as promised, and had scrupulously complied with every one of Gittel's complicated instructions. The beige carpets in the halls and living room had been vacuumed not once but twice. Every surface had been polished to a high gloss. The bathrooms gleamed and the kitchen was spotless—the counters cleared of all their usual messes. The house had never looked so good.

The Russian maintenance worker from the synagogue had come over precisely at ten o'clock to chip the last ice off the sidewalk and steps so that no one should slip. And he had brought over the two hot water urns and forty folding chairs that the synagogue generously lent out to houses of mourning—lugging them out of his van armful by armful and carrying them carefully into the house. It had taken him eight trips up and down those steps to do it.

Gittel's two brothers-in-law, Uncle Yonatan and Uncle Shlomo, had caught the morning shuttle from Cleveland with their wives to arrive comfortably before eleven. Gittel's two older sisters had driven in from Long Island—husbands in tow—pulling into the driveway just minutes after the uncles' taxi had pulled out. They scrambled into the house and immediately began making sure that everything was in place.

And the rabbi had come two full hours early to offer some special words of comfort and to personally take responsibility for covering all the mirrors with cloth so no one would be tempted to indulge in vanity at such a sad time.

By three thirty, Serach's mother and her four younger sisters had arranged their mourners' boxes in a neat line on the floor of the hallway so as to be appropriately seated when everyone else began arriving. And, in fact, no sooner than they had settled in on them than a stream of men began pushing through the unlocked front door with their prayer books while a similarly robust group of women began swinging open the back door to the kitchen, bearing their platters of food.

"The best thing about a shiva," Gittel had remarked as she lowered her bulk carefully down onto her box, "is that there are no surprises. Everyone knows exactly what to do. And everyone does it."

"The best thing about our *whole religion*," the rabbi had responded with his kindly smile, "is that everyone knows exactly what to do. And everyone does it. I don't know how the rest of the world manages."

Only Serach's baby brother, Shmuely—lone male of the immediate family—was behaving out of character. He had spent the afternoon peering anxiously through a crack between the curtains of the living room window. And as soon as he spotted the first community members converging on the front steps, he had grabbed his mourner's box and scuttled up into his room.

Shmuely was ten years old—old enough to have sat with the men during prayer services. And he generally took great pride in doing so. But today he was so terrified he would burst out crying in the middle of everything, he was willing to forego the privilege. And fortunately, everyone was so focused on *davening* that his absence was not noted till much later.

The service began precisely at four thirty-three, the moment when afternoon services begin across all of Boro Park at that time of year. The men *davened* in the living room, their voices ebbing and flowing as they stood and sat, bowed and paced, and came to stillness again. And in the meantime, their wives and sisters and daughters laid out the food, prepared the coffee, and heated the water for tea.

And no one—not a soul—as much as whispered Serach's name during the service or at either end of it. And since that crowd could so easily have been buzzing with talk of the scandal, the total and seemingly unspoken agreement to remain silent represented a true sign of collective respect.

And Serach herself? What was Serach doing while the community marked her precipitous demise with such impressive tact?

She was sitting quietly at the kitchen table of her new home, barely more than a mile from all the commotion.

Absent-mindedly letting her own cup of tea grow cold.

Patiently waiting for Paloma to return home from work and gather her into her arms.

PART ONE: SERACH'S TALE

"She is a tree of life to those who hold fast to her."

Proverbs, Chapter 3, Verse 18

1

The concept of the real number line has always intrigued me. The idea that the infinite set of rational numbers and the infinite set of irrational numbers can somehow fit neatly together on the same line without either set having anything to do with the other and without either set elbowing the other one out of the way.

My two universes—Boro Park and Prospect Park South— coexist in similarly complicated fashion. There is no conjunction between their vastly divergent realities. They are governed by completely different rules. They are impossible to consider simultaneously. And yet they remain tight neighbors—a mere twenty-six blocks away from one another on the map. And obstinately side by side within my heart.

Some people call the approach that I take to life "compartmentalizing." I call it torment. Not that I'm always consumed with it. Generally, I can make it all work. And, in fact, in the early hours of that fateful Sunday morning, I was feeling particularly well-adjusted. Comfortably ensconced at the desk of my snug little study. Happily contemplating how best to preface my client's thoroughly-parsed tax returns. Prospect Park South was holding steady. Boro Park was holding its peace.

And then everything shifted.

"Serach!" Paloma called, bumping the half-ajar door open with one softly curved hip and stepping into my space. "Turn off your computer!"

"Paloma. I'm working."

"Serach, trust me. You're going to be very glad that I interrupted you. Rise out of your chair and come with me!"

Reluctantly, I logged off, stood up, and trailed her down the two flights of stairs to the living room.

And there with his hat and coat still on, pressed flat against the wall like a post-it and peering apprehensively into the room, stood my baby brother Shmuely.

Throughout Shmuely's childhood, Mama—ever practical, ever aware that her son's clothes would never be passed down from sibling to sibling like our pleated plaid school skirts— avoided buying anything the right size for him. Shoes, okay, they always fit. But everything else remained far too large for him for at least a year and sometimes two. Poor Shmuely was obliged to wear each outfit as it passed from huge to well-proportioned to stretched-out and threadbare, singlehandedly impersonating the string of brothers who would never follow him.

And clearly things hadn't changed very much in the time I'd been away. Even with my two married sisters and me out of the house and Mama's business thriving (for news like that still reached me) maternal frugality prevailed. So there he stood, taller than I had ever seen him but still drowning in his enormous coat and with his hat falling down on his brow. Nothing interrupted the familiar head-to-toe swath of black cloth save the thin vertical triangle of his white shirt and his beautiful porcelain face.

"Shmuely, Shmuely you've come to see me at last! Shmuely my angel! Come here, let me look at you! Let me hug you!" I moved toward him, arms outstretched.

But he flinched away from me, shaking his head. "Don't touch me, Serach."

He looked so severe—so pinched and white—that I stepped back. I waited. "Okay, Shmuely. Never mind. I won't take offense. I know it's been awhile. I know I look different. I suppose I've become quite the *apikoris* in your eyes. But I promise you: I'm no different than I ever was. Not inside. Not where it counts. So, come on into the room. Sit down. Take off your hat. Show me those pretty curls of yours. And let me get you something to drink. Some water? Some juice?"

More shakes, and I felt Paloma gently touch my elbow. I had completely forgotten she was there. "Shush, Serach," she whispered, gliding behind me to exit the room. "Just let him alone for a moment."

So there we stood for a good long time, Shmuely and I. He still wouldn't as much as look at me full face. Those glinting, shielded eyes—those turquoise eyes—fixed themselves on our rug, on all those green and gold roses twirling around in garlands on their wine-red background. His gaze traveled across the parquet floor and up the walls on which our paintings hung—oh dear, the paintings!—before finally landing on the piano.

Only then did his expression change from stolid blankness. Recognition, resistance, and then that marvelous little half-smile of his. He looked straight at me at last, and our eyes locked into the complicity that we had shared for so long.

"So that's where Zayde Izzie's *tallis* went! We went crazy looking for it! You stole it!"

"Yes, I did! Stuffed our grandfather's prayer shawl in my bag like Ruchel with her father Laban's idols. Took a little bit of him away with me when I fled."

"And you draped it on that piano!"

"All grand pianos need a fringed shawl, Shmuely. Surely you know that. And Zayde's prayer shawl is one beautifully-fringed specimen, you must admit. Nothing but the best—very Paris circa 1928, don't you think? Or don't they teach you that sort of thing in that *yeshiva* of yours?"

"Ruchel paid dearly for taking those idols, Serach! And a *tallis* on the piano! It's blasphemy." But traces of the smile persisted.

"Oh Shmuely, it's not blasphemy. It's just a little repurposing. I bet if Ruchel had openly set up those idols on her patio like garden gnomes instead of trying to hide what she'd done, nothing bad would have happened to her."

"I'm not listening to you!"

But it was too late. He was caught up in my mischief as he always was. I was the only one he couldn't resist. He pulled off his hat, his sweet head bare but for the *yarmulke* beneath it. And then he walked toward one of our needlepoint-covered chairs and dropped into it.

I waited some more. I came no closer. I watched quietly while he stroked the rim of his big round hat as it sat in his lap. I choked back my impulse to rush to him, grab him, yank him out of the chair, and smother him in my embrace.

"Frayda told me where you were," he said. As if I didn't already know.

2

Early death runs in my family. My Tatteh's mother, my grandmother, died of cancer when Tatteh was just a little boy. And his father had his first heart attack when Tatteh was barely twenty. Mama's father, Zayde Izzie, lost his first wife ten years into their marriage and his second wife, Mama's mother, when Mama was a teenager.

Thus it was not entirely unexpected when Tatteh got the call about his father on that hot afternoon, the summer that I turned ten. Nor was it so unusual for Mama to respond by announcing that Tatteh would have to make the trip to Cleveland alone. That it was too hard to pack us all up. That she couldn't abandon her business. That she wasn't feeling so strong.

Mama does not deal well with bad news.

Fortunately for us, she had never been close to Tatteh's father. We had only gone to Cleveland to see him once, when I was very young. And he had never come here. So her reaction was not as severe as it might have been. She kept up appearances in the outside world for the full week that Tatteh sat shiva with his brothers. She dropped Chava and Shayna off at day care while the rest of us traveled to day camp on the yellow school bus. She navigated her usual seven-block walk to work. And I suspect that once she was in her shop she was fine. Selling wigs seems to revive her.

The evenings, however, were a different matter. By the time the school bus dropped us back home at six o'clock, her mood would have darkened. Her expression as she opened the door to us would be both belligerent and spent. There would be no food cooking, and the table would not be set. She would hand Chava and Shayna over to me before I'd even put down my backpack and lumber into the living room to sink into a chair with the lights out.

I quickly developed a workable routine. I would place Chava in her high chair with a bunch of cookies. I would arrange Beile, Mierle, and Shayna with their dolls on the floor in one corner of the kitchen, where I could keep an eye on them. And then I would get supper ready for everyone. "Spring Valley Frozen Beef Kreplach in Broth" is my specialty.

I couldn't tell you whether or when Mama ate that week for she never joined us. Yet she somehow always seemed to know when we were finished and would come in to gather Chava out of her high chair. And then she would trudge upstairs with all my sisters in tow—a large lump surrounded by her smaller lumps. Bedtime was not always easy in our house. But when Mama was having one of her episodes, everyone tended to fall into line. And so as soon as I saw that slow procession moving upward, I would permit myself to linger in the peace of the kitchen for a little while, cleaning up.

Which is why when Tatteh pushed himself and his bags through the back door and into the kitchen, he found me standing by the sink with a pot in one hand and a sponge in the other, wondering what to do next. He spun me around, took everything out of my hands and kissed the top of my head. He looked smaller than I remembered.

"Serach," he said. "Mameleh. What's happening? Where is everyone? Where's your mother? Why are you in here doing the dishes all alone?"

"Everyone's upstairs. But don't worry, Tatteh. It's okay."

"Things bad with her again?"

"They're okay."

"Well don't *you* worry, Mameleh. I'm home now and I'm definitely fine. A little sad, of course. Who wouldn't be? But guess what? I've been thinking about something. Something that would really help me. And I bet you'll like it, too. How would you like to come to *shul* with me when I say *Kaddish* for my father?"

"This *Shabbos*?"

"Every morning. Seven days a week. All summer. We can be a little creative since you aren't in school. I can take you to camp myself when we're done with services. It won't matter if you are a little late from time to time. What do you say?"

But by then Mama had heard the cab pull into the driveway and the door click open and shut (she hears everything, even when she is in one of her moods) and had rushed down the stairs. She loomed in the doorway in her big flowered housecoat with Chava in her arms and the three other girls scurrying out from behind her in their pajamas to grab Tatteh by the legs and waist.

"Asher! Asher! You couldn't phone when you landed? You just sneak into the house like a mouse? And what is this about taking Serach to services? She's too old to be sitting downstairs with the men. Someone will say something. And what do you mean you'll take her to camp? She goes with Beile and Mierle every morning on the bus. We've already paid for it."

Tatteh walked toward Mama, took Chava out of her arms, and bent down to kiss each sister in turn. "Hello, Gittel. Hello, girls. It's good to see you. Don't worry, Gittel. No one will say anything about Serach if she's with me. And I'll call the bus company in the morning to explain that she will only be traveling with them in the afternoon. Maybe they'll even give us a refund for her morning pick-up. And if not, it's not the end of the world."

But Mama had already turned her back on us and had begun straightening out something on the counter.

The next morning when I sped downstairs to set things up for breakfast, I found Mama already in the kitchen pouring out everyone's cereal. I bolted down a glass of orange juice, grabbed my own handful of Cheerios out of the box, and merrily waved goodbye to everyone. And then I took Tatteh's hand and walked the five blocks to *shul* with him.

"Is Mama right, Tatteh? Am I too old to sit downstairs with you?"

"Don't worry. I'll handle things with your mother. And meanwhile, here's something nice to think about. Remember what I told you about the first Serach? About how she was the only one of Yakov's granddaughters to be mentioned by name in the Torah? Well now, my modern-day Serach, you will be the only granddaughter of my father of blessed memory to be honoring him in this very special way."

He had missed my main point. "Tatteh, listen to me. Are other people going to think I'm too old to be sitting with the men? Will anyone say something mean to me?"

"No, no, no. No one will even notice you. You're still just a little string bean. Stay close to me. Don't call attention to yourself. No one will say anything, and you'll see just how much you'll learn."

In *shul* we sat between Mr. Birnbaum who dozed and Mr. Lesser, the jeweler, who chatted on and off with the man on his left. Directly in front of us were five boys whom I recognized from the *yeshiva* down the street. I would sometimes see them walking home together in the dusk, bumping and poking each other. But here in *shul* they acted differently. They *davened* with total concentration, bobbing back and forth in vigorous syncopation.

Tatteh also moved while he prayed, but his moves were less frantic. More graceful. And he stopped from time to time to bend down and explain things to me. Sometimes he was called up to say the blessings over the Torah scroll. And a couple of times he was called to read one of the portions. He did it very well, his cadence neither too fast nor too slow. And afterward he talked to me about what he had read and explained how the pattern of his chanting helped to clarify the story.

"Study Torah and you will never be lost in life, Mameleh. There is a tale for every occasion, every situation. And how wise you'll sound when you quote just the right thing at just the right time!"

Best of all were the points in each service when the mourners read the *Kaddish*. Tatteh would stand right up. He would speak the words softly and distinctly. He would remain very still until that part near the end when you're supposed to bow first to the left and then to the right and then straight ahead. And when he was finished he would sit right down again and squeeze my hand.

And as for me, I would chime in with all the "*brikh-hus*" and "amens" that mark the end of certain phrases. Right along with everyone else.

"Don't say it too loud," Tatteh had warned. "Girls are only supposed to listen." But he never actually asked me to stop. I think it helped cheer him up when I did it.

One of the *yeshiva* boys seemed to be in mourning, too. He stood whenever Tatteh did. I wondered who had died. One day when I must have said one of my "amens" a little too enthusiastically he turned around part way and gazed at me briefly. His expression wasn't exactly disapproving, either. I stared back.

And then, on the way to camp, Tatteh and I would talk about what we'd seen and heard. Sometimes what I said would make him smile. The little vertical lines on the sides of his mouth would grow so deep that I could see them through his beard. But sometimes it would produce this kind of dark-green tint in his eyes, and I would have to stop talking and pat his hand a bit till the bright clear blue came back. It became a game, testing when I would hit that wall that only Tatteh was allowed to perceive.

"Why does Mr. Birnbaum always fall asleep in *shul*, Tatteh?"

"It's because Mrs. Birnbaum keeps him up all night. Oy, oy, oy, how she complains! She complains about how little money he makes, she complains about her daughter-in-law, she complains about how the butcher always slices the salami too thick no matter what she tells him. How can he possibly sleep? *Baruch HaShem*, he can come to *shul* and catch up on his rest a little before he has to go to work."

"And Mr. Lesser…why does he talk to his friends instead of to *HaShem*?"

"It's because he feels at home, Mameleh. Like he's at a family gathering. Sometimes he talks to *HaShem* and sometimes he talks to someone else. If you come to *shul* every day with me, soon you'll feel right at home too."

"And when I have to go to the women's balcony…."

"When you have to go to the women's balcony?"

"Will I still feel at home?"

"Well, for women other things become more important than feeling at home in *shul*. We men are commanded to pray three times a day. But you don't have to do that because you take care of our families. You watch over our community. You make sure our little ones grow up to be good Jews."

Mama and her four lumps.

"But I *like* going to *shul* every day with you. I'd like to learn to read Torah like you."

And I don't want lumps.

"Hush, Serach. Girls can't read Torah. You know that. Look, you can come with me now because you are still just a little bean. But believe me, once you are older, all that won't matter so much to you anymore. You'll want other things."

"No, I won't."

"Enough, Serach. Some things just are what they are."

And, in fact, when summer ended and Rosh Hashanah rolled around, neither Tatteh nor I had the strength to oppose Mama's convictions. I was bustled up the backstairs to a seat in the middle of the women's balcony and assigned the task of keeping my sisters occupied. I sat there docilely for at least an hour, reading them the books that Mama had brought. But when the Torah service began and a large new wave of women and children climbed into the seats around us, I seized the opportunity that their distraction provided and scuttled away.

I didn't go downstairs, of course. But I snuck down to a place in the bottom row of the women's balcony right by the curtain where I could pull the velvet folds apart a few inches and finally see what was happening on the floor below.

It was an excellent strategy in many respects. As any seasoned theater-goer will tell you, front row center balcony seats offer the best sightlines in the house. I could take in the full choreography of all those undulating black hats. And I could also zero in on the activities of any individual whom I cared to observe. There was Mr. Birnbaum dozing and startling and dozing again. There was Mr. Lesser leaning toward his neighbor to talk business. There were my five *yeshiva bochers* in their endless back-and-forth dance. There was Tatteh.

The acoustics, however, were another story. It had been hard enough to follow the prayers when I had been sitting right in the midst of things next to Tatteh, who spoke so clearly and pointed in his prayer book whenever I lost my place. Ten feet up and with all the women and children babbling behind me I heard nothing but a throbbing drone of voices. There was no way I could make out anything but the most familiar prayers.

Unsurprisingly, I got bored after a while and went back to mid-balcony to sit with Mama and my sisters. And after the High Holy Days were over, I didn't return to *shul* for quite some time.

3

Not two years after my grandfather's death—just past my twelfth birthday in the third month of Mama's last pregnancy— Tatteh suffered his own heart attack and died. It was all unimaginably swift and cruel. He never even made it to the sonogram stage of his first and only son's gestation. Never even got to glimpse the precious shadowy proof that he had finally sired a boy.

And this time my mother plunged into a place so dark and frightening that it left no room for anyone else's sadness. I was seized with panic. How on earth was I going to manage with no Tatteh to come to my rescue?

I had not, however, reckoned with the formidable internal machinery of our community. For no sooner than I had realized how scared I was, an entire crew of first responders materialized on our doorstep.

The first to arrive were Tatteh's older brothers, Yonatan and Shlomo, along with their wives and all their unmarried children. They flew in from Cleveland as soon as they heard about Tatteh, jamming themselves and their belongings into every corner of our house where they provided all the diverting chaos I could possibly want.

They were followed by three of Mama's six sisters. They drove in from Long Island every morning and promptly began battling my other aunts for the right to take care of my sisters, the laundry, and the food shopping.

And, of course, every morning and every late afternoon, at least twenty men from our *shul* took over the living room to conduct the services at which my uncles said *Kaddish* for their brother. And finally, along with the men came a bevy of neighborhood women all elbowing their way into the kitchen to slice bagels and lay out platters of cream cheese and smoked fish.

In the end, the hardest thing was simply staying out from underfoot.

I would walk into the living room where the men were hunching over their prayer books, and someone would seize me firmly by the elbow and usher me out. I would wander into the kitchen to help put out the food, and someone would tell me to go into some other room and sit on a box. "Mourners aren't supposed to do anything except mourn, Mameleh."

I would enter my mother's darkened bedroom where she sat surrounded by sisters, sisters-in-law, and children, and, having no words to say to any of them, I would walk out again.

I would open the front door to take in a breath of fresh air, and a crowd of new arrivals would push me back in, saying: "And where do you think you are going, young lady?"

It took until the third morning for me to finally think of a place in which I would be in no one's way. A place in which I could do something to ease the huge tightness inside me.

I dawdled in the foyer till I saw the men gathering in their usual positions. Then I swiped a prayer book from the front hall table, ducked into the half-bathroom near the living room, and pulled the door nearly shut. And in that safe little spot—seeing but not seen, hearing but not heard—I was able to follow along with the service. I could respond in all the right spots to the morning blessings. I could speak the *Sh'ma* out loud. And when my uncles recited the *Kaddish*, I could join in. And not just with the amens and *brikh-hus*. I could say all the words of that ancient text like the mourner that I was.

Like my Tatteh had done for his father.

When shiva was over, the Cleveland contingent departed. The *davening* men evaporated. Mama was still in a daze. And a new wave of panic settled into my heart.

Once again, however, my worries turned out to be premature. For on the very next morning two neighborhood women knocked on the door. And every day thereafter, summoned through that mysterious central management system of ours, a shifting crew would arrive to help get us through the day. Someone would appear at seven o'clock to make sure that we all had breakfast and that Chava got off to day care. Someone else would cover the evening pick-up and would greet Shayna, Mierle, and Beile when the school bus dropped them off from their *yeshiva*. One person would see to it that our kitchen was stocked with basic provisions while another would bring over brisket and carrots and potato kugel for dinner. And someone would slip Mama the occasional check to make sure her bills were paid while her business remained on hold.

Best of all as far as I was concerned, two or three women would sit with Mama every day to fill her in on neighborhood events. They would envelop her in their chattering, boldly treading right up to the border of that forbidden sin—gossip—in their fierce determination to spark some sign of interest in their once-indomitable friend.

For a long time, their efforts made no visible difference. Mama sat wrapped in her tight cocoon nodding blandly and looking away again, only occasionally joining in with some non-committal comment.

But they never gave up. Not for a single day. They held us together. Women's obligations.

And then one afternoon I came home from school to find a huge commotion going on in the dining room. My mother was standing on one side of the table and Frayda Goldblatt—a childless older widow known for keeping tabs on everyone—was standing on the other side, looking back at Mama with a mixture of defiance and fear.

"That is *lashon hara!*" yelled my mother. "That's an evil rumor! Take it back!"

"All I said, Gittel, was wasn't it odd how your niece had those three miscarriages and now when she finally gives birth she's going to that group for women who don't like their children?"

"Shush, Frayda," said Bertha Weinstein. "It's not for women who don't like their children. It's for women who have—what is it called? Post-partum depression? It's got a name."

"I don't care what it's called!" barked my mother. "It's none of her business! She should leave my niece out of it! She's just fine."

But in the midst of the shouting, all I felt was a tidal wave of relief. My mother was back!

After that, things smoothed out quickly. Mama got through Shmuely's birth with little fanfare. After you've already done it five times it's no big deal. Or so she explained it. And then next thing we knew she was sitting up in her hospital bed, Shmuely tucked casually in the crook of one arm and phone lodged between her shoulder and ear, arranging plane tickets and hotel reservations for the relatives who would be flying in from elsewhere for the *bris*. Planning the extravagant feast, the *seudis mitzvah*, with which the whole community would celebrate the miracle of Shmuely's circumcision.

4

For any observant Jew, every circumcision—every *bris*—is cause for rejoicing. It reenacts and re-confirms the covenant that *HaShem* made with our forefather, Abraham. It proclaims that we Jews are still alive, well, and flourishing despite all the world's efforts to wipe us out.

But for our particular family and community, Shmuely's *bris* went far beyond all that. It was proof positive that life and hope can triumph over death, despair, and five unsuccessful attempts to produce a boy.

On the way to *shul*, I found myself bursting with excitement. I was thrilled to be part of something happy again. And I'd begun to miss the buzz of worship, even if all that was now available was a long-distance view of all those bowing black-hatted figures.

I bounded up the stairs to the women's balcony, quickly peeling away from my mother and sisters. There would surely be enough aunts around to relieve me of my childcare duties for a while. I ran down to claim that promising central front row seat. I parted the curtains the necessary amount and leaned in to watch the action below.

But this time I wasn't alone. Loping down the aisle right behind me was Frayda Goldblatt, the woman who had shaken my mother out of her catatonia. She didn't take a seat near me. She slid off to the left into the shadows by the wall. Nor did she use my particular approach to managing the curtains. She drew herself up to her full exceptionally tall height and simply gazed over the top. But clearly she had the same intentions that I did. She was not about to miss a trick. How curious.

There are three main players at any *bris*. The baby boy, of course. The *mohel* who carries out the procedure. And the *sandek*—the man who holds the baby while the whole thing takes place.

There had been a brief to-do about who should serve as *sandek*. Traditionally, the honor is given to the boy's grandfather, so Mama's father was the obvious choice. Not only was he Shmuely's only living grandfather, he had once been a great scholar and was widely respected in the community. On the other hand, he was neither so alert nor so sturdy anymore. He had prematurely aged. He had become almost entirely deaf. He wasn't always sure where he was. He rarely spoke.

Given the situation, a few of Tatteh's relatives had very gingerly suggested that Mama turn the honor over to Uncle Yonatan. But Mama unsurprisingly ignored them. More than ignored them. Shouted them down. Her father was fine. He could handle it. What were they talking about?

And thus, when the moment for the *bris* arrived, it was my Zayde Izzie who was escorted down to the Elijah Chair at the very front of the congregation to tenderly gather Shmuely onto the special pillow on his lap.

Uncle Yonatan initially seemed to accept Mama's edict with good grace. But it quickly became apparent that he was not going down without a fight. For as soon as Zayde Izzie was seated, Yonatan planted himself directly in front of him. Broad and awkward as my father had been small and lithe, he swayed left and right, back and forth, flaring his *tallis* in such a way as to both claim center stage and block the view of everyone around him.

The *mohel* stepped up and leaned over. Shmuely yelped pathetically. And then there was a fearful crash. Yonatan had keeled over and a huddle of black-coated men had rushed in to surround him.

"What is it, what is it, what is it?" cried my mother, who until then had been sitting in the very back of the balcony with her arms around my sisters and her face averted, in the manner of generations of mothers-of-the-*bris*-baby.

"It's Yonatan; he's fainted!"

"He's a diabetic; he faints all the time!"

"Someone should get him some grape juice!"

"Someone should call for medical help. Is the Hatzolah coming?"

"He doesn't need an ambulance. He just needs some grape juice—I'm telling you, it happens all the time. He doesn't monitor his sugar, he just injects himself with insulin whenever he feels like it. And so he faints. Get him some grape juice!"

Eventually, Yonatan was revived. The blessings were said. And Shmuely's name was publicly announced for the first time. Tatteh's other brother, Shlomo, retrieved Shmuely from my grandfather and carried him triumphantly into the social hall followed by all the men. My mother rushed in to kiss Shmuely over and over again. My sisters fought to do the same. And everyone else swarmed to the food table to fill their plates.

Only Frayda stood in a corner, clutching a single dry bagel, shaking her head and muttering. "It wasn't kosher! I saw it all! The *mohel* didn't perform the *metzitzah b'peh*! There's a curse on that family! It's the evil eye! There's worse to come!"

I ran up to her and pinched her. "You be quiet! You and your *lashon hara* and your superstitions. Don't you dare let my mother hear you after everything that she's suffered! And don't you dare ever tell anyone else."

Frayda was so startled that she didn't reprimand me. She gave me a dirty look and moved away, gnawing on her bagel and mumbling to herself.

The problem was that Frayda was right. In the midst of all the chaos, the *mohel* had not in fact completed the *metzitzah b'peh*—the oral suctioning of a drop of Shmuely's blood. I had seen the omission as clearly as she had from my similarly advantageous perch.

Before Yonatan's crash the *mohel* had managed to make the cut and pull the thin sheathing membrane off of my brother's tiny member. And after the turmoil settled down, he had somehow managed to place a bandage on the wound. But had there been any direct mouth-to-penis contact? Had that precious definitive drop of covenantal blood been drawn out orally, in accordance with all the dictates of our tradition? No, it had not. The most crucial part of the whole process had not taken place.

The image of my poor bewildered grandfather, staring down at his grandson's genitals and back up again at the *mohel*—looking around for help, seemingly unable to say a word—remains permanently etched into my brain.

5

My mother's main concern as she finally got her business back on track was who was going to keep the books that Tatteh had always kept for her. Begrudgingly, she reached out to one of Tatteh's synagogue buddies—a man who handled that end of things for a few other local businesses but whom she had never held in much personal esteem. For two years, he kept my mothers' books in order while keeping my mother in a state of constant irritation.

"I can't keep paying that Nissin Belsky, he's robbing me blind—he's such a *gonef.* But what can I do?" she would periodically explode. "I can't do it myself. You know I have no head for numbers. Who can do everything? What I know is selling and I do that very well, if I do say so myself. But numbers? Fffeh! Asher, how could you leave me with this mess? He was so good at it! What am I going to do?"

One evening as I was cleaning the kitchen stove and Mama was sitting with her friend Bertha, drinking tea and kvetching, I couldn't take it anymore.

"I can do it for you, Mama," I said. "I can keep your books."

"What are you talking about? You're a fifteen-year-old girl. What do you mean you can keep my books?"

"How hard can it be? Numbers in columns. I'm good at numbers. A lot better than I am at doing dishes. Didn't Mrs. Silverman say that I was the best math student she'd ever had? Arrange for Mr. Belsky to show me what he does for you. I'm sure I can pick it up. I like putting things in order. I could come to your shop every Sunday and help you out. Let me do it, Mama!"

"Let her try, Gittel. You won't be any worse off than you are now."

"If she messes me all up, of course I can be worse off."

"Let her try."

At first Mr. Belsky was no happier about my proposal than Mama was. A job is a job, after all, even if it means dealing with my mother. But as we sat side by side at the table in his dim office on the second floor of a building on 15th Avenue with his secretary-wife keeping one eye on us from her catty-corner desk, he began warming to my barrage of questions. Who doesn't like talking about his work? By the end of the fourth session (for which my mother reluctantly paid him his usual hourly rate) he was not unimpressed with what I had learned and pronounced me ready to go.

"Okay, String Bean—isn't that what your Tatteh used to call you? Now you know everything. Now you're a big shot. Now you're on your own. Unless of course you tangle everything up. And then you know where I am."

And so it was that I began walking with my mother to her wig shop, *Sheitls for the Discerning*, every Sunday. It was a nice walk. Our paces matched. Like me, my mother is a very fast walker. We invariably attracted admiring stares from neighbors who were not accustomed to seeing us out and about together.

And then talking about business with her was a relief from our usual bickering. My interest was unfeigned, and so was her pleasure in my interest. As soon as we arrived, she would install me in a corner and rush off to the more important task of arranging the wigs on their Styrofoam stands and welcoming in her customers. But over time as I made order out of all her books and bills and scattered receipts, it became clear that she was beginning to trust me.

"Serach, I have to admit it, you are as fast and accurate as your father."

"Faster, Mama. I used to watch him. He was never as fast as me."

"Don't disrespect your father's memory, Serach."

"It's not disrespect, Mama. I'm glad to be carrying on his tradition. He would be proud of me."

But unlike my father, I wouldn't just close up the books and go home as soon as I had finished my calculations. I would stay and watch. My mother was a queen within the confines of her store. And a savvy queen at that. She would survey her customers (almost invariably mothers and their teenage daughters), make a split-second assessment of their tastes and situation, and plunge right into action.

Seeing her so gloriously competent tickled me.

"A *sheitl*," she would say to a woman whose daughter was flying around the shop with excitement, picking up wigs and placing them helter-skelter on her head, "can make the difference between a good marriage and a bad one. Once a girl puts on her first *sheitl* as a married woman, she becomes a different person. And believe me, the way she sees herself sets the tone of the marriage for the next fifty years. If she's happy with how she looks, the marriage is happy. If she's discontent, it shows up in other ways."

And once that incontrovertible initial pronouncement was made, Mama would gauge the impact of her words and take off from there.

"When I first got married, I never had anything but trouble with my *sheitls*," the teenager's mother might confess.

"Trouble? What kind of trouble?" My mother would arch an eyebrow, one hand on her hip.

"None of them ever really fit properly, no matter what I did."

"*Sheitls* were different back then. Not so well made as now. And of course, I bet you had no one like me to help you. They didn't make them like me in those days, either."

"And my kids were impossible when they were babies. They could never get enough of my face and my jewelry and my hair.

They would reach up and grab whatever they could. Nothing I did would stop them. They would snatch at my *sheitl* and pull it to the side. Never fully off, *baruch HaShem*, not in public at least. But off to the side. I looked like a crazy person half the time."

"And was it this lovely young lady who did all that?" my mother would ask, pointing a thumb at the daughter spinning around the room. "This pretty little thing who's messing up all my wigs now?"

"No, never her. She was always my angel. Sweetheart, come here and let Mrs. Gottesman get a good look at your face, touch your hair, see what would be best for you."

"I like these, Mama," the girl would say, whirling over to them with a honey-blond wig on one fist and a paler blond one on the other. "Can I have one of these, Mrs. Gottesman?"

"Never. Never. All wrong for your skin color. You'll be so sallow your husband will turn his face away. Try this one. Rich, coffee brown is what you need. See what it does for your skin tone?"

"But that's just like my regular color! Can't I be a blonde? Isn't marriage the time to try out something new, something exciting? A time to...reinvent myself?"

"Of course it is, darling, but not with a color that makes you look like your Bubbe's faded tablecloth. *HaShem* always knows best. He gives you the hair color that goes with your skin. You want to be glamorous for your husband, not washed out."

"Just don't tell her what you told me, Gittel."

"Tell—tell!"

And my mother would stand up very straight to deliver her second signature speech. "Here's what a *sheitl* is, Mameleh. It's the way we women stay gorgeous while also honoring *HaShem*."

"That's not what you told my mother. She's blushing. What did you say?"

"Okay. Go ahead and tell her, Gittel. Eventually she'll figure it out for herself."

"All right. All right. You're old enough to know. Here is the true deal with *sheitls*. If you get a really beautiful *sheitl*, it becomes like your real hair. But when you take it off and you actually *are* just in your real hair…it becomes like being naked. And so your husband sees the *sheitl* and he thinks about what is underneath and when you take off the *sheitl*, it's like…a little bit of pepper on his eggs."

And the girl would dissolve into giggles. She would put on the coffee-brown wig and begin to spin around even more than ever.

"All human hair, all European. Only the best. Look how gorgeous she looks!"

"Really? It's European? With these darker *sheitls*, who knows what you're getting? Could be from some Oriental."

"No way. Genuine European. Only the best. Well, maybe Eastern European. What French girl is going to sell her hair? But who cares, it's definitely not from some Indian—you can't get color like that, all those rich auburn highlights, with Indian hair. Look how adorable she looks. Just a little snip here, a little snip there, and it will be perfect. And listen: here's the full package. The guarantee. The cherry on top. For the first three months, she can bring it back any time and I'll trim and wash and set it for her. Free of charge. Gratis."

"But how can I bring it in for a setting?" the girl would say. "What will I wear in the meantime? Will I need a second *sheitl*?"

"You're making your mother very nervous, darling. Let's not talk about getting a second *sheitl* right now. Listen. This is like a private women's club, this store. You come in, you take off your *sheitl*, you relax, you drink a cup of tea—the tea also is gratis—and while you relax, I do everything you need. Often it takes some time for a *sheitl* to settle in—for the *sheitl* to adjust to the woman and the woman to adjust to the *sheitl*. And no one but the other women in the store will see you until you are ready to walk out again, all beautiful, all set. In a couple of years, if you want a second *sheitl*, you can come back... we'll see what works. And then it's your husband's headache. Right, Mama? No worries."

The girl would look at her mother and her mother would nod.

"You'll never regret it. It's the most beautiful item I have in stock, that *sheitl*. And you can carry it off. You're a beautiful girl. You've got the bone structure and the skin for it."

And they would go home with the most expensive wig in the store.

One day, however, things played out differently. The bell rang and a mother-and-daughter duo entered. The mother was angry. Everything about her was angry—from her sour expression to the perfectly straight line of her shoulders. The girl was exquisite, with dark red hair water-falling down her back. But her face was totally impassive. She neither ran around nor giggled. She stood dead center in the middle of the room showing no interest in the wigs, in her mother, or in Mama—who is generally the star of the show.

"Do you think you can get a *sheitl* the right color for this one? Will it have to be custom-made?" asked the mother.

"I admit it's quite a color. Buuuut.... I have one *sheitl* in the back that might just work. Come here, sweetheart, let me see your skin in the light."

The girl didn't move. She stared straight ahead. Finally she spoke, in a voice so soft that I almost couldn't catch her words. "What about that wig?" She pointed at a mouse-brown wig perched on a stand close to her mother. "That wig would be all right."

"Don't be silly, Mameleh. She just points? She says it doesn't matter? A face like yours deserves the very best. This is the most important decision of your marriage. By the way, where are you holding the wedding? Who's the photographer?"

"We're holding it at Jewel Caterers of the Five Towns. And Glittering Video is handling all the photography. Prints *and* video."

"Jewel Caterers! I'm dying! Young lady, do you know how lucky you are? What do you mean it doesn't matter? Your parents are spending a fortune. And your *chossn* deserves a beautiful *kallah*. Let me go in the back and get that very special red-haired *sheitl*. You won't regret it."

"Tamar—thank Mrs. Gottesman; she's really going out of her way for you."

"Thank you, Mrs. Gottesman. I appreciate it." And Tamar went back to looking at some object in the distance.

Her cheekbones were like scimitars. Her stance was like a dancer's. And she didn't want to get married. I could see it. I watched her like a hawk, like a knight in shining armor, wishing I could carry her off.

My mother returned from the back room, holding the wig aloft as if it were a trophy.

"The most beautiful *sheitl* in my shop. Six weeks it took to make this *sheitl*. Everything by hand. A *sheitl* that any girl would be proud to wear if only she had that lily-white skin of yours."

Tamar mustered a small smile. She slipped on the wig and glanced in the mirror that my mother held up to her face. "That's fine. Thank you, Mrs. Gottesman. That will be just fine."

Her mother took my mother aside and they spoke in low voices for a moment while I sat and pretended to do my calculations.

"…mth…ft…the same. Absolutely the same. Worse. I can't tell you how many times someone has approached me to talk about her future. Good prospects, all of them. My father is a great scholar, you know. We've got *yichus* up to here, our family.

And she's not so hard on the eyes, either, though you'd never know it from the way she carries herself. Why does she shlump her shoulders like that all the time, like she's ashamed of her breasts? Sure, of course, a woman needs to be modest, but does she have to be all caved in like that? She comes here every Sunday and has the store to herself for a couple or hours. And has she ever even wanted to try on any of the *sheitls*? Her hair is nice enough—my Aunt Seidel of blessed memory had golden-brown curls like that—but wouldn't you think she'd want to see what she'd look like as a real blonde? What girl wouldn't be tempted? Not my Serach. No, at least yours is safe and sound and on her way to getting married; you should count your blessings."

Eventually the wig was packed up in its special box and Tamar and her mother left. On the way home, Mama began telling me a long story about one of her dealers, a Romanian man who always gave her good prices. Ordinarily, I would have been engrossed in her tale. I always enjoyed hearing about her wheeling and dealing and often had good ideas to contribute. But on this day my thoughts were far away.

It wasn't that I was angry at my mother's poorly-muffled outburst. I'd heard it all before. No, my silence came from another spot. A deeper spot. A sadder spot. I was lost in a potent fantasy in which Tamar was standing stock-still in a big white room while someone clip-clip-clipped at that incredible mass of hair, preparing her for that wedding that she dreaded so much. I was waiting until she and the unnamed barber finished, until she strode out of the premises with her shorn head and that aloof sad walk of hers, so I could gather up that blood-red cascade of discarded curls—those wounded, cut curls—and bury my own face in them.

6

My mother was possessive with Shmuely in ways she had never been with any of my sisters. She rarely asked me to manage the tasks associated with his feeding and hygiene. And she placed him in my total care only on those rare occasions when someone else needed attention that no one but she could provide.

But none of that mattered. She couldn't keep us apart. We had a steel-strong bond from the outset. It was to me that Shmuely ran for a kiss when he fell down. It was my bag that he pilfered when he needed one of the sweets that he knew I always stowed away for him. It was into my lap that he crawled when he needed a story read over and over again.

I arranged my affairs so I could pick him up from school every day. Even my mother couldn't argue with the fact that it made sense. When I was in sixth grade I had switched to a girls' *yeshiva* that had a much better math program than the one that my sisters attended (my math teacher, Mrs. Silverman, had helped me apply), and it turned out to be right across the street from the boys' *yeshiva* in which Shmuely eventually enrolled. And when I started college, I scheduled my classes so I could still wait at the door for him most afternoons.

Shmuely was the most serious little thing. So as we walked home every day, my central goal was to steal a grin from him. If I couldn't do it by feeding him chocolates or tossing a snowball at him or tickling him, I would do it by asking him odd questions about what he was studying.

Did the two elephants have to stay on opposite sides of the ark so the whole thing wouldn't tip over? Did the Tower of Babel sound like our house with all our sisters yelling and no one understanding what anyone else was saying? Did the angels' feet smell like stinky old fishes when Abraham bent down to wash them?

Shmuely would start off protesting but inevitably would fall in with my nonsense and begin adding his own sly humor to the mix. Yes, the elephants' activities posed a terrible problem. It was all Noah could do to keep them apart because they loved to sit together and bicker like Mr. and Mrs. Birnbaum. The Tower of Babel was far worse than our house. It was like Mr. Singh's variety store, filled with South Asians and Russians and Israelis and Mexicans all talking at once. The angels' feet did smell horrible. Thank goodness no one expected us to extend foot-washing hospitality to Uncle Shlomo when he came to visit, since his unclad feet were the worst of the worst—if our cousins were to be believed.

"So, what did you learn about today, Shmuely?"

"We learned about how Yakov stole Esav's birthright and his blessing."

"Oh, that's tough stuff. Nothing funny about *that* story. So. How did he do it? How did he steal Esav's birthright?"

"Esav was very, very hungry. So hungry that he didn't care about his birthright. So he sold it for a bowl of beans."

"Silly Esav. Not such a good thing to get that hungry, is it? Perhaps you should have another chocolate."

"Good idea."

"And then how did he steal Esav's blessing? Did he take advantage of Esav's hunger again?"

"No. He pretended to *be* Esav. He dressed up like Esav and put animal skins on his arms so they felt hairy like Esav's arms. And when he heard that his father Yitzhak wanted some meat—the kind of meat that Esav always used to bring him—he brought it to him just like Esav would have done."

"And did it work? Did he fool his father?"

"Yes. It worked. Yitzchak was almost blind, so Yakov was able to fool him."

"So Shmuely, if Mama couldn't see…."

"Don't say things like that!"

"It's only pretend, Shmuely. Don't worry. Honest. So if Mama couldn't see, do you think she would ever confuse Beile with me?"

"Never! You can't fool Mama. She would always know who was who."

"So how did Yakov do it? Was it because Yitzhak was so hungry, like Esav? Was it that dangerous hunger thing again?"

"Do you think I should have another chocolate?"

"Yes. You should. Here. Finish it up before we get inside. So was it because Yitzhak was so hungry?"

"I don't think so."

"How then?"

"I don't know."

"Shall we look at the text? Shall we see if we can get a clue?"

A nod. We climbed the stairs to his bedroom and he pulled the book out of his backpack.

"So. What does it say? Read it exactly. And then translate it for me."

"It says," Shmuely squinted at the page. "'*Va-yagesh-lo va-yochal va-yaveh-lo yayin vayesht*,' which means, 'So he served him meat and he ate and he brought him wine and he drank.'"

"So. Yakov didn't just serve his father Yitzhak the meat that he had asked for, did he? He served him wine, too."

Shmuely said nothing. He just looked at me.

"So, do you think that might have had something to do with it? Do you think that maybe Yakov was trying to make his father a little drunk?"

"That he was trying to make him a little drunk? My teacher didn't say anything about making him drunk."

"But do you think it is possible? And that Yitzhak, being drunk, was easier to fool? You know how silly the grown-ups get at Purim when they've had too much to drink. When they get to the point that they can't tell Haman from Mordechai."

"I guess. But that's awful."

"Yes, it is."

"But, in the end…in the end it was okay because it helped fulfill the prophecy. *HaShem* wanted Yakov to get the birthright and the blessing, not Esav. He wanted Yakov to be our forefather, not Esav. So it was okay, everything that Yakov did. That's what my teacher said."

"Humph."

"My teacher *said* it."

"Hummmph. And do you believe it?"

"Yes."

"And would you ever have done that to Tatteh? Would you ever have gotten him drunk just to get what you wanted? Would you have played such a bad trick on him?"

"Never!"

"Humph."

"Serach?" Suddenly he looked more serious than ever, and this time I sensed I shouldn't push it.

"Yes, Shmuely?"

"What was Tatteh like? Did he ever get drunk?"

This was new territory. I had often talked about Tatteh to him but he had never spontaneously asked me anything about him.

"Tatteh was wonderful. He was twinkly. But he was also dignified. And no, I never saw him drunk. He didn't even drink much at Purim."

"And…. And what did he look like, Serach? Mama doesn't hang pictures of everybody on the wall, the way Aunt Idy does. I only saw a picture of him once and she put it away again as soon as she showed it to me."

"Humph. I don't have any pictures of him, either."

"But you remember, don't you? What he looked like?"

"Of course I do. He looked…he looked…." I sprang up from the bed where we had been sitting to examine the text and ran to the bureau—to the little stand on which Shmuely had resettled his big round black hat as soon as we had entered the room. I picked up the hat, put it on my head and spun around.

"Serach—take that off! Girls aren't supposed to wear boys' clothes!" Shmuely covered his face with his hands but his blue eyes showed through thin fingers.

"*Look at me*, Shmuely!" I commanded as I stood there bold and straight, amazed at how suddenly powerful the hat made me feel.

"No! Take it off!"

"Look at me, Shmuely!"

Slowly, he pulled his hands away. I walked up to him and held my face close to his so that he was forced to see it.

"He looked like this. He looked like me."

"Take it off!"

"Okay, okay." I took it off. "But guess what else?"

"What?"

"Come!" I took him by the hand and led him into the bathroom where I put the hat gently on his head and turned him to face the mirror over the sink.

"This is also what he looked like. He looked just like you. Except he smiled more. He smiled all the time. It's why I tickle and tease you, Tatteleh. It's so I can see his face."

We were silent for a moment while he thought.

"You loved him a lot, didn't you?"

"I loved him a whole lot and he loved me a whole lot."

"And would he…would he…?"

"Would he have loved you?"

A nod.

"He would have loved you more than life itself, Shmuely."

I caught the expression on my brother's face and quickly turned away. He had his dignity too.

"I better go downstairs before Mama has a fit that I haven't started supper."

7

For a long time, it seemed as if Frayda had been wrong. Our family had finally escaped the evil eye. Things were good. My sisters were obedient daughters and solid students. Shmuely was the smartest, sweetest, and most beautiful boy in the world. I continued to do as well as ever in school and I kept the books for Mama's flourishing business in tip-top order.

Negotiating the whole college thing had not been so easy, of course. I rarely took on Mama in a full-frontal attack. It was generally best to try to side-step her wishes. But in the matter of higher education, I was ruthlessly direct. So despite her reservations about my attending college at all (and despite her insistence that if I absolutely had to study I should limit myself to one of the two main institutions serving Orthodox women), I prevailed. I enrolled in Brooklyn College with its outstanding Computational Mathematics program.

At first, everything seemed to hold together. The major really suited me in its orderliness and its ability to explain things. Math is the closest thing to perfection that I can imagine. In my mind its elegance—its mystery—is proof positive of the existence of *HaShem*.

And the commute wasn't half bad either. I was able to complete at least one assignment on the 45-minute bus ride home every day, and my sisters graciously took over some of my household chores so I could complete the rest of my work by a reasonable hour. And, of course, I found a way to keep picking Shmuely up from *yeshiva* on most afternoons.

Early in my senior year, however, things began falling apart. I was suddenly overcome with exhaustion. So tired that I sometimes fell asleep in class. I struggled to get out of bed every morning and was utterly drained by the time I arrived back home. I reluctantly asked Beile to pick Shmuely up from *yeshiva* in my stead so I could just slink into the house as fast as possible and lie down.

The verdict was not good. Evidently, not only did I look just like Tatteh. Not only had I inherited his mathematical gifts. I also had inherited his family's propensity for poor health. It wasn't my heart, like Tatteh or his father. It was my bone marrow that wasn't working right. And it was almost certainly destined to get worse.

What followed is a bit of a blur. It seems that we had to work quickly and that I needed two things: blood transfusions to strengthen me and then, in all likelihood, chemotherapy.

It also quickly became apparent that it was all too much for Mama. Four other girls to look after—not to mention her precious Shmuely. A business to run. And a daughter who insisted on doing things her own way. A daughter who was now flirting with death. With the thing that Mama feared most in all the world.

She didn't take to her bed or even to a darkened room. And she did get someone to sub for her at work on the days when I had my appointments so she could deposit me at the hospital while she ran some errands and then swing back again to pick me up. But she absolutely refused to talk with me about what was going on. And she never once sat with me during my procedures. She abandoned me. There is no other way to put it.

Waiting for that first transfusion was terrifying. We got the time wrong. Mama dropped me off a full half-hour early and I was left to sit all by myself in the procedure room for what seemed like forever while my mind spun out endless dire scenarios.

I was weak, alone, and cold—so cold. I hunched over myself and hugged my shoulders tightly with my hands.

Finally, the doorknob turned, and in walked the most beautiful woman I had ever seen. More beautiful than Tamar, the girl in Mama's wig store. More beautiful than that girl on whom I had briefly fixated in statistics class.

Dressed in green scrubs whose square cut could not obscure the luscious curves beneath, skin gold as honey, she moved toward me and placed one warm hand on my shoulder.

"Hi, I'm Paloma," she said. "And I'm going to help you get through all this."

I had been just sneaking sideways peeks at her, but upon hearing her voice, I lifted my eyes and looked directly into that wonderful face. She met my gaze. More than met my gaze. Returned it.

Two whole pints of blood dripped into my veins that afternoon. But I was blessedly oblivious to that whole scary process. I was too caught up in trying not to swoon every time Paloma came close—so close—to adjust this or that, or to ask how she could make me more comfortable.

On the second visit, there were two other women already in the room receiving transfusions, but Paloma was nowhere to be seen. When she finally arrived, she went about her tasks in total silence while I sat in painful exhilaration, wondering whether I'd been imagining things.

Eventually, however, the others cleared out and she approached my chair and gave me that bemused, seductive smile of hers.

"So, Serach," she said. "Tell me. What do you like to do when you're not battling cancer?"

I had no idea what to say. No one had ever asked me that question. What *do* I like to do? Math? Should I say "math"? Would that sound silly to her? She watched me struggle for a moment and then relented and gently rested her hand on my shoulder.

"Well, never mind. You'll tell me another time. Instead, tell me about that woman who brings you in and then leaves without saying a word."

"That's my mother."

"Your mother? And she doesn't stay with you?"

"She's a busy woman. She runs her own business. She has five other children to look after."

"Five other children! Even we Latinas don't do that so much anymore. Brothers? Sisters?"

"Four younger sisters and one younger brother."

"And are you close to them, all those siblings?"

"My sisters…my sisters are kind of…they're always kind of bunched up around my mother. So it's hard to get close to any of them. But my brother, Shmuely, he's my angel."

"I have a brother whom I adore as well. But…heh, heh…he's no angel. And your father?"

"My father's dead."

"I'm sorry."

"So am I. Every day of my life."

"Still, six kids. And she's not that old. They must have started young."

"That's what we do."

"But not you, eh? No husband, I presume? No kids? No starting young?"

"*Baruch HaShem* I didn't start young. How would they cope, now that I'm so sick? Who knows where this disease is taking me?"

"It's not taking you anywhere, Serach. You're going to lick it. But still…no husband? No boyfriend even? Such a pretty girl? How do your people put it? Such a *sheyn meydl*?"

I don't blush so easily, but I must have blushed deeply because Paloma began to hum. And to smile her wickedest smile.

"Don't answer. We'll pick up the next time we convene. Two weeks? Same time same place?"

The second blood bag was empty. Paloma unhooked me. And a few minutes later Mama arrived and I trailed out after her, trying hard not to look back.

When the next appointment rolled around I would have skipped into the room like a girl but for my illness and my mother. Forced to exhibit a degree of restraint, I made my way to my seat. My mother nodded briefly at me and left. Paloma moved in and attached all those tubes and bags. And then she pulled over one of those little hospital stools-on-wheels, sat on it, and got right down to business.

"You know, Serach," she said. "I spend a lot of time managing other people's body fluids. Emptying bedpans. Changing diapers. Inserting catheters and blood drips. You can tell a lot about people by the way that they react to that kind of intimate work. Some look right through me like I'm not even there. Some apologize. Some lash out at me. But when I help you, it is as if I were watering a flower. You suddenly sit up straight. You look up at me with this expression…how can I possibly describe it? It's so beautiful. So radiant. So sad and wise and sweet."

What do you say to something like that?

"Actually, I do know how to describe it. Do you know what I thought the first time I saw those deep grey eyes of yours? That pale, smooth high forehead? That mysterious, barely-curved smile that hints of things that no one else can ever know? I thought, 'She looks just like the Blessed Virgin Mary.'"

This was definitely not what I was expecting.

"How can you say that? Like the Blessed Virgin Mary! *Chas v'cholileh*! I can't believe I just spoke her name. I'm not even supposed to think about her. She and her son! And anyway, how can anyone possibly know what she looked like?"

"Ah, Serach. I knew there was a sharp tongue lurking somewhere under that saintly exterior. Thank goodness! Now listen. *I* don't believe you guys killed Jesus. So you needn't shout at me. And we know what Mary looked like because all the greatest artists have painted her. I'll have to bring you in my print of Bergognone's *Assumption of the Holy Virgin*. It's hanging in the living room just where Judith left it. Like so many Jews, Judith loved Renaissance art. All the best art historians were Jewish, you know."

"Not my kind of Jew. Not Haredi. And don't even *think* of bringing that print in here! What if my mother came in and saw me looking at it? She'd yank the transfusion needle right out of my arm."

And who's Judith?

"Quite an image, Serach. Your pretty white arm spurting blood. A martyr for modern times."

I relocated my voice. "And who's Judith?"

"Judith Skollar was my employer. I was her home health aide. She was an ailing former opera singer—missing one leg and confined to a wheelchair. I lived with her and took care of her for nearly a year and a half. I wasn't quite truthful when I implied that you were the only patient who has ever responded to my help with sweetness. Judith treated me with exceptional warmth."

What was she saying?

"But with you, it's so much more than with Judith. You make my head whirl. Who are you, Serach? So mysterious, all covered up top to toe like a nun. What goes on in that wise little head of yours when I leave the room? And who takes care of you when you are out of my sight?"

"I've always taken care of myself." The blood pouring into my veins made it difficult to speak. "Until now, I guess. Look, Paloma. You can tell me I remind you of whomever you want. I'll try to digest it. Just promise me you won't bring in that picture."

"You're right. God forbid—a picture of the Madonna in Maimonides Hospital."

She leaned toward me and flicked a recalcitrant wisp of hair back behind my ear.

"Such lovely curls. The chemo will rip them all away, you know. Save one for me."

Did she know what she was doing? I have to assume that she did, even that early on. Tease. Temptress. She stood up and moved away. Became engrossed in hauling some terrifying piece of machinery from one side of the room to the other. But before she exited, she turned back to face me.

"So, Serach. Clearly if you're ever going to get to see my Madonna, you're going to have to come visit me. I don't live so very far away, you know. I'll draw you a map. But I can tell that you're someone who really thinks about things before doing them. Therefore, I'm not going to pressure you. I'll bide my time till you're ready. Still...perhaps I won't have to wait so long? Hmm?"

I sat and shivered, thinking about what she was asking of me.

8

I felt immediately stronger after each transfusion. Not strong enough to go back to school—I had to take a leave of absence. But enough to behave almost normally at home for a week or so. Until the effect gradually wore off and I found myself spending a lot of time in bed again.

It wasn't long before my doctor said the words I'd been dreading: "Time to start the chemo."

I'm not sure just how much my sisters thought about my situation. They were totally caught up in school and chores and incipient crushes. But Shmuely felt it all deeply. One day he slipped into the girls' communal bedroom when no one was there but me. Eyes big, face pale, he blurted out, "Serach, are you going to die?"

"No. I'm not going to die. I promise. The blood transfusions have kept me going. And the chemo will cure me."

"Can I do anything to help?"

The poor soul was only nine. What could he do? But I thought of something. "I tell you what. You could do something that Tatteh started to do with me. You could teach me to read Torah—to chant the way they do in synagogue."

"I could never do that! Girls have their own special tune for the Torah, which you already know. You're not allowed to use the real one!"

"Yes, that was what Tatteh said too. At first. But then he saw the light. He saw that I could do whatever a boy could do. He accepted that he might never have a son. He knew that the tunes they let girls use are not as good as the real thing. That they don't convey the same sense of what's going on. So he gave in. We did it in secret. Can you do it in secret with me?"

"There are no secrets in our house," he said, wisely. "Walls too thin. Spies everywhere. How could we do it?"

"We could do it while I get my next transfusion. You can ask Mama to pick you up from *yeshiva* after she comes to get me. You can tell her you'll do your homework while you sit with me. Do it for me, Shmuely! Torah is the tree of life, isn't that what we say?"

We only did it once.

But for those few glorious hours I had Paloma bustling in, surreptitiously stroking my neck as she passed and smiling that incredible smile. And I had Shmuely sitting right beside me with one sweet hand on my shoulder, listening to me chant with all his luminous concentration. Solemnly and patiently correcting my intonation.

It was the happiest day of my life.

9

According to the much-creased map in my coat pocket, the distance between my home and Paloma's—between the intersection of 13th Avenue and 45th Street and the spot marked on Marlborough Road—was twenty-six blocks.

It was a damp, grey early afternoon when I set out to cover that distance. Nothing showed green yet and there were still leftover drifts of snow on the ground. But there was enough warmth in the air to suggest that winter was finally on its way out. Good walking weather. Except for someone who was deathly afraid of slipping on some unexpected ice patch and shattering her treacherous bones.

If I'd chosen to take the bus as Paloma had suggested, it would have taken no more than ten minutes from the stop nearest my house to the stop nearest hers. On foot, still wobbly-legged and fuzzy-headed from my recent bout with chemo, I figured it would take three times as long. Or maybe four or five. Or six.

Okay, the truth of the matter is that I had no real idea of how long it would take. And not just because I was dealing with a body that kept failing me. Because even at my healthiest I had never walked along that part of Church Avenue. I had barely ever ventured out of my community before. For all my pretensions of worldliness, I only knew one route out of my neighborhood— the bus route to Brooklyn College. And I had never even paid much attention to the length or landmarks of that route. My head was generally buried in math assignments the whole way there and the whole way back.

It was clearly a stupid idea, walking all that way. But I was determined. My fevered reasoning went like this: An exodus should involve lots of effort and risk. It should be done on foot with no short cuts. If I made it, then I deserved it. If not, well then neither did most of the Children of Israel. At least not the first time around.

The only way in which I consciously attempted to ease my journey was by traveling light. All I took was what I was wearing—skirt, blouse, coat, shoes, head-wrap covering my stubbly scalp—plus one small bag filled with a spare skirt, two blouses, some underwear, and two pairs of stockings. And Zayde Izzie's *tallis*. And three wigs.

If Paloma really was going to take me in and help me rebuild myself, she was going to have to do so from scratch.

Here's what I saw along that trek: Kosher butchers yielding to *carnicerias*. Round black hats yielding to red, green, and black crocheted hats. Sidelocks yielding to dreadlocks. *Shtieblech* to storefront Evangelical churches.

Of course, I didn't really know what all those things meant at the time. That came later. But I was very much aware that the world was shifting before my eyes.

At Marlborough Road, the map instructed me to go right. I turned the corner and passed between two neat columns bearing stone plaques that read: "Prospect Park South." And as I crossed that last line of demarcation, the most startling vista of all appeared.

On either side of the street were enormous houses—fairy-tale houses—with turrets and gables and porches and ornate wooden doors and neat little front yards in which withered grass patches alternated with piles of dirty snow. The street itself was lined with stately trees and divided in two by a series of islands that undoubtedly bloomed heartily in summer. There was no traffic. There was no one on the sidewalk. It was as quiet and deserted as Shapiro's delicatessen on *Shabbos* afternoon.

This was New York? This was Brooklyn? This all existed within the same universe as the teeming lively stretch of Church Avenue that I had just traversed?

Well, *baruch HaShem*. There were things in this world marvelous enough to distract me from my self-pity. I took heart. Picked up my pace. Walked till I reached number 98—the house that Judith Skollar had bequeathed to her home health aide. Mounted the steps, crossed the porch, and rang the bell.

And within moments there stood Paloma, resplendent in a royal blue track suit. She took my bag, put one strong arm around my shoulders, and drew me from the front hall through the living room to the kitchen.

"Brava, Serach!" she said. "Welcome home."

Paloma's kitchen had five sides. Emerald green tiles stretched above jet-black marble counters. Walls shone in a shade of yellow brighter than anything I'd ever seen outside a cereal box. There was a big picture window covering much of one wall. And in the center of the room was a big oak table with six not-quite-matching chairs.

Paloma sat me down in one of those chairs and poured me a glass of water.

"We can drink something tastier later, but for now let's just rehydrate you. You look so—what do you guys call it? *Shvach*? And anyway, you can't drink too much water when you've just gone through chemo."

"Paloma, you're not my nurse right now." But I drank.

We sat in silence for a moment. She was good at that. And then she leaned forward. "What tipped the scales? What was the final blow? Don't answer if you don't want to, but perhaps it would be good to talk?"

"It was the wigs," I said.

"The wigs? I'm listening."

"When my hair began falling out in clumps with the chemo, Mama would come over to me every time she saw my balding head and stroke it and cluck. It was the only time she touched me during this whole ordeal."

"I'm listening."

"And then last night she came home with three big boxes and placed them in front of me with this really excited expression on her face. Inside each box was a wig. Each was a different color. I'd been perfectly happy to just wrap up my head in a scarf when I went out in public, but she clearly had other ideas. She lifted the wigs out one by one and began telling me all about their care and virtues. No blushing bride ever received so loving a set of instructions. She made me try each one on and oohed and aahed about how it looked. I wanted to throw them all at her."

"Maybe it's the only thing she felt she could give you. Don't get me wrong, Serach! I know she was never so great in the maternal love department. But perhaps this was the only way she could show you her concern."

"No, Paloma! You're wrong. You should have seen the predatory longing with which she looked at me as I tried those wigs on. She wasn't trying to help me. She was living out some delusional fantasy in which she was finally decking me out for matrimony. She's never forgiven me for not wanting those boys she set me up with. The one who sat with me in that hotel lobby talking about his father's dental practice. The one who took me to a video arcade and said, 'Let the fun begin!' The one who smelled so bad I almost fainted when he leaned close. Yes, it's funny. I agree. But Paloma, bear with me. When she brought me those wigs and looked at me in that horrible eager way, she proved to me that she had never known me. Never cared about me. Not the real me. Not the person that I am."

It was a long speech and it winded me. We sat in silence again.

"And did you say something to her?"

"Yes. I said far too much. I did it quietly. I didn't want the whole house to hear me. I told her she didn't care if I lived or died but only if I got married. That even if I recovered I would never wed—that she should get that rotten hope out of her mind. That I was going to go live with a woman. That that's what I wanted. Something inside me just snapped. And you know what? It was really strange. She didn't scream back at me. Didn't say a single word. Just left the room. I packed my bag, called you, and went to sleep for one last time in my childhood bed. When I awoke, everyone was already gone. I pulled out your map. And here I am."

"And you're okay with your decision?"

"Yes, of course, I am. There was really no other choice for me. It's just...."

"Just?"

"It's just that I'm worried about Shmuely."

That was it, of course. I was ashamed of how I had spoken to Mama. But Shmuely was at the core of the turmoil that remained in my heart.

"You mean your kid brother? That little boy who came to sit with you that day?"

I nodded. Yes, my kid brother—the little boy who came to sit with me. The only person who ever came to sit with me.

"He'll never forgive me. I didn't even get to say goodbye to him. I left before he came home from school. I think I was afraid that if I saw his face, I wouldn't go."

"And yet how could you stay?"

"I couldn't. And I couldn't unsay what I'd said. Paloma, I've never been that mad. It frightened me how mad I was. How could I say such things to my mother? I guess I figured I'm going to die soon anyway. So what did I have to lose?"

Paloma let go of my hand and poured me another glass of water. I tilted it back and forth gently, not spilling it but not drinking it either.

"You're not going to die, Serach. I've tended enough patients to know a fighter's heart when I see it. And you did the right thing. You were finally true to yourself. Still, I can't even begin to imagine what it took out of you. I've never had to cut myself off from everyone and everything because of who I am."

I stayed very quiet.

"But Serach, don't you worry about Shmuely. I saw you together. Love that deep doesn't just disappear."

"You don't understand, Paloma. In our little universe there are no grey areas. And Shmuely's acquiescence to its assumptions is bone-deep. It would take an earthquake for him to accept what I've done."

"Love *is* an earthquake, Serach. It overturns all sorts of assumptions. You'll find a way with him. But for now, put it out of your mind and get yourself some rest. I'll show you upstairs."

She picked up my bag and led me through the central hall to the main staircase, where she began wending her way up and around to the third floor as I carefully trailed behind.

And then suddenly, as we climbed, some switch deep inside me turned on and my every sense was electrified. Paloma's sweetly reassuring voice became utterly provocative right in mid-sentence. The whiffs of perfume rising off her body became unbearably intoxicating. And that perfectly-shaped bottom undulating steadily in front of me—so near my hand, just inches away—*hob rachmanus*! I nearly collapsed as I realized that if I reached out just the tiniest little bit I could be stroking those glorious curves.

But I couldn't do that. Could I?

"One of these doors leads to your bedroom, one to your bathroom, and one to your study," Paloma was saying as she led me onto the landing, seemingly oblivious to the fact that I was melting away behind her.

She stopped in front of the first door, opened it, and motioned me in.

I will admit that for one small moment the treasures in that room distracted me. A four-poster bed covered in a white and gold comforter. A big wooden wardrobe and a five-drawer dresser topped by a brass-framed mirror. A little wing chair covered in rose- and gold-striped silk. Paintings that I didn't quite understand (Matisse prints, I later learned) on the walls. Two windows with nine beveled-glass panes apiece. It was the prettiest room I'd ever seen.

Within seconds however, the only thing that mattered about that room was that I was all alone in it with a woman who had the most beautiful ankles on earth. I knew all about those ankles. I'd seen them stretching gracefully above her purple sneakers as she climbed up all those stairs.

"This was where Judith slept when she was growing up," Paloma continued as she gestured around the room. *What on earth was she talking about?* "It's basically stayed the same all these years. The only thing I did when you called to say you were coming was to change the bedclothes and get rid of all the stuffed toys. Judith was crazy about Steiff bears, but I've always found them pretty creepy."

Forget Paloma's ankles. Forget her hips, even. Look at those lips as she talks. Oh, let her kiss me with the kisses of her mouth!

Yet what on earth was wrong with the woman? How could she possibly still be talking about bedclothes and teddy bears when I was radiating nuclear-force waves of energy right at her? Didn't she feel all those waves?

Or had I completely misread her intentions? Had I been so wrong about everything? Was her goal in luring me to her house simply to make me safe and comfortable after the long ordeal I'd been through? Was I being consigned to an upstairs bedroom like some recuperating aunt?

All right. Leap-of-faith. Big one. I had to know.

"I thought…. Paloma, I thought I'd be moving in with you. *Really* moving in with you. Into your bedroom."

She spun right around and stared at me with those velvety black eyes as wide as I'd ever seen them.

"Well, I'll be damned! Little Serach!" And then she laughed her marvelous deep laugh, took me into her arms and let those hands find all the spots I could ever have wanted them to find.

I would have wept, except that I was gasping too hard.

"Well, my darling," she said when we finally broke apart. "As you can see, you needn't fear a thing. My bedroom is your bedroom, as we say in the old country. I'm as hungry for you as you are for me, trust me. But don't you also want a little bit of space that's all your own? Haven't you shared a dormitory room with four whiny little sisters for long enough? Don't you want somewhere to retreat from time to time as you digest all the *patitas de chancho* I'm going to feed you?"

How did she get so wise? How did she know everything—absolutely everything?

10

"Okay, Serach, it's time to start bringing out the 'inner you,'" Paloma announced on the third morning of my new life. She then produced a plastic bag from somewhere that I hadn't noticed, pulled two pairs of jeans out of the bag, and tossed them onto our bed.

"Let's liberate those lively little legs of yours from their many years of bondage."

When had she bought them for me? When she went out to buy the groceries? And how did she know my size? She was the most enterprising human being I'd ever met. The jeans glided over my bare legs as if they were made for me.

"And we're going to ban those awful blouses forever and get you into some T-shirts," she continued, casting a few soft white garments onto the bed beside the jeans. They were tiny things, barely there. How would I ever fit into them? And yet, somehow, I did.

"See? See what happens when you show off that lovely throat of yours? And those graceful arms? And those deliciously subtle breasts?"

I peeked in the mirror and then stared at myself in full-out wonder. In those new clothes, my whole body felt fresh and bright—fresher and brighter even than when I found myself naked with Paloma for the first time.

"Wow, Serach," said Paloma, narrowing her eyes as she looked me up and down. "You're even standing up straighter."

Which I was. Well, I finally had reason to.

It took a couple of weeks for my hair to start really growing back, but it finally did. And when it got long enough to be brushed, Paloma took on the task. She fiddled with it, ruffled it, parted it one way and then another and then stood back to survey the results.

"There," she said when she got it just the way she wanted it. "Perfect. We'll keep it like this—never let it grow any longer. You look so exquisitely ambiguous." And then she laughed. "Blessed Virgin Mary no more. Now you are my slender, curly-headed young Jesus, bathing in the river or leaning tenderly on his mother's knee in the days before he got all tall and bearded and bossy and started wearing all those awkward long robes."

As usual, I only understood half of what she was talking about. But what I did know was this: my head finally looked right. Light and free. No braid, no wig, no scarf, just a bunch of short-cropped curls. As the months went by, I would use Paloma's nail scissors to continue snipping away at it, whenever the fancy struck me. Sometimes I'd just give myself a little trim and sometimes I'd clip it all practically down to the scalp. My appearance was finally within my own hands—no longer the property of my religion, or of the cancer, or even of Paloma—and it felt grand.

The other thing that Paloma did with me was "attend to my education."

The way that she explained it, her employer Judith Skollar had given her "the grand tour" of Western art, history, and literature. That—without budging from her wheelchair and using nothing more than the resources available in her father's home library—the ailing former opera singer had managed to give her home health aide a basic liberal arts education.

And so now Paloma had big plans to pass on all that enlightenment (and more) to me.

"The entire universe is right here on our doorstep," she remarked. "New York City is the best classroom on earth. So hurry up and get all your strength back so we can go out and sample everything that's out there!"

It didn't take all that long, as it turned out. Just being with Paloma made me feel stronger, and before I knew it we began heading out on expeditions.

We spent our weekends walking around neighborhoods with architectural guidebooks. We toured major museums and tiny galleries, viewing whatever they were showing.

We spent our evenings going to concerts. We heard Evgeny Kissin and Jorge Drexler in Carnegie Hall and lots of little choirs in Greenwich Village churches. We saw the Alvin Ailey Dance Company perform Judith Jamison's creations. We went to recitals by Savion Glover—whose tap-dancing feet produce patterns as balanced and elegant as any mathematical equation.

And even on those nights when we were forced to stay home by virtue of exhaustion or inclement weather, Paloma remained relentless in her quest to keep opening doors for me.

"We'll do what Judith and I did," she announced. "We'll read aloud to one another."

We began by sampling the "great works" contained in Dr. Skollar's library—a trove of volumes that I reluctantly admitted was even larger than Zayde Izzie's. But even all those books were not enough to satisfy my indefatigable Paloma. She began culling the resources of the Brooklyn Public Library at Grand Army Plaza to "round out" what we were reading.

"Dr. Skollar's tastes were admirable, up to a point," she'd say as she emptied works by Colette, Audre Lorde, Jhumpa Lahiri, and Kay Ryan…Amy Tan and Elizabeth Bishop and Emily Dickinson—into my lap. "But his perspective was somewhat limited. Shakespeare and Melville and Proust are all very well and good. But old white men aren't the only ones with stories to tell. Let's mix things up a bit."

I will confess that I was not a fan of everything that we sampled. My artistic preferences seem to be much narrower than Paloma's.

I fell deeply for certain poets (Kay Ryan—spare, clear, and sharp—was my absolute favorite) and for certain Renaissance artists. To Paloma's great delight, I grew to love many of those pictures of the Virgin Mary that meant so much to her. And I was also absolutely entranced by certain modern artists. The first time that I saw Kandinsky's lovely little rectangles and squiggles and dots, I laughed out loud.

But I will never like Picasso.

Paloma can stand in front of some painting in which the head is going one way and the shoulders another and there is this cardboard guitar stuck in the middle with a piece of newspaper glued on top and she'll be all sighing and shivering and saying: "Oh my God, the genius of the man!"

And I'll be thinking, "Send him back to drawing school."

"Just what do you see in Mr. Picasso, Paloma?" I once asked her.

"It's his—it's his *joy*, Serach. And his energy! And his imagination! He can't stop himself from seeing far, far more than what's actually there. From turning things upside down. From creating something out of nothing! He looks at a bicycle seat and a handlebar and sees a baboon! He contemplates a naked woman and he says, 'She's beautiful, okay, but I bet she'd be even more beautiful, if I put both of her eyes on the same side of her nose.' He's...he's like God. Don't you see it? That unstoppable, irrepressible drive to create? I'd give up a year of my life to have that vision and power and creativity for just one day."

"I don't get it."

"I know you don't. And neither did I. At least not at first. But then Judith helped me."

The most disturbing experience by far, however, was the night that Paloma took me to hear *Carmen* at the Metropolitan Opera House. At first, I thought it might be lovely. It's a really impressive building with all these gorgeous chandeliers. And when that curtain goes up and the music begins, it is like being in the midst of a fairy tale.

But as the story progressed, I began to feel troubled. And when it launched into that scene in which Carmen is showing off everything *HaShem* has given her—taunting and dazzling her suitors like some modern-day Jezebel—I was truly unnerved. I know I sound like a prude. I'm not. Well, maybe I am. It's just that...I don't think a woman's sexual powers should be so blatantly, so aggressively, so *publicly* flaunted. What it called up in me frightened me. And what it called up in Paloma frightened me even more. For when I glanced to my right, I saw Paloma looking down at the stage in a way that I thought belonged only to me.

She was leaning forward in her seat, breathing hard. Eyes half-closed. Cheeks burning. Chest heaving. She was somewhere far, far away from me. She was right up there on the stage with Carmen, drinking it all in.

And all I could think was: "I may be enough for Paloma for now. But what if someone like *Carmen* were to come along and sweep her away? I could never be like that. I could never provide all that fiery music and high drama. I may be sassier than I used to be. I may have finally come out of my shell. But I am no match for all that color. I'll never be everything that Paloma really wants. Carmen is what she really wants."

I sat on the subway submerged in deep sadness. Paloma kept putting her hand on my arm and I kept shaking it off. Until, when we got home, she finally confronted me.

"What on earth is wrong with you, girl? You look like you've been hit by a truck and left for dead."

"Paloma, I don't think you understand. I love it that you are treating me to all of this artistic stuff. And I love it that you love it. That it makes you so happy. And some of it...a lot of it....I also like very much. But, Paloma...."

"Yes, my darling?"

"I sometimes feel like...I sometimes feel like I can't reach you when you go there...to that place where all the music takes you. That I can't reach you, when you are...in the power of all that glitter. Like tonight…when you were so completely under Carmen's spell…when it was so clear that she was getting to you in ways that I…."

"Serach—you poor creature! Are you jealous? Do you think I was feeling *love* for Carmen? How could I possibly love Carmen? Carmen totally reminds me of my mother! She doesn't enchant me. She makes me feel furious and helpless. And homicidal. And then when she gets herself killed off for that behavior, it makes me feel even worse. I feel like she deserved it and then I feel like a complete beast. But, Serach…." She took my hand, and this time I let her hold it. "That's not even the point! Don't you know that what I feel for all that music and drama and bright lights and theater is nothing compared to what I feel for you? That you are the ballast and the serenity of my soul! That listening to Carmen gives me this marvelous catharsis—that's what art is for, after all—but that it is *you* whom I love. That it is *you* who help me make peace with my whole crazy past simply by being there for me…Serach, don't you understand anything at all about love?"

"Perhaps not, Paloma. What should I understand about love?"

"Don't you understand that love surpasses everything else? That it surpasses all art, all music, all faith—all human creation? That it is the only true source of all joy, the only true source of all healing?"

And then she closed her eyes and began to recite.

"'If I speak in human and angelic tongues but do not have love,'" she began, "'then I am nothing but a resounding gong or a clashing cymbal.'"

"What on earth is that?"

"Hush!" She held up a hand and then placed it back gently on my shoulder. "'And if I have the gift of prophecy and comprehend all mysteries and all knowledge—if I have all faith so as to move mountains—but do not have love, I am nothing.'"

"Paloma?"

"Just hush. Just listen. 'And if I give away everything I own, and if I hand my body over so that I may boast but do not have love, I gain nothing. Love is patient, love is kind. It is not jealous, it is not inflated, it is not rude, it does not seek its own interests, it is not quick-tempered. It does not brood over injury. It does not rejoice over wrongdoing but only rejoices in the truth. It bears all things, believes all things, hopes all things, endures all things. It is the only thing that never fails.'"

And then she opened her eyes and gave me that thousand-watt smile of hers.

"Paloma, what on earth was that?"

"Corinthians," she said. "First Corinthians. You forget that I was basically raised by nuns. And that then I was tutored by an opera star who really knew her way around the Bible. And so one way or another, I ended up memorizing whole chunks of the New Testament. You may think that the Old Testament is the whole story. The beginning and the end. The alpha and the omega. But there is much more to life than the Old Testament. More to life, even, than art or music. First and foremost, there is love."

"Paloma, you confuse me."

"There is nothing to be confused about, my darling," she said. "I'm just being your *Rebbe*, like Judith was mine. Isn't that one of the mandates of your religion? Teaching and learning? Passing on what you know and believe to the ones you love?"

"I'm not sure my *Rebbe*s would be happy with all the stuff that you've been teaching me, Paloma. But I suppose that you're right."

"You tell me that you love me, Serach. And I know that I love you. Don't you trust me?"

I nodded. I trusted her. Hadn't she, in fact, been the one to heal me when I came to her all broken into pieces?

I will always remain a little wary of Paloma's mischief, I'm afraid. Of the ease with which she seduces. Of the ease with which she is seduced. And of her need to always be a bit subversive, particularly when anything Jewish comes up. I mean, I get that way too. At least I used to, with Shmuely. But she goes far further than I would ever have dared. Boundaries are so totally at the heart of Jewish practice that there are some that I could never breach. But there is no border that Paloma doesn't feel entitled to cross.

Still, on that evening at least—after the episode at the opera—I began to relax a little bit. Began accepting what she said to me without constantly worrying about hidden meanings. Began enjoying our trips into the city a little more freely. Began thanking *HaShem* for the power of vision and hearing, so I could appreciate all that Paloma was showing me.

I even agreed to go back to the opera and found that some of it appealed to me. I've seen *La Bohème* twice. It's very beautiful.

For hasn't part of the thrill of Paloma always been that she is so fierce and brave and dramatic and receptive? That she's so determined to pull back every curtain and take a good hard look at what's going on behind it?

And hasn't that been what I've been craving all my life?

11

"What have you done to my brother Manny? Have you cast a spell on him?" Paloma put down the phone and looked at me in amazement.

"What are you talking about?"

"I just finished speaking with him and he couldn't stop talking about you. Said you were 'cute.' Gave me his seal of approval. He actually said it like that. 'Okay, Hermanita,' he said. 'I approve.' What on earth did you do to him?"

"I didn't do anything. I just kind of followed him around and watched him and asked him questions about what he was doing. Why does it surprise you that he liked me?"

"Well…I don't know. I mean…he knows we're gay. And he's okay with it, more or less. So it's not that. It's more that…. Look, he's a typical, old-fashioned Latino man. He thinks that women should be nice and curvy. Which you aren't. And that they shouldn't show off their brains too much. Which you do. All the time. And that they should show deep appreciation of his *machismo*. Which I can't imagine you doing. I'm surprised he even knew what to make of you."

"Well, I *was* very appreciative of his *machismo* as a matter of fact. I was very interested in what he had to say about the work he was doing—and very impressed with how he went about it. Isn't that what men like best?"

For the first several months that we'd been living together, Paloma had talked a great deal about her late employer, Judith. And she also spoke frequently about Judith's former piano accompanist, Frank. She warned me that he would be coming to stay with us from time to time. It was part of the deal of inheriting the house, evidently.

"The bedroom on the left as you go up the stairs? The one that we never use?" she'd asked. "Well, it's his. That's where he sleeps and parks all his stuff when he's performing in New York. But I must warn you: he uses up a great deal more space than just that one room when he's around. He basically takes over the whole house. Still, I think you'll get a kick out of him. He's an experience unto himself. And once he's played the piano for you, you will never be able to refuse him anything."

When it came to talking about her own family, however, Paloma was exceedingly—and curiously—reticent.

What I'd managed to pick up from the "Carmen" episode (and from certain other comments that Paloma dropped) was that her mother had been a truly terrible person. So it was understandable that she would avoid discussing her. She'd never mentioned a father at all in those early days, and I'd never asked about him. I knew she had a grandmother in Colombia to whom she sent a letter and a check every month. But even that grandmother came up in conversation very rarely. And there was never any mention of traveling to see her.

It was clear, however, that Paloma and her brother Manny were still very close, both emotionally and geographically. He lived up in the Bronx somewhere. She was constantly on the phone with him, and she occasionally went off to see him. But she never suggested that I go with her. And she never invited him to our house, either.

It wasn't as if I obsessed about all that. We were still in a kind of honeymoon period, after all. We didn't really need to bring anyone else into the picture. Nonetheless, if Paloma and Shmuely could have been with me at the same time every once in a while—as they'd been on that one blissful afternoon at the hospital—it would have made me happier than anything. So I did sometimes wonder.

But then that Thursday morning in mid-November arrived and everything changed.

Paloma's colleague Shaneequa had called her shortly before seven o'clock that morning to say that she was sick and could Paloma please fill in for her. And my accounting professor had sent out an email blast announcing that his morning class had been canceled.

So when the back doorbell rang, it was I who was home and available to answer it.

I ran down the two flights to the ground floor, opened the door a crack and looked out.

"Yes?"

"I'm here to fix the sink," said a gruff voice.

Our sink had been lightly leaking for a couple of days. We'd stuck a pail under the leak but it was clear that something more would have to be done fairly quickly. The leak would only get stronger, or we'd forget to empty the pail, or no one would be home for too many hours and we'd have a flood.

Paloma had promised that she would call in a plumber. She hadn't told me exactly when she was going to do it, but evidently she'd made the call and here he was. I opened the back door wide to see a dark burly man in navy blue coveralls, carrying a toolbox.

"Oh!" I said. "Thank goodness! I didn't know you were coming this morning, but I'm sure glad you're here. The drip is becoming impossible. Here, let me show you where it is."

If he was perplexed at my being there instead of Paloma, I didn't catch it. If he was upset that I wasn't greeting him differently—that I wasn't introducing myself and saying hello nicely—I didn't see it. I was far too preoccupied with just getting him to attend to the problem.

I led him through our kitchen with all its gleaming tiles and antique wood furnishings and hanging copper pots and bent down to open the cabinet under the sink. Just in time, too. The pail was already growing full despite my having emptied it earlier that morning.

"Man, this is some place," he said, shaking his head as he followed me. "Paloma doesn't appreciate what a gold mine she landed in."

This was not, in my opinion, the way a plumber should be talking about his client.

"Excuse me? Paloma? You call her *Paloma?*"

"What else should I call my sister?"

"You're Manny?"

"No, I'm Santa Claus. Of course I'm Manny. Mr. Fixit, always ready to lend a hand. And where is Paloma, anyway?"

"She's at the hospital. One of her colleagues called at the crack of dawn to ask her to fill in for her and she left in a cloud of smoke. Fortunately, however, *I'm* here…."

"Yeah, right. Fortunately. What the hell would I have done if you *hadn't* been? It's not like she's ever given me a key."

I looked hard at him, trying to calculate just how deep his resentment went, but he wouldn't catch my eye.

"Well, Manny," I finally said. "It's all worked out, hasn't it? I *was* here and I was able to let you in. This is an odd way to meet, it's true, but it will have to do. Let's not be strangers. I'm Serach. And I'm glad to meet you."

And then I held out my hand.

Shaking hands with a man was still a very novel idea for me. And shaking hands with his sister's girlfriend was probably even more of a stretch for Manny. So the transaction took us each a little time. Eventually, however, my hand was encased in his big brown callused grasp. And after a moment, he even looked me in the face.

He was very handsome in his way, though very fat and very fierce.

"Hello, Sara," he said slowly. "I'm glad to meet you, too."

"It's Serach," I said, smiling at him. "With a 'ch'—like you're clearing your throat."

"Hello, Sara with a 'ch' like you're clearing your throat," he repeated. And then, suddenly—almost as if he couldn't help himself—he grinned.

And the face that had glowered so ferociously at first (it had been quite terrifying, really) turned surprisingly welcoming and sweet.

"You have Paloma's dimples!"

"No," he said. "She has mine. And we both have our mother's."

"I didn't know you were a plumber."

"I'm not. I'm a car mechanic. But…I'm pretty good at fixing just about anything. And Paloma knows it."

"So how do you fix a leaky sink?"

"Come watch me, if you're so interested."

He knelt down heavily with his tool box by his side, and I knelt right down beside him.

"The main thing to do is to figure out where the leak is coming from," he said, pulling out all the detergents and cleaning products that we keep in that cabinet and carefully stacking them behind him. "It could be a lot of different things. The valve stems sometimes get loose from…" he stuck his head deeper within, "from expanding and contracting over the years. Or it could be the gaskets or the 'O' rings that have…" he pulled his head out again and started fishing around in his bag to pull out a flashlight and some frightening-looking tools, "that have deteriorated and have to be replaced. Or maybe it's that the retention nut needs to be…tightened or…."

He looked in one more time and then pulled his head out entirely.

"No, it's the pipe. It's completely busted through. See? Right here? It's really good quality, this pipe. Copper. The stuff you find in these old houses can be really fine." He sat back on his heels. "Unlike what they use in newer places. Most new plumbing is made of plastic. So it breaks more quickly. But it is also…more fixable. You can just kind of…well, never mind. When a pipe this good finally gives out, you have to replace it altogether." He rummaged around in his box, found a metal tape measure, took some measurements, wrote something down with a pencil on a scrap of paper and stood up.

"Where's the nearest hardware store?"

"Well, there's a really good one on Coney Island Avenue," I said. "It's not far. I'll show you. I love hardware stores. So many interesting little gadgets. Everything so shiny and well-organized. I can easily amuse myself while you pick out what we need."

By the time we got back with the piece of pipe and all the trimmings, we had become friends. I spent the rest of the morning watching him as he worked and asking him all sorts of questions. And though some of what he explained was incomprehensible to me—he was actually pretty talkative once he got going—a lot of it made sense. I love seeing how things fit together—how things work. And I love watching people do what they love to do.

When he had finished his repairs and cleaned up (he was particularly meticulous about the clean-up) I offered to make him some coffee. I'm no cook and I prefer tea, myself. But I'd watched Paloma often enough to approximate what she does with that big shiny espresso machine of hers. And evidently what I managed to do met with Manny's approval, for he drank it all down with gusto and ate all the cookies that I put in front of him.

Finally, he stood up from his chair. I thanked him again, and once again we clasped hands. I caught him shaking his head one more time as he walked toward the door, but just before he reached it he turned back to me and gave me his big, slow grin.

"So long, Sara with a 'ch,'" he said. "And thanks for all your help."

So I figured I'd done the right thing.

"Not only does Manny think that you're really cool," continued Paloma, "but he's invited us to his house for Christmas dinner." She looked at me sideways. "Are you game?"

"Why, Paloma, since when do you ask whether I'm game for one of your adventures? Generally, you just drag me along. And anyway, this is your brother. This is your family. Of course, I'll go. I'm very glad that Manny likes me. But do tell me about what I may find there, so I don't make any terrible mistakes."

12

Paloma was unusually thorough in her preparations. She says that, as a rule, she likes to "wing" things—that improvising makes for more excitement. But she really wanted this Christmas visit to go well. She was therefore finally willing to fill me in on a whole range of family details so I would know what to expect.

She explained that Manny was married to a Dominican woman, Beatriz, who had come as a package deal with two sons and then had a third one with Manny. Beatriz had been Judith's home health aide before Paloma. She'd turned the job over to Paloma when the third child was born and, simultaneously, Judith had begun needing round-the-clock help.

"She switched over to being a housekeeper rather than a home health aide, and it was a very smart move," Paloma remarked. "There are only so many diapers you can change in a day. And patience isn't Beatriz's thing. She's much better off just vacuuming and dusting."

Manny's oldest son was now twelve. His name was Oscar, but everyone called him "Negrito"—"Little Blackie"—because he was so dark-skinned. Paloma had evidently never realized how strange it was to call someone that till she caught the expression on my face when she told me. And then she'd laughed and assured me that giving nicknames like "Negrito" is common practice among Latinos. That they are "given with love" and never taken badly.

The middle son's name was Roberto but everyone called *him* "Gordito"—"Little Fatty"—because he was so fat. He was ten.

And the littlest one's name was Ramon but everyone called him "Anteojitos"—"Little Glasses"—because from a very young age he had needed to wear corrective lenses.

"Anteojitos has some pretty serious problems," Paloma had explained, in a slightly less breezy tone than she'd used to describe everything else. "Though Beatriz and my idiot brother have refused to do anything about it. Which is sooooo Latino! I tell them: 'Take him to a specialist!' And they say: 'Stop being such a nurse! Specialists are quacks—they just want your money. Leave him alone—that's just how he is.' And so they do nothing for him. But I can tell that my brother is worried, despite all his scoffing at my suggestions."

"Well, what exactly is wrong with him?"

"He's like…this little bag of bones. His brothers will be speeding around the house like cannonballs, and he'll be sitting in a corner looking at the TV or just staring into space. He doesn't eat much. And he doesn't speak a word, yet—*not a word*. And he's almost *seven*. He's been left back at least once. He's still in kindergarten, I think. And the school does nothing for him, either."

"But haven't they given him a special plan and a special aide? In our community, kids like that get all sorts of supports."

"We're talking about the Bronx, Baby. If a kid is hurling things around the classroom and hitting people, the teacher will send him to the principal's office or suspend him till he can be shipped off to the appropriate juvenile justice facility. But if a kid is simply very subdued, the teacher will generally just heave a sigh of relief and happily leave him alone."

"Paloma!"

"It's true! Or maybe I'm being unfair. Maybe the school *has* tried to do something, and my stupid sister-in-law has resisted. I don't know. It's none of my business, really."

"Is there anything that Ramon really likes to do?"

"Well…computer games, of course, though I'm not sure he really understands what they're all about. But he watches over his brothers' shoulders when they play and that seems to make him happy."

"Does he like books?"

"I don't know. I've never seen him with a book."

"I'm going to get him a book. I'll get them all books. That little bookstore on Cortelyou Road can probably advise me as to what might appeal to them. That's the main thing you do at Christmas, isn't it? Give gifts?"

Which is why when Paloma and I arrived at Manny and Beatriz's apartment up on East 205th Street on that snowy early evening, I was bearing three gifts wrapped in bright red and green Christmas paper for my... nephews...I guess you'd call them. A big book about soccer for Oscar, a big book about baseball for Roberto, and two Dr. Seuss books—*Hop on Pop* and *Red Fish, Blue Fish*—for Ramon.

"If he's a quiet little boy and very young for his age," the bookstore owner had told me, "he'll love Dr. Seuss. I've never met a kid who didn't."

Paloma dolled herself up in a red dress with a black patent leather belt and high red heels. I'd asked her whether I had to do the same, and she'd laughed.

"Maybe I'll tie a red ribbon around your head," she'd said. And then she caught my horrified expression and got serious. "Just put on your best white shirt and your best black pants, Baby. And your new white parka and that adorable white hat that I bought you. Don't worry. You'll be fine."

Manny's apartment was on the third floor of a big red brick building with a little courtyard out in front. When the elevator door opened, the entire hall smelled of cooking. Most of the apartment doors had wreaths on them. Manny's had a giant paper candy cane.

We rang the bell, someone opened it, and then Paloma took my arm and drew me inside. There must have been thirty-five adults crammed into that tiny space, speaking loudly in Spanish and English—and at least ten kids jumping and yelling and climbing all over. There was Christmas music playing and a big

Christmas tree with toys and wrapping paper strewn all around underneath it, standing in one corner.

Paloma took our coats and stowed them away someplace and then introduced me to a few people as her "friend, Serach." Everyone said "Hi," but no one paid us much attention. They were all drinking this thick white concoction—Paloma called it "*ponche*" and told me that it had more rum in it than the whole island of Cuba. Beatriz was nowhere in sight, but Manny appeared quickly at our side and gave us each a big hug.

Paloma pointed out Oscar and Roberto among all the other children. At first, we couldn't locate Ramon, but Paloma finally spied him sitting by himself in a corner on the floor, moving a toy truck back and forth, back and forth. She nodded her head in his direction and whispered his name to me.

Within minutes, Manny began herding everyone toward a dining table that was actually a long string of card tables cobbled together and covered with overlapping Christmas-themed paper table cloths. We'd evidently arrived very late. Paloma had insisted on taking me on this long detour beforehand to look at Christmas decorations, and we'd lost track of time.

The smells coming out of the kitchen were powerful. I wondered whether I would be able to eat anything. I'd become more open about food during the prior nine months—stopped insisting that Paloma use kosher meat, for example. But there were some things that I still had trouble putting in my mouth.

Paloma had laughed at me for weeks after seeing me cringe when she served me a glass of milk with my roast beef sandwich. Well, giving up kosher meat is one thing. You can't really taste the difference. But mixing meat and dairy is something else. It's obvious that you are breaking a prohibition so deeply-ingrained that it is impossible to ignore.

To her credit, Paloma never made that mistake again. Nor did she ever serve me those pigs' feet that she kept threatening to prepare for me. I was never convinced that she really "got"—or even fully respected—my food restrictions. But she did try. And when it came to the upcoming Christmas dinner, she was absolutely determined to protect me from anything that might disturb or offend me.

"There's bound to be pork tucked away in several dishes," she'd told me as we'd approached Manny's apartment. "It's kind of a staple ingredient of our cuisine. But I'll stay very alert and make sure you don't eat any by accident. And the, uh, main swine event—the suckling pig that is the centerpiece of any self-respecting Latin-American Christmas dinner—well, there is no way you will be able to mistake it for something else or eat it unknowingly. So no problem."

The first course consisted of these bricks of thick greyish dough wrapped in banana leaves.

"*Pasteles*," Paloma explained as she leaned over my plate to pull off all those leaves. "It's a Dominican specialty. There are these little pieces of pork inside, but it's pretty obvious where they are so you can just pick them all out."

I spread the contents of the *pastel* out on my plate. I moved all the bits of meat and all the olives (I don't like olives) to the side. I briefly contemplated the dough that Paloma had told me was made of green bananas and then took a small bite. It was sour and salty and starchy and greasy all at once. Rather like stuffed derma, actually.

After the *pastel* there was salad and rice and beans, all of which were fine with me, so I ate some of each.

And then, finally, Beatriz emerged from the kitchen with the pig. It was the most horrifying thing I'd ever seen—pink and brown and shiny, with its eyes and ears and snout and feet and tail intact and with this big apple stuck in its mouth.

Paloma had specifically placed us near the foot of the table to be as far away as possible from the seat at which, evidently, Beatriz always sat to carve.

This year, however, Beatriz clearly had other ideas. She walked right up to us and plopped the platter down directly in front of my seat with a big flourish.

"Dig in, Sara," she said to me with a grin that I didn't like.

Paloma put her hand on my shoulder and squeezed hard.

The platter provoked a huge commotion and a roar of admiring comments. The man sitting next to me sprang out of his seat, pushed Beatriz out of the way and grabbed the carving knife and fork from her.

"I'm carving!" he announced. "And I'm taking the biggest piece for myself!"

"Just as long as I get some of that *chicharrón*!" said the woman across the table. "I'm drooling. Hurry up!"

What on earth was a "*chicharrón*"? A whole lot of this experience seemed to be flying right by me. I no longer felt Paloma's hand on my right shoulder. She had managed to leave her seat without my noticing. I sat very still, wondering what I should do.

And then I saw that little Ramon had also left the table and I had an idea.

"I'll move out of here so you have more room to carve," I told the man as he continued madly slicing meat. He didn't seem to hear or care and neither did anyone else, so I slipped out of my place, grabbed my bag, walked over to Ramon and crouched down beside him.

"I have a present for you," I said. "Would you like to see it?"

He looked up at me. Brown eyes, sad eyes—enormous eyes magnified even further by those glinting thick lenses of his.

"Come, let's take a look at it," I said, holding out my hand. He took it and we stood up together. His own hand was tiny and hot, with thin little fingers.

"Let's go sit down on the couch," I said, "and I'll take off all the gift wrapping."

He held my hand tighter and allowed me to lead him to the couch and to pick him up and place him down right beside me.

"It's a book called *Hop on Pop* and it's by a man called Dr. Seuss," I said as I ripped open the paper and showed it to him. "Isn't that a funny name for an author? I don't think he's a real doctor, do you?"

Ramon didn't answer. He just nestled right up close against me.

"Let's see what story Dr. Seuss has to tell us," I said, putting my arm around him. And then I opened up the book and began to read.

It was a truly delightful little work. Such clever, rhythmic, funny little rhymes! I'd never read it before. I don't think it's ever been very popular in the Haredi community. It may not even be available there. Pity.

When we got to the last page, I closed the covers and prepared to pull the other Dr. Seuss book out of my bag to unwrap it. But Ramon took his hand off my knee, placed it on the book and looked up at me imploringly.

"Do you want me to read *Hop on Pop* to you again?"

A nod.

So we read it again. And then a third time.

"Come on, Ramon, let's be adventurous!" I finally said. "Let's look at the other book I brought you. It's called *Red Fish, Blue Fish*. And I bet it's really good, too.'

But Ramon put his hand down on the book even more insistently and shook his head. "Hop on Pop," he said. And then he said it again, louder. "HOP ON POP!"

"Okay, okay, we'll read *Hop on Pop* again."

"Hop on Pop!"

However, no sooner than we had begun than I heard a noise a few feet in front of us and saw that Paloma and her brother were striding toward the couch. They both looked really upset.

Manny's face was deep red and Paloma's even redder. She had our coats draped over her arm.

"Yes?" I asked.

It took a moment for anyone to reply but Paloma finally did. "I think it's time for us to leave, Serach," she said.

"HOP ON POP!" said Ramon again, as loud as he could, and this time he banged his hand down on the book so hard you could hear it across the room.

"What was that?" asked Manny. "What was that? Did my son just say something? Did *Ramon Rodriguez* just say something?"

"He said: 'Hop on Pop,'" I answered. "He wants me to keep reading to him. So that's what I'm going to do. And please stand back a bit, both of you. You're making us very nervous."

Manny didn't budge, but Paloma grabbed his arm and dragged him backward a few steps, while Ramon snuggled further into my side and put his hand back on my knee.

"Hop on Pop," he said again. "Hop on Pop."

And so I resumed my reading.

When I had finished the story for the fourth time, I gave him a kiss on the top of his curly head. How could I resist? He was so sweet. And then I motioned for Manny and Paloma to come back.

"Here," I said, reaching up and handing Manny the book. "Your turn. Give it a try."

I pulled *Red Fish, Blue Fish* and the other two still-wrapped books for Manny's other two sons out of my bag and put them down on the couch. I ruffled the top of Ramon's head one last time. And then I stood up.

Paloma helped me on with my coat, slipped into her own, and began maneuvering us toward the door. But before we reached it, I felt someone grabbing my shoulder from behind. Manny had left Ramon and all the books on the couch, had run right up to us and was turning me around to gather me in his arms. He gave me a hug that was warmer and stronger than any hug I had ever received from any man in my whole life.

"Thank you—Sara with a 'ch'!" he finally said, letting go.

I looked up at him and I could swear that there were tears in his eyes. And then he swiftly ran back to Ramon, put him in his lap, opened up *Hop on Pop*, cleared his throat and began to read.

I waved at them, but by then they were too deeply ensconced in their reading to look up and see me. And then Paloma and I continued walking toward the door, took the elevator down to the lobby, and walked out of the building into the still-falling snow.

We walked for a while in silence. I don't know about Paloma, but I was suddenly having a lot of trouble thinking straight and needed to be very quiet. Just before we reached the stairway down to the D train, however, Paloma turned to me, put both hands on my shoulders so I couldn't avoid looking at her, and began to speak.

"Serach, we're not going a single step further without my offering you an apology. I can't tell you how sorry I am."

"Sorry about what?"

"About my sister-in-law! About that damned pig!"

I started to protest but she held up one gloved hand. "No," she said. "Let me finish. I had no idea Beatriz would behave like that. She's never exactly warmed up to me, nor I to her—despite the fact that Manny seems to think that she is all that and a bag of chips. Still, I never thought…. I never knew that she was such a *bigoted* bitch. I would never have exposed you to that, if I'd known. Please, please, *please* forgive me for not protecting you."

I leaned over and gave her a small kiss on her cheek.

"Don't worry, Paloma," I said. "It's okay. Really, really. I didn't like what she did, of course, but…I'm well aware that attitudes like that exist. Your brother really likes me, and he's the only one who really counts. It made me very happy when he gave me all those big hugs. And it made me very happy that Ramon liked his present."

"*Liked his present?*" Paloma switched gears quickly. "Liked his present? Anteojitos was *talking*! That present wrought *miracles*! *You* wrought miracles! Beatriz should have been kneeling at your feet, not behaving like a bitch."

I don't recall what I answered her. All I know was that Beatriz's nastiness hadn't been the main thing on my mind. Even Ramon's "miracle" hadn't really registered very deeply.

No, the thing that had been overwhelming me, paralyzing me—unleashing emotions so fierce that I was having trouble breathing—was the visceral memory of that trusting little boy leaning up against me. Of his small thin hand on my knee as I read.

The feeling of loss that it stirred in me made me want to howl. It lasted deep into the night.

13

It took a full ten days for the little signals in my head to reach a fever pitch. I tried valiantly to push them away and was almost convinced that I'd mastered them. But then that cold late Tuesday afternoon arrived when my gaze landed on that young *yeshiva bocher* all in black with a big black hat scurrying down Ocean Avenue, and I found myself walking straight into the pole of an apartment house awning. At which point, I knew it was a lost cause.

I went straight home to Judith's former bedroom, opened the wardrobe in which my old clothes still hung and checked to see whether the skirt, blouse, scarf, and seamed stockings were still passable. I laid them out on that little canopied bed and contemplated them for a long time. I wasn't planning to try them on right then. I was a bit frightened, I think, of what it would be like to have that skirt swirling around my legs again, the scarf wrapped around my head. Would it feel like bondage, the way Paloma had said? Like an embrace that I'd both craved and fled? Finally, I decided to see for myself. I had to know. I stood up and started pulling off my boots and my jeans.

And as it turned out, all I felt was numb. Numb and determined. If this is what it was going to take, I told myself, then this is what I was going to do. I buttoned the blouse as if I were dressing someone else, and then I picked up my phone and called the one person whom I knew might be able to help. And when I hung up, I shook out my head and felt it clear. It was all going to be okay. I was going to get through it, and I was going to get what I wanted.

I slipped back into my real clothes and went downstairs again.

The following Sunday came quickly, and—decked out like a proper Haredi lady (and it wasn't so very hard to put all that stuff on the second time)—I walked briskly back along Church Avenue to that little kosher coffee shop in Kensington, just over the border of Boro Park, found a booth and sat down.

When Frayda arrived, she looked just as she had always looked. Tall, skinny, slightly lopsided and dressed in a navy-blue coat, with a navy-blue hat of a slightly different shade perched on her wig.

I waved from my seat. "Over here, Frayda!"

She spotted me but remained hovering in the vestibule between the outer and inner doors, scanning me up and down.

"Over here!"

She stood for one minute longer. And then she opened the second door, marched up to my booth and slid in.

"So, I'm here. So, what do you want?"

"Frayda, I can't thank you enough for coming."

No answer.

"No, really. I know it must have been hard for you to agree to this. I'm sure I'm a sinner in your eyes."

"You're not a sinner. You're dead. Your mother sat shiva."

Ah, Frayda. Definitely unchanged. But at least the bluntness of her statement knocked the unnaturally sugary smile off my face. I sat very still for a moment.

"Did she take to her bed?"

"Your mother? Take to her bed, why?"

"You know my mother. Death, funerals, shiva…all that stuff usually sends her straight to her bed."

"Not this time. This death—this shiva—was entirely her party. She was in charge. You know she does just fine when she is in charge."

So as I'd suspected, Frayda and I shared some world views. Or at least some views about my mother. All to the good. I tamped down the pain that her revelation had caused me and forged ahead.

"Frayda, I can't hope to explain why I've done what I've done. But I can tell you that it wasn't an easy decision."

She gave something between a sniff and a snort.

"Well, some of it was easy. I am living as I've always wanted to live. And that feels good."

"With a woman." No hair on Frayda's tongue, as Paloma would say.

"With a woman."

"So, what are you, anyway? *Milchig* or *fleishig*?" And not without a sense of humor. Who knew?

"Perhaps I'm *parve*. I can go on a plate with dairy or I can go on a plate with meat."

"So…you like both men and women?"

"No, no, no. I only like women. In fact, I only like Paloma. But I seem to be very comfortable being with men and doing what men do." I was suddenly emboldened. "And I don't want what women are supposed to want. I have never wanted children, for example. It gives you a certain freedom as a woman, doesn't it, if you choose not to have children?"

She looked at me steadily. I had never really observed her face. I doubt that she'd ever been pretty, but in her lined and sober features I saw an intensity that might once have been attractive.

"I never had children because I couldn't, Serach. Not because I didn't choose to. I married too late. I took care of my father till he died and then I married too late. And then my husband died. It wasn't a choice."

"I'm sorry."

"Don't be. You didn't know. And you're right in a way. It *has* given me a certain freedom, not having anyone but myself to worry about."

And so what, exactly, *did* she do with all her time—skinny old Frayda with her uncoordinated navy blue coat and hat? I had never really ever thought about it. You don't, as a child.

Did she do volunteer work? Did she read? Did she eat her every meal alone, every single day? What on earth does a pious Jewish woman do with all her time, when she finds herself husbandless and childless? When all her natural functions have been derailed? Was Frayda such a gossip—so keen on absorbing the details of everyone else's comings and goings—simply because she was lonely?

I shuddered for a moment, thinking of that truncated life. And thinking of what might have become of me, had I not found Paloma.

But then—just as suddenly as I'd swooped down into all those grim contemplations—I yanked myself out again.

I was there for a reason, after all. I'd invited Frayda there for a reason. How rude I was being, just staring into the void like that! I snuck a peek back at her face, scared of what I might see. But she didn't actually look annoyed. Or no more than usual, anyway. She was gazing right back at me as impassively as ever. Perhaps she was used to being tuned out by those around her. Perhaps she hadn't even noticed my discourtesy.

I launched back into my task.

"Listen, Frayda," I said. "I want to tell you something and I want to ask you something."

No response—just that calm, uninvolved stare.

"First I want to thank you. I never did, you know. You didn't say a word to anyone about... about what you saw at Shmuely's *bris*. It would have killed my mother if you had. And yes, she and I don't generally see eye to eye, but she's still my mother. Or she still was. Or, or...what can I say?"

Still, not a word. Just a small nod.

"And then I also wanted to ask you a favor."

That finally got her. "What?"

I opened my handbag and pulled out the much-folded piece of paper. The map with a single sentence scribbled at the top.

"I wanted to ask whether you would give this to Shmuely for me. He goes to *Yeshiva Machzikei Hadas of Belz* on 16th Avenue. He gets out every day at four o'clock except on Friday when he gets out at two. I used to walk him home but I suspect he's on his own now. I started going home alone when I was about eleven. And besides, he's a boy. Mama probably started letting him do it by the age of ten. Would you be willing to wait till a day when he's not surrounded by his friends and then slip this to him and tell him it's from me?"

She took the paper and unfolded it. No couth. Who opens someone else's mail? Still, I needed her help, so I bit my tongue.

She glanced up from the paper to give me a hard look. "Just a map with: 'Here's where I am—come when you can' written on it?"

It had been all that Paloma had given me and it had worked. "What should it say?"

"It should say: 'I love you, Shmuely. I miss you. Please come visit me.' And you should sign it: 'with love from Serach.' This is your little brother you're writing to!"

What other surprises dwelt inside this strange woman?

She opened her own bag, pulled out a pen and handed it to me along with the map.

"So write!"

"I don't want to pressure him."

"He needs to hear it. Write!"

I did what she said and then handed the pen and map back to her. She took a good look at what I'd written to make sure I'd followed her directions, folded it up again and put it in her purse. And then she began to stand up.

"And just one more thing, Frayda?"

"Yes?"

"About that whole *metzitzah b'peh* thing. When you said that my family was cursed. That it was the evil eye. That more bad things would happen to us because the *bris* wasn't done exactly right. Did you really believe that? Or were you just being mean?"

"You can hardly deny that bad things have happened."

"It took a few years. There may have been no direct cause and effect, Frayda."

"When you don't follow the commandments exactly, bad things happen. They don't always happen immediately—it's not always like when Miriam the Prophetess was covered in white scales the moment *HaShem* heard her gossiping about Moses. But eventually they happen."

"So tell me, Frayda. How do you avert the punishment? Or end it, if it's started?"

"You make up for it, of course. You go back and do the right thing. *HaShem* forgives. Didn't He take away the scales once Miriam went into solitude for the seven prescribed days?"

Frayda smiled, unexpectedly. And was unexpectedly lovelier.

"But surely I don't have to tell you any of this, Serach. Surely you still remember it. By my recollection you used to be fairly attentive in *shul*."

And then she stood up definitively.

"Thank you, Frayda."

"Don't mention it," she said. And she was gone.

14

"So Frayda came through for me! Well, hurray for Frayda! I thought she might!"

"I don't understand," said Shmuely as he continued fiddling with his hat and looking surreptitiously around our living room. "Why did you bring her into all this? She's not a nice person."

"Here's the story, Tatteleh. When I first moved out of Mama's house, I couldn't bear how much I missed you. So I got in touch with Frayda and asked her to contact you. After all, whom else could I turn to? Mama sat shiva when I left the community, did she not? And anyway, I had reason to trust her. It's a long story but let's just say that she once did me a good deed—kept her mouth shut about something important. And also I figured she might like being asked for help. She's left out of things a lot, you know."

"But it still wasn't very nice for me, Serach. Having her take me aside on that day. Having her hand me that piece of paper with that knowing look. Learning where you were and not being able to tell anyone for all that time. I *didn't* tell anyone, you know."

"My poor Shmuely. I guess I took that for granted, didn't I? I shouldn't have. But I never took it for granted that you'd come see me. On the contrary. I can't begin to tell you how much it means to me that you've finally come. You brave, brave boy!"

I waited for him to melt. To run to me. To give me that hug that I wanted so much. But he didn't. He fell silent again, looked away again. Finally he met my gaze.

"But I'm not here for you, Serach. I'm here for me. I had no one else to turn to."

And then he began to cry.

15

"He told you what? And that it's happened twice? At the same time of month? Well, it can't be what he thinks it is. It's just not possible. And whatever it is, he needs to go to see a doctor. Pronto. A bleeding penis is nothing to mess around with, even if it only lasts a few days and then seems to clear up again. Eventually it won't, you know. And who knows what damage will have been done in the meantime. Serach—you have to do something!"

Paloma was sitting on our bed, facing me, with her back pressed up against the foot-board while she carefully polished her toenails. The vehemence of her words took nothing away from the concentration with which she approached her task—her commitment to those shapely feet of hers runs deep. She keeps her overall makeup within reasonable boundaries (mostly). She keeps the nails of her hands (those capable nurse's hands) pristinely naked. But she gives full vent to her inner flamboyance when it comes to her toenails—painstakingly shaping them and then coating them in violet, metallic-green or Marilyn-Monroe-red enamel, as the fancy strikes her.

"Well, Paloma, he *said* it was at exactly at the same time of month, and it's clear that it's the timing that is bothering him the most. What's more, I have no reason to doubt that he is right. He's very precise, my brother."

"Serach, you're missing the point. You can't possibly agree with him that he's menstruating. So whether the bleeding re-occurred at precisely the same time of month or a week later is totally irrelevant. The important thing is that it shouldn't be happening at all. And therefore that *he needs to see a doctor.*"

"Yes of course, Paloma, yes. But it isn't all that easy with a person as stubborn as Shmuely. When I suggested that he go see someone, he began shuddering so hard he could barely speak. And when he finally calmed down, all he could do was to repeat: 'No one must know that I'm bleeding like a girl! No one! Ever! No one!" Eventually he paused long enough to say that he's been stuffing his bloodstained underpants in the trash-can behind the house but that he couldn't keep doing that because Mama keeps meticulous track of everyone's clothes. Of course, it never even occurred to him to try washing them out, himself. But that's another story. Paloma, I swear, it's not the pain that bothers him—and evidently there's been some pain. Nor the fact that something might be wrong enough to require medical attention. It's the gender thing."

Paloma kept her eyes on her toes as she shook her head. The back-and-forth sweep of that silky-dark hair momentarily distracted me.

"And so what did you reply to all that?" she asked, finally satisfied enough with her efforts that she could look up.

"I held my tongue till he stopped ranting. And then I got up to give him a hug. But he immediately thrust out his hands and told me to stay away. Said that he'd only just stopped bleeding. That he was still 'untouchable.' That he was dirty and disgusting. It was a real little window into how our men think about us. Into the real reasons for all those laws of *niddah*—those laws of family purity. About not touching a woman for all the days that she's menstruating plus an additional seven days for good measure. They say that it's to keep the sex fresh between married couples. But that's baloney. Our bleeding frightens and repels them."

"You said it, Serach. Not me. And so?"

"Well, it took me some time to calm myself down after he'd said all that. But, in the end, I remembered that he's spent his whole life being praised for parroting those ridiculous beliefs. And that he was totally terrified. And that it was my job to comfort him, not to lecture him."

"Naturally. Of course. Your baby brother who has always walked on water."

"And then I told him that I could take him to a specialist in Manhattan if he didn't want anyone in our neighborhood to know. But that just started him shaking again. He said any doctor he went to would feel obliged to tell Mama about it. And then she would tell our sisters. And then the whole community would find out."

"And so?"

"And so I bought some time. Said it probably wouldn't come back again, and that there were ways he could manage it better if it did. That he could pilfer the family's communal supply of Kotex and swaddle his penis with the help of some adhesive tape. That no one would think that the used pads were his, since someone else would inevitably be bleeding at the same time as he—and probably more than one person, since women living together tend to get into synch. Told him that cold water takes out blood stains and Midol takes away pain. And that gin works even better than Midol does, so he can use that when he's older."

"In short, you went along with all his nonsense."

"Well, Paloma, there was no reasoning with him. And I'm not a doctor, after all. What do I know about what he really has?"

"Serach, for such a smart woman you sometimes act in ways that completely confound me."

"I know my brother, Paloma."

"Okay, okay. So what did he respond to all that?"

"He started sniffling again when I began talking about women 'getting in synch'—and by the time I got to the part about the gin, he was crying inconsolably. I had to tell him I'd only been teasing him about that. To assure him that I didn't consider him part of the 'women's group' in our family and that there would be no 'older.' That we'd get him back to normal in no time."

"But you still didn't insist on going to a doctor."

"No."

"Serach, you are worse than he is, if that's even possible. But as you say, you know him better than I do. So I guess you know what you are doing."

"I do. And it *has* stopped on its own. Twice. I'm assuming that it probably really *is* all over."

"I hope you are right. But promise me you'll take him to a doctor if it comes back."

"Yes, I promise I'll take him to see someone, if it comes to that. It may take some doing. But I'll find a way to do it."

Paloma waved her toes around to finish drying, spun her legs off the bed, put on her flip flops and stood up. "I know you, Serach. You're scared that if he's cured he'll never return."

I spoke slowly. "Yes, of course I'm scared of that. And angry that our taboos are so strong that it took...this earthquake...to get him to visit me. But I'd never hurt him. Never."

It was an honest answer but not a full one. I pondered how much I could tell her about the idea that had begun perking in my head. The idea that had nothing to do with any known medical approach. She was a trained nurse after all. She didn't believe in spiritual illnesses—or spiritual healings. Fortunately, however, she seemed to have moved on.

"It's okay Serach," she said, leaning over to kiss me. "I'm sure you know what's best. And I know how much you love him. So just let me know if I can help."

16

The bleeding came back and so did Shmuely. He opened the conversation by announcing that he still wasn't ready to go to a doctor. And I, in turn, wasn't ready to broach my new and not-entirely-formulated plan of action to him. So instead, we talked about his studies and about what was new with our sisters. Until there was nothing more to chit-chat about and we found ourselves sitting in silence.

Finally, I took a breath. "Okay, Shmuely. I know you aren't just confused about your own situation. I know you must be perplexed by what I've done. That you must have questions about why I left. About what I'm doing here. And I want you to know that you can ask me anything. I'll answer you."

I braced for the hard stuff. To talk about love. About how unpredictable and how natural it is in all its many forms. To tell him that Paloma cared for me in ways that no one ever had. That she had saved me from both cancer and desolation. I was ready to pull out all the clichés—all the true clichés—in a frantic attempt to persuade my baby brother that what I was doing was right and acceptable. That *HaShem* had made Paloma and me just the same way that He had made him – Shmuely. And Mama. And our sisters.

Shmuely did what he always did. He looked up, looked down, and finally looked straight at me with those eyes that saw so much.

"I do have two questions. I do."

"Go on."

"Serach, how could Paloma afford to buy this expensive house with all these expensive things? The piano, the rugs, the furniture? Since when do nurses make so much money? Is, does Paloma, is she…does she…*does she sell drugs?*"

"Shmuely! What the heck *do* they teach you in that *yeshiva* of yours? Is that what you think? And is it just because she's Latina? Do you really think that all Latinas are poor? And that if they have money it's only because they deal drugs? Couldn't her father have been a rich doctor? Or an investment banker?"

He continued to look at me, unconvinced. "So, was he? A doctor?"

"No, he wasn't. She was far from rich growing up, as a matter of fact."

"And so? The house? The rugs?"

I took a breath. "Before Paloma was a nurse, she was a home health aide to a lady—Jewish, as it turns out. Judith Skollar. An opera singer who never got married or had children. It was Judith's father who was the doctor, and Judith was his only child. She grew up in this house and she never moved. Paloma came into the picture when Judith was already old and sick and had very few people left in her life. When Judith died she bequeathed the house and almost everything in it to Paloma. Plus, some cash which allowed Paloma to complete nursing school and keep pursuing additional degrees. As I am doing as well, by the way. I'm finishing up a master's program in accounting, you know. And I'm really good. I've already got a few clients who don't seem to care that I still don't have my…."

But it was obvious that Shmuely had lost interest. He was staring at the ceiling and pulling at his fingers. I closed my mouth and waited, but he said nothing. Clearly, it was up to me to get us back on track.

"And the second question?"

He snapped back to attention. He pointed to a spot behind me. "Why did you put your *sheitls* on those horrible heads? And why aren't you wearing one of them yourself, if your hair still hasn't grown back, instead of…instead of going around looking like a boy?"

I looked over my shoulder to see where he was pointing, though I knew very well what he meant. Oh, yes. The wigs. The heads. How on earth was I going to explain that one?

Here's what had happened: When I'd finally shown Paloma the wigs that Mama had given me—the wigs that had set me off on my journey, the wigs that I couldn't quite bring myself to throw away—she had seized them and waved them in the air.

"We're going to exorcise these devils!" she'd said.

And then she'd made the three women's heads out of papier maché. She'd given each one a different fiendish woman-warrior expression. She'd painted each one a different bright, tropical color: blood red, ebony black, jungle green. She'd made them all bald. And then she'd plopped the wigs onto them. The silky black one on the red head. The sexy blond one on the black head. The carefully coiffed red one on the green head. And she had set them all in the place of honor at the center of the mantel.

"There!" she'd said. "Look at them and remember with thanksgiving that you will never have to put up with any of that nonsense again!"

I glanced back at the heads again while I pondered exactly what to respond to Shmuely. I decided to deal with the second part of his remark first.

"I don't look like a boy, Shmuely," I said, as gently as I could. "I look like myself. My hair actually grew back a long time ago. I'm keeping it short because this is how I *want* to look."

We regarded one another for a long moment while I tried to assess the impact of my statement, but he had resumed the impassive expression with which he always greeted information that was hard for him to process. I moved on to his second concern.

"And about the wigs? Why they're on the heads? Well Shmuely, you must know how scared I was of the cancer. Or maybe you don't. I put on a good show. But I really did, at one point, think it might be all over for me. So Paloma made the heads and put the *sheitls* on them as a reminder that I had somehow managed to run faster than death. It's our way of thumbing our noses at what almost happened, she and I. *Kenahora*, of course."

How could I tell him the truth about Paloma's intention, after all? Shmuely was Mama's pet. Her favorite. He believed that Mama's way of thinking was right. And he loved her. Could I even begin to hope that he'd understand the pain that she'd caused me? And why risk the further pain if he couldn't?

We sat silently for another moment, while I debated whether to ask him that one big question of my own. That question that had given me no peace—that had eaten away at me for so very long. Finally, I came to a decision. I would take a chance on it. He alone could provide the answer that I sought, after all. And I really needed that answer.

I leaned forward to shrink the distance between us by one small degree and took a breath.

"Shmuely."

He looked up.

"Shmuely, I have something I want to ask you, too."

He said nothing.

"May I ask it?"

He spun his hat around. He nodded.

"What exactly did Mama say about me, in private, when I left? Did she say all sorts of terrible things about me?"

Shmuely raised his head slowly and I caught such a look of sorrow on his face that I flinched.

"Mama told me that *you'd died*, Serach. And that's all that she said."

I lowered my own head as I processed his answer. It was even more terrible than I'd thought. I had simply and truly died for my mother. I was so dead for her that she didn't even bother to tell her beloved Shmuely what had really happened. So dead that she didn't care whether her unadorned announcement broke his heart completely—left him absolutely no hope of ever seeing me again. All other thoughts evaporated for the long moment that I contemplated that fact.

"And Shmuely," I finally breathed. "Did you just take what she said to be totally true?"

"Yes, of course I did. Why wouldn't I?"

"You really believed that I was dead?"

"Yes."

"And didn't it seem odd to you that there had been no hospital stay, no funeral service, no burial?"

"Serach, Mama told me that you'd died. What reason did I have to doubt her?"

"And did *no one else* say anything to you about what had really happened? At the shiva service, with everyone pouring into the house, weren't they all gossiping about what I'd done? They must have known that I hadn't really died. They must have been talking about it."

"I don't know anything about that," answered Shmuely, briefly and coldly. "I didn't stay to *daven* the service. As soon as the crowds started arriving, I took my mourner's box, went up to my room, and shut the door."

At his words, a torrent of images swept me up with him into that neat little space in which I'd taken refuge myself, so many times—grateful to be away from all the noise and mess and frilly, girly details of the room into which my sisters and I were crammed each night.

There was Shmuely's narrow, tightly-made single bed. The maple dresser with the hat stand perched on top. The towering bookcases double-stacked with all the volumes that had showered down on my brother from the moment of his birth, as every community member competed to be the greatest contributor to his inevitably-brilliant scholarly path.

And there was Shmuely seated on his mourner's box on the floor in the corner where two bookcases came together to create that little sheltered spot in which he liked to sit and study. But this time, his hands held no book. He wasn't reading. He wasn't studying. He wasn't behaving like any great sage-in-the-making. Hunkered down, arms wrapped around his thin frame, back to the door—unaware that his yarmulke was askew—he was just a very small, very scared, very lost little boy trying to steady his unruly emotions.

"And so you just stayed there?" I asked. "All that time? Through the whole *mincha* and *ma-ariv* services? All by yourself? Doing nothing?"

He sighed. "Not doing nothing, Serach. I was crying."

Worse and worse.

"And no one heard you and came upstairs to comfort you?"

"Everyone was busy *davening*, Serach. And anyway"—and for a fleeting moment Shmuely permitted himself a small look of pride—"I cry very softly you know."

"So, what finally happened? When did you finally decide to come downstairs?"

"I *didn't* 'finally decide to come downstairs.' Uncle Yonatan and Uncle Shlomo came up to get me. Uncle Yonatan came in first. He was puffing hard like he always does, and he had this big plate of food in his hand. He walked right up to me and stood there for a moment, looking down. And then he kicked my box and told me that I was acting like a girl, hiding in my room and crying. He said: 'Aren't you ashamed of yourself?' And then he gave me the napkin that he'd been using and told me to dry my eyes with it. It had a big shmear of cream cheese on it. I had to fold it over before I could use it."

"Oh, Shmuely! And then?"

"And then Uncle Shlomo stepped forward and told Uncle Yonatan that he should go back downstairs, himself. That he—Uncle Shlomo—would take care of everything. And Uncle

Yonatan said: 'Sure, fine. But hurry up. It doesn't look right for him to be up here like this. He's the man of this *farmishte* household, after all....'"

I had no doubt that the scene had unfolded exactly as Shmuely was recounting it. My brother has a memory like a steel trap. And he never says more than is absolutely necessary. He's as terse as the Holy Scriptures. If he chooses to mention something, you can be sure that it is true. And that it is germane.

"And did Uncle Shlomo 'take care of things?' Was he helpful to you?"

Suddenly—unexpectedly—the barest beginnings of a smile appeared in one corner of Shmuely's mouth. He tried to stifle it but he couldn't quite manage it. I let out my breath. Had we finally gotten through the worst of it?

"Uncle Shlomo squatted down next to me and put both his hands on the ground for balance," Shmuely said, nodding a little to himself. "And then he tried to put one of his arms around me and nearly fell over. So he asked me couldn't we please just sit on the bed."

"And you answered: 'No. I have to sit on my box.'"

"Yes. That's right. Just like you said. But Uncle Shlomo explained that his knees were giving out. That he had problems with his arthritis. And that I would be doing a *mitzvah* if I agreed to sit on the bed with him for just a little while. And that doing a *mitzvah* for someone with a disability takes precedence over sitting on a mourner's box. I don't know if that's true. But Uncle Shlomo, of course, didn't need to sit on a box. You don't have to, if it's just your niece who's died."

"Yes, Shmuely, I suppose you don't. So then what?"

"Then we both sat down on the bed and he asked me what I'd heard about what had happened with you. Just like you're doing, now. And I told him that Mama had said that you'd died. And then he said something very nasty about Mama. I won't repeat it. It's *lashon hara*."

"I'll bet it is. And then?"

"And then he asked me whether I'd like to hear some *Midrashim* about the 'other Serach.' The one in the Torah. Asher's daughter. Yakov's granddaughter. I didn't really want to hear anything about her, right then. But you know Uncle Shlomo, once he gets started."

How much sharper my brother had gotten in just two short years! He would never have made pointed comments about his uncles when he was younger. He might have giggled guiltily in response to some peculiarity that I had noted. But he would never have said anything first.

"Indeed," I said, looking at him with new respect. "So, Shmuely. Which of the *Midrashim* did Uncle Shlomo share with you? There are a lot of them, you know. Tatteh used to tell them to me all the time."

"Well, he started out by saying that Serach was the only one of Yakov's granddaughters to be mentioned by name in the Torah. Mentioned twice, in fact. The first time, when the Children of Israel were first setting out for Egypt from Canaan. And then the second time when they were on their way back to the Holy Land. 'And so clearly,' Uncle Shlomo said, 'Serach was a really special person.'"

"Oh, she was. She was just amazing."

"And then he said: 'Just like your sister Serach is really special.'"

"And you said?"

"Nothing. I didn't say anything. I didn't get it right away that he'd said: 'is' and not: 'was.' And anyway, like I said, I wasn't feeling much like talking at that moment."

Shmuely looked down at his hat again.

"And then Uncle Shlomo told me that Serach was the only person in Yakov's family sensitive enough to tell Yakov that his beloved son Yosef was still alive and not eaten by wild animals, like his brothers had said."

He stopped speaking and we were both very quiet again for a time.

"And did he tell you anything else?" I finally ventured. "There are lots of other *Midrashim* about her, you know."

"Well, yes. He told me one more thing. He said that Serach never died. Not the way that everyone else does, anyway. That she was taken straight up to heaven, body and soul. 'Assumption,' he called it. And he said that she was the only woman—and one of only three people—who was ever brought to heaven in that way. First came Enoch. Then came Serach. And then came the Prophet Elijah. And then that was that. It never happened again."

I just barely stopped myself from blurting out something about the "Assumption of the Blessed Virgin Mary" that Paloma was always going on about. Definitely no future in that.

"And that's when Uncle Shlomo told me that *you* hadn't actually died, either. That you'd just run away. That you'd always had your own ideas about things. And that now you were acting on those ideas."

Shmuely looked me full in the face for the first time that day. "And that's when I got really mad at you, Serach. I'd already been mad at you for dying. You'd *promised* me you wouldn't, you know. You'd *promised*. But then it was *even worse* to think that you'd just run off like that. I told Uncle Shlomo that I would never forgive you. Never."

His remembered anger made him look more masculine, somehow. Handsomer. He really had matured since I'd gone away. I could see a flash of the man he would grow up to be. But then—just as quickly—his features crumpled and he looked young again. Very young.

"Serach, how could you abandon me?" he said, those blue, blue eyes filling up with tears. "How could just leave me all alone in that house...*that house full of women?*"

I clamped my hand over my mouth, but it was of no use. My laughter spilled right out. I took my hand away and grinned right at him.

"But Shmuely," I said. "But Shmuely—was I not also one of those women?"

"Yes, but you were…."

"Different? Were you going to say 'different?' Well, yes. I was. Still am. And that's the whole point, isn't it? It's why I had to leave. There was no place for me in that family or that community. I just didn't fit in. And I never would have. Never, ever."

He remained silent, but I finally knew exactly what I had to say to him.

"Shmuely, listen to me. I can't begin to tell you how sorry I am for having caused you even one single moment of grief. Or anger. Which, by the way, you have every right to feel. But here's the thing. I'm still Serach. I'm still that 'different' sister of yours. And I'm still totally here for you. There's nothing you could ever say that would shock or alienate me or make me love you any less. And I have to believe that—somewhere in that brilliant little mind of yours—you've always known that. Or else you wouldn't be sitting here entrusting me with your deepest, darkest secrets in the full knowledge that I'll do whatever it takes to help you."

Shmuely shook his head out vigorously. I couldn't tell whether he was denying what I'd said or simply coming to terms with it.

He finally stopped. "I checked out everything that Uncle Shlomo told me about Serach. And it's all true. She really *was* assumed. She really *did* go straight up to heaven."

"Well, Shmuely, I don't know if you'll ever fully understand or accept it but moving in with Paloma has put me closer to heaven than I ever believed possible. I love her. And she loves me. She's my life partner—my true life-partner. And I'd never thought I'd have that. The only terrible thing about moving in with her has been losing you. I don't know what I'd have done if I'd ever really thought you were gone for me forever. But I've always known that...."

"Uncle Shlomo told me something else," Shmuely interrupted me. "He said that *HaShem's* greatest attribute is the attribute of mercy. He asked me who was I to think that I was better than *HaShem*—to think that I could sit in judgment of you like that?"

I held my breath. "And?"

"And then he said I'd better hurry up and join everyone else. That the last time he'd looked, there were only a few pieces of herring in cream sauce left."

Shmuely finally gave me his full-out, beautifully-lopsided grin. How I'd missed it!

"So," he said. "So, I went downstairs. And there *were* a couple pieces left, *baruch HaShem*. Uncle Yonatan hadn't demolished them all. And I grabbed them."

Did I honestly think my stubborn little *yeshiva-bocher* brother would give me the response that I'd craved? That he'd extend himself that far toward comforting his wayward sister? Silly me. And yet, despite all his nonsense, I knew him. I knew that grin. And I wasn't greedy. And thus I found myself feeling truly at peace for the first time in a really long time.

17

The third time that Shmuely came over he got right to the point.

"Serach, it's happened again. This is the fourth time. I can't go on like this much longer. In July, I go off to Camp *Romemu*. Mama insists. And my friend Moishe is going so he's insisting, too. How can I take care of...of all this stuff...in a boys' bunk?"

"True."

"And then there is next November, when I become a Bar Mitzvah. How can I stand in front of the congregation and hear everyone say that I'm taking on all the obligations of manhood when I am such a fraud? How can I read from the Torah—from the sacred Torah—when I'm as impure as any woman?"

Well, clearly my brother was still as far from enlightenment as ever. I clamped my lips shut before I could say something I'd truly regret, but he must have caught my horrified expression.

"Serach, it's the *halacha*! Women can't read Torah. It's the law!"

"Shmuely, it may be the *halacha* but it is *wrong*! All that stuff about women and bleeding and being impure and not being permitted to do what men do is just plain *wrong*!" I breathed in and out several times. "All right, look, let's just not talk about it. We'll never agree. Meanwhile, we have a problem to solve and I'm going to help you solve it. *You* certainly shouldn't be bleeding. I've been thinking about it for a while and I have some ideas about what it is and why it all started. And about what you may have to do to stop it. It's a long shot and it won't be any fun. But I don't see any way around it."

I laid out my plan. He winced at first, but then he agreed. I let him out the front door and went quickly back upstairs.

18

And thus it was that on the following Sunday, Shmuely and I met on a street corner in Boro Park not too far from my old home. I had donned the long black skirt and long-sleeved shirt with which I typically ventured out to meet Frayda. This time, however, I had replaced that old head-wrap with a big hat that looked very chic on my closely-cropped curls.

We walked briskly to the little red brick building with the white porch. I rang the bell. The door opened and we were ushered into the living room by a small woman in a kerchief. It hit me in the gut—it was all so familiar. The glass table placed in the same position as in the front hall of my old home. The inoffensive paintings of shtetl life on the tan walls. The chairs covered in beige upholstery. The vases of artificial flowers and bowls of individually-wrapped hard candies on the end-tables.

Eventually, a door at the end of the living room opened and Rabbi Lev Schneider—*mohel* to all the best families of Boro Park—emerged and motioned for us both to enter.

"No, it's just me," I said. "Shmuely is staying in the living room for now."

The rabbi smiled at Shmuely, motioned me inside, and left the door ajar. A Haredi man doesn't spend time with a non-related woman in a closed room. When he had closed the door as much as seemed appropriate and no more I pulled off my hat and looked at him, full face. He hadn't changed a bit. Short, stubby, grizzled, tough. He looked at me once and then looked again. And then he blanched.

"Okay, Rabbi. It's not what I told you when I called. It's not Mierle paying you a friendly visit now that she's pregnant and knows that it's a boy. We have the same voice, she and I, but that's as far as it goes. This is that old Biblical trick. One sister for another. Leah for Ruchel. Yes, I'm Serach Gottesman. Yes, I'm dead as far as you are concerned. Yes, you shouldn't be talking to me. But you *need* to talk to me. You are *going* to talk to me."

Rabbi Schneider turned from white to bright red. "Out of my study! Out of my house! How dare you come in here under such false pretenses? And how dare you drag your poor brother in here with you under such false pretenses—such a good boy, the pride and joy of your family? How dare you force him to associate with you?"

"Rabbi, stop shouting and listen to me. I have a duty to my brother who will become a Bar Mitzvah in six months and who—talk about false pretenses—shouldn't be going up to the Torah if he's not in full compliance with the law."

"What on earth are you talking about?"

"You didn't do your job when you circumcised Shmuely. You never completed the *metzitzah b'peh*. You never sucked out the drop of blood. I saw and, what is more, Frayda Goldblatt saw. We never said a word at the time because we didn't want to worry Mama after all the *tsuris* she'd been through. But eventually I felt I had to let Shmuely know. You know how he is. How committed to keeping all the commandments. And now he refuses to go up to read the Torah for the first time unless you make it right."

Rabbi Schneider looked at me sideways, his mouth slightly open.

"And if you don't figure out what is necessary—and do it—I'll unleash Frayda on you. I'll give her permission to tell the world what she saw. And where will you be? You with your unblemished reputation. You with your devoted following! How will anyone ever trust you to perform a *bris* again?"

The red face turned to white once more. "Yes, of course, sure. But what can I possibly do? This is a very unusual case. I can't do the circumcision all over again! That's over and done with."

"Well, what would you do for some other person who was already circumcised?"

"Well...if the person were—say—a potential convert, first I would make him study. And then I'd do the *hatafat dam bris* with him. A little pinprick on his member, to make him bleed, followed by the *metzitzah b'peh*, followed by submersion in the *mikveh* and an appearance before a tribunal of three rabbis—a *Bet Din*—to make sure the whole thing is Kosher."

Rabbi Schneider paused and scratched his head for a moment. "Buuuuut," he said. "But when it comes to Shmuely...when it comes to Shmuely, I think we can skip almost all of that. Shmuely's not a convert, after all. He's a Jew—clearly a Jew. There's no need for him to do the studying part. He knows more about *Halacha* than many full-grown men, *baruch HaShem*, your mother should be very proud of him. And he doesn't need the *mikveh* or the *Bet Din*. Why should we get anyone else involved in any of this? No, no, no. All he needs is the *hatafat dam bris* and the *metzitzah b'peh*. And that I can do myself, right here in my study. And I'd be happy to do so, I might add. How could I not be? After all, as the Talmud says: 'a *mohel* who doesn't suck creates a danger and should be dismissed from practice.'"

"My thinking exactly. So when can you do it?"

"I'm free tomorrow afternoon as it turns out. Four o'clock, perhaps? After his classes let out?"

"Good. Thank you, Rabbi. He'll be here."

"Of course. Anything for Shmuely. He's such a good boy. So circumspect, so exacting in his practice. I wouldn't want him to worry, not for a single minute." He waited a moment, fiddled with his fingers. "And there is no question about...you won't say a word to anyone?"

"You never saw me. This never happened. I'm dead, remember? You have my word, such as it is." I put my hat back on again, shielding my face from view as I exited best as I could. "My lips are sealed."

Outside on the sidewalk I told Shmuely what the rabbi had said. He looked briefly horrified and then relieved. "And you really think it will work?"

"I really think it will work. And no one will know besides you, me, and him."

He took it in gravely. Nodded. "Okay." And then he looked at me hard. "Not even Paloma?"

"I haven't told her anything about this plan. She thinks you've been having a urinary tract infection. That you didn't want to worry Mama about it and so you came to me. She knows you didn't want to go to a doctor—but she did say that sometimes these things clear up on their own. I won't have to tell her exactly what we did."

And in all my web of lies and counter-lies, those sentences at least were true. I had concluded that I could never tell Paloma anything about this whole *meshugge* strategy. Couldn't begin to explain to her about *metzitzah b'peh*, or *hatafat dam*. Her response would have been too scathing for me to bear.

Shmuely stood very still, considering what I'd said. "But is that all right?" he asked. "Is it all right to keep secrets from your...is it all right for a...for a...couple to keep secrets from one another? To not tell the full truth?"

A couple. My eyes filled with tears so fast that I couldn't avert my face in time. They popped out and dripped down my cheeks onto that long-sleeved blouse.

"Sometimes, Shmuely. Sometimes it is." I kissed him quickly on the forehead, turned on my heel and walked away swiftly. As we had agreed. A necessary precaution, given all the potential spies—all the thin walls—of our community. But then I stopped in my tracks. Turned back to him. Called out: "And may *HaShem* bless you, Tatteleh! Courage! You'll be okay. One hundred percent okay. In more ways than you can know. I promise!"

19

Shmuely continued to visit me from time to time. He never said anything about his second visit to Rabbi Schneider and I never asked. But he did go to Camp *Romemu* and he did become a Bar Mitzvah, so I assumed that all was well. What is more, barely a month after passing that major milestone, he applied for a scholarship to attend the prestigious *Yeshiva Mir* in Israel—the same *yeshiva* that our cousin Reuven had attended—was accepted almost immediately and began making plans that couldn't possibly be followed if he were still in trouble in any way.

Mama wept a great deal at the thought that he might make *aliyah* and never come home again, the way that Reuven had. That she might lose Shmuely for good. But Shmuely held his ground and she finally accepted it. Or so he explained it to me, with a touch of self-satisfaction that he rarely permitted himself. "A good excuse for all of us to go visit the Holy Land," he reported her as saying.

And so now Shmuely Skypes with me on every third Monday. Even the most observant community has had to make certain concessions to the modern world. *Yeshiva Mir* actually makes official time for well-monitored family Skyping. Even provides the students with a special room in which to do it. And I, in turn, make sure to don my head-scarf before signing on, so my face on the screen will not cause a ruckus if anyone happens to be looking over my brother's shoulder.

Shmuely doesn't talk about himself very much, and I remain circumspect in what I ask him. But he makes sure to tell me that he is still okay—really okay—in a way that shows that he knows what causes me anxiety. In a way that alleviates my fears. And I can see it for myself. He grows handsomer by the month. His voice is deepening and his beard beginning to grow. My

Shmuely. And some lucky bride, some day! It's okay. I'm willing to share.

At one point I considered joining a synagogue. An egalitarian one, in which I could read Torah openly and have Paloma stand with me openly. Eventually, however, I stopped thinking about it. It wasn't what I really wanted. What I wanted is what I still seem to think of as the "real thing." What I'd had and yet never really had. And can never have again.

And so I remain unchurched. As Paloma puts it.

But every year on the anniversary of Tatteh's death I put on my long skirt and long-sleeved blouse and that new more fashionable hat. I walk to this little synagogue that I found. Not one in Boro Park, of course. One in Kensington, not too far from the coffee shop where I continue meeting up with Frayda.

I climb the creaky steps to the balcony and walk down to a center front-row seat. I pry open the curtain a bit and then I open up my prayer book. I peer down at the men *davening* below me in their black coats and hats. I feel the sweet presence of the women praying behind me. I bask in the deep faith swirling all around me in that little limbo space. I murmur the words of the Mourners' *Kaddish*. And for a little while I am comforted.

PART TWO: PALOMA'S TALE

"Heal me and I will be healed. Save me and I will be saved."
Jeremiah, Chapter 17, Verse 14

1

When my mother first arrived at the Bronx Convent of Good Hope, my brother Manny was already firmly lodged in her belly. "Luckily for me," she told me in one rare burst of woman-to-woman intimacy, "the postulants were never allowed to be naked—not even when we showered. And the habits we wore were so shapeless that you couldn't see anything going on beneath them. So I had time to pick up some English and get to know Joe before the nuns finally caught on and kicked me out."

Joe himself was let go from his post as convent porter shortly afterward. And Mama would periodically bring up that fact. It used to puzzle me. What was she so concerned about?

"You know, Joe," she would start out, musingly, as if the thought were just occurring to her. "I'll never understand it. There's no way you could have been fired because of me. I never told anyone about our goings-on. And anyway, even someone with half a brain could have just counted the months and figured out it wasn't you who'd knocked me up. So why *did* you get the sack, Josecito? Did you take up with some other postulant—some even younger and prettier little postulant—when I was gone? A postulant who couldn't keep her mouth shut, like I did? After all, they say a man who likes tender meat…is always on the look-out for even tenderer meat. Do I have to start keeping my eye on you?"

And that lovely mouth would pull downward and Joe would begin swearing to the Virgin and all the saints that he had always been true to her. That the nuns had fired him for other reasons. That they were biased against Latinos. That someone's brother had arrived from Ireland and needed a job. That once he'd laid eyes on Mama he'd never wanted anyone else.

Mama would just stand there, hand on waist and seductive little half-scowl on her face, till he ran out of things to say. And then she would pivot on one high heel and walk off into the other room, swaying her blue-jeaned hips. And he would follow her.

I eventually figured out that Mama wasn't actually worried about Joe. She just liked to see him jump. After all, what other postulant would have looked twice at him? He had to have been a good thirty years older than any of them. And he is absolutely to the left of zero in the good looks department.

No, only my disgraced, pregnant, sixteen-year-old Colombian-immigrant mother would have been desperate enough to put in all the effort to snag him. Just as only Joe would have been dumb enough to become so totally involved with my mother.

On certain rare occasions I would get a glimpse of the affection that might also have been a factor in Mama's calculations. She would run one hand softly across the back of Joe's neck in a way that was bound to send shivers down his spine. Or she would call him *"Manitas"*—Handyman—with a sly smile.

Mostly, however, she didn't bother with any of that extra stuff, at least in front of me. And I suspected that even the *"Manitas"* thing was more a reference to his professional skills than to what they did when they were alone.

But in the end, what does any of that matter? The main thing was that Joe remained obsessed with Mama no matter what she did, and that his *locura* stood me in good stead for a long time.

What I managed to piece together from the things they said to one another is that when Mama was kicked out of the convent, Joe found her a one-room apartment—Mama always called it "that rat hole"—in a building on Featherbed Lane where his cousin Felix was the super. ("All those damned Puerto Ricans are related," Mama liked to say.) Joe couldn't join her at first, owing to some complicated previous family *congojas*. But he paid the rent and brought her food and visited her often. And when Manny was born he brought over big boxes of diapers and formula and regular *ayuditas* of cash.

And finally, three years later, when I arrived and Joe managed to wriggle out of all his prior commitments and land the super's job at Essex Hill—that big gated apartment complex off of Bailey Avenue—he was able to move us all into the basement apartment that came with that position so I could be raised in what he termed "better circumstances."

Mama, of course, kept right on complaining. The place was too small for all of us. The walls were too thin. The roaches marched into her kitchen from the garbage room on our left. The fumes from the laundry room drifted into their bedroom whenever more than one washing machine was being used at a time.

And Joe would sigh and respond: "Well, Dolores, what can I do? Employers like Essex Hill like to stick you in a lousy dump like this instead of giving you a decent salary. Welcome to the U. S. of A."

Still, the place was clearly a lot better than the one on Featherbed Lane. And I, for one, thought it was great. Right outside the front door was a set of swings and slides and a jungle gym that I was allowed to play on, same as all the co-op owners' kids. It had two bedrooms and Joe built a partition down the middle of one of them so Manny and I could share quarters but each still have some privacy. The partition didn't quite reach the ceiling and only extended two-thirds of the width of the room. But that was part of its charm, as far as I was concerned. I learned a lot by listening to my brother talking with his friends. And even more by walking right up to the edge of the partition and sneaking a peek at what they were doing.

Manny and Joe were never close, though they had a kind of grudging mutual understanding. And who could blame them for their occasional quarrels since Manny clearly wasn't Joe's child? But Joe was always nice to me. He hauled me back and forth to all the babysitting arrangements that Mama put together. And when no babysitter was available, he let me trail along with him as he made his repair rounds. Unlike Mama (who mostly spoke Spanish at home) he only talked English with me and Manny. And he sat me in his lap each evening to teach me words from the *Daily News* comic strips while he puffed on his smelly cigar.

One day he arrived home with a big TV set. "This is America," he announced as he placed it on the table across from our couch with a grand flourish. "If you're a Latino you're a 'nobody.' And if you can't speak English you're *really* a 'nobody.' So start watching those cartoons, Baby. Listen up and learn!"

I could never decide whether Joe really thought I was his child or if he just hoped that doting on me would help bind him to my mother. He must have known that nothing could ever really tie my mother down. And he must have noticed that I looked nothing like him. People always said I looked just like my mother—that I had her coloring and her knock-out smile. I'm not bragging, it's just a fact. So basically, while he might have been my father, it could easily have been someone else.

But whatever the truth, when I was little Joe was my mainstay. And I took what I could from him with the surefooted ingratitude that comes with youth. At least he never insisted that I call him Daddy or Papito or anything like that. He was always just Joe.

The other thing Joe did was cook for us, and he was very, very good at it. I had assumed the arrangement would always remain like that. But one late afternoon when he picked me up from school he announced that things were going to change.

"Okay, Mamita," he said. "I'm tired of slaving alone in the kitchen after a day of fixing broken boilers and overflowing toilets. You're nine years old. That's old enough to hold a frying pan and a knife. Your Mama is useless. And your brother is never around. So that leaves only you to help me."

Cooking turned out to be a lot better than homework. I quickly learned the secrets of chopping onions without crying and of boiling beans till they are just soft enough to combine with *sofrito* and of frying platanos so they leak their sugary goodness without burning. I got really good at judging how much salt and achiote and tomato paste to throw into sizzling rice without a measuring spoon.

I found that it was fun. And that it had its benefits. Like the fact that whenever Joe left it all to me—which began happening more and more frequently over time—Manny would eat his fill, pat his stomach and say: "*All right*, Hermanita! You are one fabulous chef!"

In later years, cooking became a real lifeline for me. But at the time, it was just something I did that pleased my brother. Something that was expected of me.

Mama had her bartending job in a place on 199th Street off the Grand Concourse. She worked nights and slept during the day, which kept her out of my way most of the time.

Joe fixed apartments and was there if I needed him. Which wasn't very often, actually.

And I went to school and made dinner when I got home.

If Manny was around he would sometimes let me hang out with him once I'd cleared the table and cleaned up. Increasingly, however, he would escape to the streets as soon as he'd eaten. And I would go to bed and lie there till I heard the front door click and his familiar tread making its way back into our room.

And Joe would sit by the TV with his beer and cigars listening for the second door click that announced my mother's return.

I guess we both did a lot of waiting in those days, Joe and I.

2

Why my mother enrolled me at St. Gertrude's instead of letting me go to public school with Manny was beyond me at the time. You'd think she'd have had enough of nuns after her time at the Convent of Good Hope. It probably had to do with her wanting to keep me pure. Mostly, however, it just seemed to make me a thorn in her side.

"I work my butt off to pay for your school and how do you repay me? With lousy grades! With calls from Mother Antoinette about how you don't listen to the Sisters. Lazy brat!"

It didn't take me long to figure out that Mama was just being Mama. That what she was paying in tuition was next to nothing. That her boss, Kevin McCochrane, had somehow wrested a scholarship out of the nuns for Mama in return for favors unspecified.

The way I found out was through Juana—a Dominican girl who never smelled entirely clean and who was one of my only friends.

"You know that sign outside the school," she hissed at me one day. "The one that says: 'It's not because you're Catholic—it's because we are!'? That is such bullshit. They give scholarships to girls like us because they need someone to do the scut work! Think about it! Who's always assigned to empty the waste paper baskets and clean the blackboards? Hmm? Who gets the biggest number of red marks on their homework assignments? You, me, and Brenda Sullivan. The three girls on scholarship!"

"How do you know that?"

"Don't you know anything? Sister Harold told Brenda's mother during a teacher conference. She said we three had better do what we're told or we'd all end up in public school. But I wouldn't mind that, would you? No nuns!"

Juana and I began practicing small insurrections. We'd only dump half the waste paper baskets. Or we'd leave big streaks on the blackboards. Brenda—droopy-eyed coward that she was—wouldn't participate. But Juana and I steadfastly carried out our pact for several weeks, putting up with the yelling of our home room teacher, Sister Harold, and congratulating one another afterward.

Until they decided to bring out the big guns and Juana—big-mouthed Juana—buckled after a single session with our principal, Mother Antoinette.

And I discovered that I had a backbone.

Mother Antoinette's office was on the second floor of the school and smelled of detergent. It contained two small desks and one larger one. There were crucifixes over each small desk and over the big one was a picture of the Blessed Virgin Mary (the BVM, as we liked to call her) holding Baby Jesus with the phrase: "Heal us and we shall be healed, save us and we shall be saved" printed in curly letters in a garland that hovered over her head.

At one of the small desks sat Sister Bettina, Mother Antoinette's assistant, who didn't even glance up from her work when I arrived.

Mother Antoinette's desk—the big one, I presumed—was covered with papers.

The third desk was empty.

"So, Rodriguez," Mother Antoinette intoned. "I hear you have been insolent yet again. Oh, yes, I know it isn't the first time. Sister Harold is a patient woman, but enough is enough. Refusing to do your job? Arrogance is a sin, Rodriguez. Come here."

I walked over to her slowly.

"Put your hands on the desk."

"What?"

"Now."

I placed one hand down and looked up at her.

"Sweet Jesus! Who bred such insolence into you? Both hands. On the desk. Palms up. Now!"

Five swift swipes with a yard stick. Mostly on my left hand. Not enough to disable me. Just enough to make a point. There had been some whispers around school that beating was against the law now—not that Mother Antoinette would have cared or that any of the parents would have put up a fuss. Mama certainly wouldn't have said anything. She regularly beat me, herself, except that she generally used a leather belt.

"Now sit and do your homework till that father of yours arrives," Sister Antoinette concluded, placing the yardstick carefully back in the closet and wiping her hands. "No kickball for you today. And tomorrow you'll empty every wastebasket in every classroom on your floor. Alone."

"He isn't my father," I said, *sotto voce*, as Mother Antoinette strode out of the room. And then I stood by the desk for a good long while, looking at my palms. Just as I'd feared, the welts on the left hand were steadily deepening in color and would probably be even more painful on the following day. At least that was the way it worked with my mother's whippings.

"And I don't have to clean out your goddamn wastebaskets."

I stood catching my breath. It was a windy late afternoon in mid-November. The clouds were speeding across the autumn sky and the branches of the big oak tree in front of the school kept banging up against the window pane. I could see Montefiore Hospital across the street. I glanced at my hands again and unexpectedly found myself wondering whether Mama had been beaten a lot at the Convent of Good Hope. She'd been an even bigger rebel than I was, after all. Had the nuns hit her as hard as Mother Antoinette had hit me? Had they whipped her belly when they'd learned she was pregnant? Had she learned just how to beat me at the hands of those good Sisters?

"You might want to start with your math homework," said a soft voice behind me. "Math is my forte, so you can ask me for help. I know some good tricks, if you need them."

I turned around to find myself unexpectedly swaddled in the gaze of Mother Antoinette's assistant, Sister Bettina.

"No thanks. I'm okay with math." I wasn't, in fact, but why did she have to know that?

"Well then, would you like a mint?"

I looked away.

"Hmm?"

I turned back. She had a face like the moon. Round and pale with tiny oval glasses.

"A mint?"

I walked over to her, looked down into her open pink palm, took the lifesaver she was offering and put it in my mouth. It was prickly and tasteless at the same time. Then I walked slowly back to the empty small desk. I looked down at my hands again and—as much to myself as to her—said: "And how am I supposed to do my math if all my stuff is still downstairs?"

Sister Bettina stood up. She was tiny, like her glasses. "You're in Sister Harold's room, right? I'll go get it for you. You'd best not be seen wandering through the halls right now."

And that's how I found yet another reason to rebel. I refused to do wastebasket duty on three separate occasions over the next two weeks. I endured Mother Antoinette's castigations—once on my wrist, once on my left shoulder, and once (like my mother) across the small of my back. Because after I'd received my blows, I could accept a mint from Sister Bettina's soft, soft hand and sit in that quiet space nursing my wounds and sucking slowly on her gift.

"You know, you don't have to endure punishment for the privilege of sitting in this office," Sister Bettina finally told me. "Unless you like to suffer. Some of our girls do. But you don't strike me as the type. You could even begin behaving like a total angel while I arrange for you to come here every afternoon to do your homework. Or do you really love kickball?"

"No way," I said, practically dancing with joy. "Colleen Fitzpatrick always slams the goddamn ball into my stomach."

Sister Bettina didn't blink.

I'd like to say that I became a model student. It didn't exactly happen like that. I didn't see much point in learning till much later in life, under very different circumstances. But I did, at least, begin dumping the wastebaskets without protest. And my grades went up a small notch. And true to her word, Sister Bettina fixed it so I could sit with her every day after classes.

Besides asking me whether I wanted a mint, Sister Bettina rarely spoke without my speaking first. She never asked me pesky questions about my home life or how my day had gone. She just sat there doing whatever it was she did at her desk with the slanted late-afternoon sun rays slowly fading away. At first, I sometimes asked for help with my math just for the pleasure of hearing that melodious voice and having her lean over my desk. But after a while I stopped. I found that all I wanted was to sit near her, inhaling the peace that she exuded like perfume.

So it took me by complete surprise the day she folded those little hands over her desk, turned toward me and said: "Paloma. Tell me. Who *is* that man who picks you up if he's not your father?"

"He's the super in our building."

No reaction.

"He's my mother's lover."

No reaction. Not even a raised eyebrow. "And your mother?"

"My mother?"

"Why doesn't she pick you up? What does she do during the day?"

"She's a bartender at Malachy's Bar & Grill on East 199th Street. She does the night shift and then sleeps all day. So it's Joe who takes care of me, mostly."

"Ah." Sister Bettina looked at me. "Ah. Well then, we do have something in common, you and I. I kind of suspected that we did. My mother also drank for a living."

"Mama's no drunk! She just works there." *Doesn't she?*

"Oh? Well, perhaps you're right."

We sat in silence. It was not, however, uncomfortable. Nothing with Sister Bettina was ever uncomfortable.

Finally Sister Bettina made a little noise. A little sigh.

"So," she said. "Does she spend any time with you, your mother? Does she ever take you anywhere, just the two of you?"

It wasn't something I'd thought about very often.

"Well," I finally said. "Well, last summer, she took me to Loehmann's on one of her days off."

"Loehmann's?"

Didn't she know about Loehmann's? Doesn't every woman in the Bronx know about Loehmann's? Though of course, as I thought about it for a moment, why on earth would a nun know anything about the best clothing store on earth?

I grinned to myself at that sudden insight and went on.

"Oh, yeah, I guess you wouldn't know about Loehmann's would you? Well, Loehmann's is this clothing store down on Broadway near Van Cortlandt Park. You know the Park, right? Anyway, Mama took me there one Monday last summer to buy a fancy dress for a wedding she had to go to."

"And what is Loehmann's like?"

"Well, it's really enormous inside. It has rows and rows and rows of clothes. You've never seen so many clothes. And it has this huge dressing room at the back, where all the women try things on."

Where all the women get naked. But that I didn't say.

For suddenly, my mind was swamped by that confusing thing. That confusing memory about what had happened on that day when that one particular woman had stood right in front of me and Mama, and had taken off everything, even her brassiere.

And shown me those enormous breasts. Those breasts that seemed to float straight at me, so big and white and with those pink, pink nipples. Those breasts that—oh my God—what had I wanted to do with those breasts? Touch them? Something else?

I winced as I remembered all that stuff, sitting in Sister Bettina's office. I may not have been a particularly good Catholic, but I sure knew sin when I felt it.

And I must have blushed as well.

"And are there other times?" asked Sister Bettina, finally interrupting my guilty reverie.

"Other times when what?" I stuttered. Had she been reading my thoughts?

"Other times when your mother spends time with you? Does she ever take you to work with her, for example?"

"Well, not anymore," I said, glad to be thinking about something besides that day at Loehmann's. "I can stay at home by myself at night, now that I'm in fifth grade. But when I was smaller and Joe was away…she couldn't just leave me alone all night, I guess. She could do it with my brother Manny. He's older than me, and…well…he's a boy."

I couldn't have said then—and I definitely can't remember now—how often she'd actually taken me with her. It had to have happened more than once. Joe must have been out of the house at night from time to time. She might well have brought me and maybe even Manny to the bar a lot when we were young enough to be put down to sleep on a blanket in the back while she worked.

But on that late winter afternoon, as I sat there with Sister Bettina gently prodding me, only one specific memory of being at the bar with Mama came rushing back.

And it was an even more distressing memory than the one about Loehmann's.

What was it about Sister Bettina? What was her power that she could ask me those questions so calmly and sweetly and stir up such terrible recollections?

Mama's bar was on a side street right off the Grand Concourse that was otherwise residential—all six-story red brick apartment houses. I remember that it was really cold and really dark. The City doesn't bother maintaining the lights on the side streets of certain neighborhoods of the Bronx. The only illumination, therefore, came from the big green, white and orange neon sign over the door that spelled out: "Malachy's Bar and Grill."

I was very excited. I was almost never out that late.

Mama opened the front door and we stepped inside. I remembered that there were men everywhere, sitting and standing. And that almost every man was smoking. The place was thick with cigarette smoke.

Mama and I walked to the far end of the bar where there was still one empty stool. She unbuttoned my coat, pulled it off me and stuck it on the ledge under the bar. Then she lifted me up by the armpits and put me on that empty bar stool. I felt really embarrassed and angry. I must have been at least eight. Too old to be undressed by my mother. Too old to be placed on a stool like a baby.

As soon as I was seated, the man next to me leaned over very close and said: "Well, little girl, you here for the ride, tonight? These bar stools are magic. You can spin around and around on them. I do it all the time." And then he showed me how he did it in slow motion, grinning to show the ugly gaps in his teeth.

I didn't spin. I didn't want anything to do with him. Any more than I wanted anything to do with my mother. Not that it would have mattered if I had. She was already too occupied with other things to pay me much mind.

As soon as we'd entered, a few of the men had left their posts and begun walking toward us. And as soon as I was seated, one of them came right up close to Mama, helped her out of her coat and put his arm around her waist. She pushed his arm away, but she was laughing as she did it.

The bartender who worked the shift before Mama's was a big blond woman. She had large hands with deep red nails and a cigarette hanging from her lips. She was carefully wiping down the bar all the time that this was going on and appeared to see and hear nothing.

Eventually, however, my mother reached out and rapped on the bar and she looked up. Mama pointed her thumb at me and said: "Keep an eye on her, won't you Rosie? I've got something to do before my shift officially starts."

And then Mama and that man—the one who had taken off her coat and put his arm around her—went into the room at the back of the bar and closed the door behind them.

Rosie didn't look at me directly at first. She did, however, put her cigarette down in a black ash tray for a minute and begin filling a plastic cup with maraschino cherries. Then she filled a second cup with orange slices and a third one with little paper parasols.

She put the three cups down on the dark, stained wood in front of me, picked up her cigarette again, looked at me at last and said: "Here, Honey. You can play with these till your Mom comes back."

I took the orange slices out of the cup and placed them directly on the wooden surface. I looked up to see whether it would make Rosie angry, but she didn't seem to be paying any attention. And the man sitting next to me was now too deeply involved in his drink to have anything further to do with me. So I put a cherry on top of each of the slices. I stuck a parasol in each cherry to create a fleet of little boats and then shifted them around in different patterns on the bar-counter sea.

I must have arranged and rearranged them four or five times, leaving trails of red and orange food dye on the wood beneath.

But then I got bored and began to eat them. I ate every last cherry and every last orange slice. Flesh, rinds (even though the rinds really made my lips burn)—everything but the cherry stems. I began pushing my fingers around in the puddle of syrup that the fruit left behind on the wood and then sucking on those fingers, one by one, to get the syrup off. Rosie and the man at the bar remained uninterested. Maybe they just didn't see what a mess I was making.

Finally, my mother came back. She didn't notice the mess, either.

"You must be tired, Paloma," she said. "It's so late. Why don't you just put your head down on the wood of the bar and take a little nap while I work?"

But I wasn't going to lay my face down in all that mucky syrup. Instead, I sat up even straighter. And then, suddenly, all those cherries and oranges and all that syrup and smoke—and all that Mama must have been doing in that back room, whatever it was—got to me. I leaned over and was sick all over the bar.

Rosie was forced to stay on past her shift while Mama took me home. And once Mama got me home, she'd beaten me hard.

Sister Bettina had said absolutely nothing while I plunged back into all those memories. But she must have been watching my face closely. And it must have been showing something. For when she finally spoke to me, her voice was very kind.

"And so, Paloma," she said. "Tell me. Do you pray?"

"We pray three times a day, Sister."

"No, I mean you, personally. Do you pray? Is that where you get your strength?"

"Uh, I don't know what you mean."

"I find," said Sister Bettina, "that it's sometimes hard to pray to Jesus."

I looked up to see if she was kidding. But her expression was totally serious.

"I generally prefer praying to the Blessed Virgin."

I glanced up at the picture with the curly writing. It was not much of a work of art. Even I could tell that. It looked as if it had been cut out from a calendar. There was one like it in the local pizzeria.

"Sometimes for women like us—women who never had much of a mother—it's nice to pray to another woman," she said, dreamily. "You should try it some time."

3

By the time I was in sixth grade, I was not only staying home alone at night when necessary, I was making my own way home from school every day. Joe was around much less, in general. Wednesday nights, in particular, were his nights to go bowling and he was never home before ten. Dinner, therefore, was entirely up to me. And Manny began bringing his friends over to take advantage of my skills.

"Hey, Hermanita, can you handle a few more mouths to feed?"

Of course, I could. I loved his friends. I loved it that they ate my food and asked for seconds. That they didn't mind me hanging around them, listening to them curse and smoke and talk about girls. Chico was small and skinny and smoked the most. Bernie was fat and slow and drank the most. And Fernando was dark and lean and had muscles that showed through his T-shirts. Several girls in the neighborhood credited him with giving them babies. He tossed their names around but didn't really seem too interested in them.

One day I walked in from school to find the three friends already seated at the kitchen table and Manny leaning over Fernando with the closest thing to concern that I'd ever seen on his face.

"Hermanita, hurry up and give this poor man some food. He's in a bad way."

"Shit, Manny," said Fernando. "No food. Just another beer. I can't eat, man, I'm in pain."

"What? What's wrong?"

"Stay clear, Hermanita. Just go mind the stove. You're too pure for this."

There's nothing worse than telling me not to do something. I ran over to see what Manny was staring at. The top of Fernando's head was gashed down the middle—a purple, pus-filled stripe wending its way down a mass of black-and-blue flesh.

"Oh my God! What happened?"

"It's better than it was yesterday, but I keep seeing double and the pain is a bitch-and-a-half."

"*What happened?*"

"His old man whacked him with a baseball bat."

I leaned over. "You should go to the emergency room. It looks infected."

"Fuck emergency rooms. If I tell them what happened, they'll send the child welfare police to my house and that would be even worse than my father."

"Well, at least let's put some alcohol on it. Manny?"

"What alcohol? We have no alcohol in this house."

"So I'll use some beer."

"Shit, that's funny," said Bernie, giggling. "Why didn't I think of that? Give me some more beer, too. Internal medicine."

"No really, Manny," I said. "Give me some beer to use on this thing."

He handed me his open bottle. I tipped some onto a napkin and carefully swabbed Fernando's head. Fernando winced and then relaxed.

"Hey, you've got some touch, Paloma."

My brother sprang up. "Don't even think about it, shit-head."

"Shush, Manny," I ordered. "Shush, Fernando. Let me just look at this." I concentrated on the gash and imagined what it might feel like. I stroked it with the tip of my finger. And then, very softly, I said the Blessed Virgin's words. "Heal me and I'll be healed. Save me and I'll be saved."

"Jesus, Hermanita. Those nuns have you brainwashed."

"Shut up, Manny," said Fernando.

"What?"

"Shut up, Manny. It feels better. Shit, Paloma! You've got healer's hands, you know that? Touch me again. *Shut up, Manny. I mean it.* All I want is for her to touch my head. I'd never hurt your sister."

But at that moment, the kitchen door opened and in walked an apparition. Mama is usually long gone by the time Manny's crew arrives but evidently this day she was on a later shift. Sleep-blurred, one strap of her nightgown hanging off her shoulder— brushing a hank of night-black hair off her face with one hand— she looked like a young girl. Well, she really wasn't that much older than Manny when you come right down to it.

"Well-well-well, what do we have here?" When she spoke Spanish, her voice would go a good half-octave lower than when she was struggling through English. Sometimes it got so sultry that I thought Joe would melt. "A whole collection of young studs right in my own kitchen. You never told me you bring all these handsome men into the house when I'm away, Manuel. How long has this been going on?"

She strutted directly over to Fernando, swinging those hips. "And who's this particularly gorgeous thing with my slutty little daughter's hands on his head?" She winked at Fernando and then, in a switch so smooth it took my breath away, she reached over to pinch my shoulder hard between her thumb and middle finger and hiss: "I didn't realize you were growing up so fast, Palomita. I hope you're not getting any ideas, *muchachita!*"

And then she slapped me.

Manny had leapt up as soon as he saw Mama moving toward me and managed to swipe at her arm as she swung. But his reaction was too late and her palm made solid, noisy contact with my cheek.

He did, however, finally manage to grab her by the wrist and yank her sharply away from me. And as she stumbled sideways she looked down and caught sight of Fernando's wound.

"Oh my God—ugh! What's all this?"

No one answered. Mama regained her balance. And then Manny sat down again heavily and cleared his throat.

"Okay, guys," he said in a voice that held just the slightest trace of menace. Or maybe it was shame. It was one thing to experience my mother when it was just us. Quite another to deal with her when other people were watching. To realize how she must look to them. "Time to get out of here. And Mama—time for you to get dressed and go to work."

Manny's friends stood up in a single motion and made their way to the door. But once they got there, Fernando turned briefly back around again and offered me a little half-bow and one of those grins that made all those other girls swoon.

Well, hell, his father had just smacked him on the head with a baseball bat. I guess he understood about parents.

4

In the picture that I kept—God knows why—of my 8th grade graduation from St. Gertrude's, I'm sitting between Mama and Joe, and Manny is nowhere to be found. Mama is in a purple pant suit and a white blouse with a big bow and she is smiling as wide as can be. Even when she is in a rotten mood, she remembers to flash her dimples for the camera. And on that day, she was positively twitchy with excitement.

Joe is in a black shiny suit with his tie tied too tight and an even tighter expression on his face. He has bad teeth and is very self-conscious about smiling. I am looking uncomfortable, still in my graduation gown. The cap that I had tossed in the air at an earlier point in the day is back on my head, as per Joe's request. We're in a dark red crescent-shaped booth with a big Red Lobster logo on the wall behind us.

Joe tipped the waiter immediately when he took the picture—tipped him well—and then ordered margaritas for Mama and himself, a Shirley Temple for me, and butterfly shrimp appetizers for everyone.

"We'll live it up, since we've all got things to celebrate," he said, taking the Instamatic camera back from the waiter and handing it to me. "Here, Paloma. You can have it. Use the rest of the roll for your own pictures. Big things ahead."

The drinks came, the shrimp platters came, and not ten minutes later we had that fight that left me pushing Mama out of the way and hysterically dashing toward the door.

"Let her be," was the last thing I heard from Mama as she resumed her seat and took a swig from her glass. "She's pretty emotional right now."

5

The graduation itself had been staged for maximum drama. It took place in the church of St. Nicholas of Tolentine—the Cathedral of the Bronx, as it is known. A fat sweating Monsignor conducted a ten o'clock mass. Seventy-five fourteen-year-old girls decked out in nylon gowns of St. Gertrude's cobalt blue knelt for Holy Communion with their two hundred very dressed-up family members following close on their heels. We heard speeches about how these had been the best years of our lives and speeches about how the best years of our lives were still ahead of us. We chirped through the school song. And then we lined up to receive a blessing, a hearty handshake and a diploma before rushing down to our beaming relatives and beginning our lives for real.

When they got to the "R"s and my name was called, I walked up briskly. Mother Antoinette gave me a hard look and an even harder handshake—we'd settled into a kind of peaceful coexistence over the years—and I accepted the diploma she gave me as quickly as I could and descended the steps to my abbreviated group of kin. Gradually, the crowd made its way toward the church vestibule and out the front door. Juana hugged me shyly and a number of other girls said goodbye. And that was that.

Here's the truth: I had never really clicked with that crowd.

It wasn't the fact that I was on scholarship. As it turned out, there were a lot more kids in my position than I'd thought. And every student—scholarship and non-scholarship alike—was assigned to a few months of cleaning blackboards and dumping waste paper baskets at some point. So it was simply Juana stirring up trouble when she said it was just her, me, and Brenda doing all the dirty work.

Nor was the exclusion due to my peculiar family situation. Very few students actually had two married parents, though most had substantial extended families of one sort or another and almost no one had a mother as totally uninvolved as mine. And I never really was bullied. Not like poor Juana. I was actually accorded a kind of respect after word got out that I hadn't cried over Mother Antoinette's lashings. And once I started working with Sister Bettina, my math abilities caught up with my English skills and I swam along in the middle of the grade academically, attracting neither accolades nor reprimands.

No, it was just that I kept to myself. I never seemed to get into the fads that swept through the grade each year. Not kickball nor My Little Ponies. Not Barbies. Not hiking up my plaid skirt as high as possible as soon as we left the premises. Or seeing just how much jewelry I could get away with before the nuns began preaching about vanity and confiscating everything.

Most of all, I never found myself giggling over the boys at St. Michael's—our brother school. And I never made a chewing gum wrapper chain to give to that one special boy.

No, all I really wanted was to sit in Sister Bettina's office and then go home and make dinner for Manny and his friends and laugh at their jokes and scold them for their escapades and then retire to my room.

And when Sister Bettina was transferred to a Yonkers school at the mid-point of my graduation year ("The Archdiocese is a goddam corporation, same as any other," Joe had commented when I told him. "What do you expect?"), all I wanted to do was go straight home.

And finally, when Manny began working in Fernando's father's auto shop and coming home for dinner less and less frequently, all I really wanted to do was to sulk.

And so I sat through the graduation ceremony stony-faced, waiting for it to be over and praying that Mama wasn't hung-

over or saying inappropriate things to the other mothers. She
had gotten only four hours sleep that night, after all. She hated
churches. And she got really nervous in most social situations.

"So," said Joe, as we sat in our booth, picking at our
celebration lunch. He was really nervous too, for some reason—
sweating worse than the Monsignor as he twirled his margarita
glass back and forth in his hands. "So, I've been offered a new
job." He dipped into the drink and then put it down. Mama put
one hand on his. "I'm going to be the caretaker at a fancy hotel
in the Catskills. It comes with an apartment."

"A very small apartment," said Mama.

"And it also comes with a salary high enough so your mother
won't have to work anymore and can finally begin taking care of
herself."

I had no idea where he was going with this but I knew I didn't
like what I was hearing.

"Manny is going to go live with Fernando. He spends all his
time there, anyway."

"His dear little friend, Fernando," said Mama.

"And you…."

"And I?"

"Are going to live with your grandmother."

"What grandmother?"

"Your grandmother Isabel. My mother. In Antioquia."

"In *Colombia*?"

"Well, Paloma, you're a big girl now. Too big, if you ask me."
Mama picked up a shrimp and nibbled at it. "Don't think we
haven't noticed the way you can't keep your hands off Manny's
friends. Though it seems he's not letting you do that so much
anymore. But who knows when you'll start hitting the streets?
Getting yourself in trouble. Lord knows, we don't need another
mouth to feed."

I couldn't digest any of this. The main points kept sloshing
over my head. Instead, I remained stuck on the stupid details.

"I thought you hated your mother! I thought you never spoke to her. I thought you never wanted to go back there."

"It's true, I don't speak to her. It costs a fortune to call Colombia. And I certainly don't want to go back there. But I do write to her from time to time. Send her little *ayuditas* on the off-chance that I might need to cash in on her good will someday. Like now."

I finally pulled my thoughts together and got to the core of things.

"But I don't want to go. I'll hate it there. I'm an American! I'm going to De Witt Clinton High School, like Manny did. I'm not going to some third-world country. I'll run away!"

"Paloma, be reasonable," said Joe. "Manny dropped out of De Witt Clinton. It's become a lousy school. And we can't keep paying for a parochial education."

"And you have nowhere else to go," said Mama, shrugging.

"We can't bring you with us, Honey," said Joe. "When I told them that we had a teenager they said that bringing you was out of the question. It's just a tiny apartment in the back of the hotel lobby. And we have to live there so I can be available whenever they need me. No, your mother and I have to go alone. This is my big chance. This is your mother's big chance."

"Yeah, but it's not *my* big chance! You're ruining everything! God, I hate you! I hate both of you! And you are really, really stupid, Joe, if you think Mama's going to get better in the mountains doing nothing all day! She just wants to be in a fancy hotel so she can meet some fancy new man."

"Paloma, that's no way to talk about your mother."

"Joe! How can you be so blind? She's got you…she's got you by the…." But I couldn't say it. He'd always been kind to me.

Still, why wasn't he standing up for me? And how could he be so stupid about my mother?

And where the hell was Manny? Why had everyone deserted me?

6

I went where I always went when I needed to think: Orchard Beach. You walk along Fordham Road to the bus stop and wait for the Bx 12. There's a street vendor in front of the bus stop selling mango slices doused in salt and hot sauce that I normally find irresistible. But this time I had no appetite. I took off my blue nylon graduation robe, balled it up and threw it in a garbage can along with the cap. It was all rented. Let Mama pay for replacing it.

I fished my MetroCard out of the pocket of the jeans I'd been wearing underneath the robe and pulled the hood of my sweatshirt over my head. I rode the bus out in silence, my fist pressed up against my mouth.

That beach has never failed to soothe me. It was unusually blustery for late May, so the whole place was practically empty. I walked the length of the section that Manny and I and Fernando usually hung out in (the "young people's" section as it's called) where you can smoke and blast music and toss garbage on the sand without worry. It looked completely different than it would a scant few weeks later when everything would be jumping. But some things were the same. The rolling waves. The gulls swooping here and there. The garbage cans bobbing in the water. The bathrooms with the drippy sinks and the rolls of sodden toilet paper unfurling on the ground.

I bought a coke from the single concession stand that was open that early in the season—I was suddenly thirstier than I'd ever been in my life—and walked and drank and thought.

When Sister Bettina left St. Gertrude's, I'd thought I would die. She'd told me before she told any other student. That much she gave me. But still I cried bitterly.

"I have to go where my calling takes me, Paloma," she'd said, looking at me with that peaceful face that had always calmed me down but was now making me frantic. "I don't expect you to accept it right now, but some day you will. And know that I'll always remember you, Paloma. I'll always pray for you. And the Virgin will always be there for you. You are a very strong girl, and I expect to hear great things from you."

What kind of answer was that? She was my mother, my sister, my friend, my protector. How could she be so blasé about breaking my heart? For several months I mourned.

And then there was Manny spending all his time in the *Los Milagros* Auto Shop. "Hey, Hermanita. This is a way out for me, don't you see? I can't keep wasting my time in school. I can make some real money this way. I'm really good at it. Even Fernando's sonofabitch father says so."

So this was the last straw, for sure.

And yet.

As I paced my mind whirled. Maybe it was all for the best after all. Maybe I was better off without with my mother and that dumb old fool, Joe. And who wants to live in upstate New York—the middle of nowhere? It couldn't be any worse in Colombia. Manny I would miss. I'd miss him with all my heart. But everything else? The hell with it. I'd go.

7

Still, I had scores to settle.

Manny was home when I got there and Mama and Joe had the good sense not to be. I lit into him.

"Where the hell were you? Why didn't you come to my graduation? Why weren't you there when they told me they were shipping me out? You knew, didn't you? And you never told me!"

"Yes, yes, Hermanita. 'Yes' to everything. Shit, Paloma. I just couldn't sit there while you were getting your diploma, knowing what was coming."

I'd never seen him look so sheepish, and I played it for all it was worth.

"Coward! Coward! You may have fourteen-inch biceps but you're nothing but a coward! I needed you, you sonofabitch, and you weren't there!"

"Hey," he said, catching me by the arm and looking at me with those big black eyes of his. "Hey. I'm here now. And I'm the one driving you to the airport tomorrow."

"Tomorrow!"

"Yeah, Hermanita. Tomorrow. Well, what is it that Joe always says? You've got to pull off the Band-Aid in one motion? The flight won't take off till late, but I'm going to have to drive you out first thing in the morning so I can get back to work on time. And it's not like you have a whole lot of people to say goodbye to before you leave."

I winced.

"Anyway, everything is ready. That passport that Joe got you last winter? All that talk about a family vacation in Aruba? He was already bargaining for the job at that point. There's nothing you can do. Nothing. *Nada.* It's a done deal. But cheer up.

Fernando is driving out with us. He's the one who can swipe the car from his Dad's shop. He's the one with the license, in case we need to switch seats all of a sudden. And he wants the chance to say goodbye to you, too. You're his favorite girl, he says."

"Yeah, right. What he means is I'm the only one who isn't jumping into bed with him."

"He likes that, Hermanita. He respects that. Plus, he knows I'd beat him black-and-blue if he ever tried anything with you."

We were silent for a good long time while I worked up the courage to ask what I'd been aching to ask him for so long.

"Okay, Manny. Answer me this. Is Mama right? Am I a *putita* because I like to hang out with you and Fernando?"

"A *putita*? Don't make me laugh, Baby. You—a *putita*? You're one of the guys. No, Baby, what you are is an *arepera*."

"What the hell are you saying, Manny?"

"Come on, Hermanita. The fact that you've never actually fallen for Fernando? That crush you had on that dried up old nun of yours? It's clear as day. You like girls."

I felt a shock wave flooding me from top to toe. Oh. Oh. Oh. Oh my God.

"Okay, Hermanita. Enough talk. Let's get you packed. Fortunately, you don't have too much stuff. I'm giving you the duffle bag Joe bought me when he thought the only thing I was good for was the army. It should all fit. Let's go."

We walked into the room and began piling things on top of the bed. I was still in a daze—a triple or quadruple daze—but he was right. It had to be done.

"Hey, what's this?" His foot had hit a shoe box.

"Nothing," I said, kicking it back under the bed.

"Hey—no, really. What is it?"

"It's nothing, Manny. It's garbage. Let me take it into the kitchen and throw it out."

"No way, Hermanita. You're blushing bright red. What is it? Dirty pictures?"

"Hell, no Manny. Give it to me! Give it to me!"

He pried it away from me and opened it up. Twenty-five Milky Way candy bars, still in their wrappers, stacked in neat rows in a shoe box.

"What the fuck is this? Is this what you do with the treats I bring you every week? Are you some kind of nut case?"

I closed my eyes.

"Answer me! I spend my money bringing my little sister the thing she likes best to eat and she sticks it in a goddam box? Don't tell me you're on a diet—I'll kill you. Your new curves are nice, even if they're going to go to waste."

"No, it's not a diet."

"What then? Paloma! What then?"

"I…I gave them up."

"Yeah, duh. Gave them up, why?"

"I…I promised the Virgin I would never eat another Milky Way if she would only bring Sister Bettina back to St. Gertrude's."

I thought Manny would explode. He grabbed me by the arm again—hard—and slapped my face.

"You idiot! Doesn't God send us enough sacrifices without you giving up something you really love for the goddam Virgin? Don't we have it hard enough? Aren't Latinos treated like shit in this city? Don't we have a fucking drunk for a mother? Aren't I losing the sister that I love so much? Idiot! Idiot!"

He was holding me for all he was worth, and—yes—he was crying. I let him collect himself. I forgave him for the slap. I forgave him for not going to my graduation. Manny really loved me! Manny was going to miss me. Nothing else mattered.

Finally he drew back but kept holding both my hands tightly.

"Paloma, promise me something! Promise me that you'll

never again make a goddam sacrifice that you don't have to make! Promise me that when someone offers you something nice you'll grab it with both hands! And that you'll enjoy every bit of it! Promise me!"

"Okay, Manny. I promise."

8

Serach once told me that the hardest thing about her first transfusion was how cold we kept the procedure room. She said that something about that cranked-up blast of air-conditioning froze her through and through. And that the uncontrollable chattering of her teeth frightened her even more than the thought of the needle or the idea of being infused with a stranger's blood. Even more than the cancer itself.

I shivered a bit myself when she told me that. It struck a chord. For as soon as the delight of Manny and Fernando's big farewells had ebbed from my mind, it was the airplane's bone-chilling cold that most occupied my thoughts. The three one-hundred-dollar bills that my brother had pressed into my hand before I left did nothing to warm me up. The cardboard-like blanket that the flight attendant handed me was of no use. I shook all the way from New York to Medellín.

When we disembarked the next morning, we passed briefly through some deliciously humid tropical air on the tarmac only to be quickly reembraced by refrigeration once we filed back inside the airport itself. I figured I would never warm up again till I got outside for good so I rushed at top speed through Baggage Claim and Customs and onto the curb where—as Manny had promised—someone was waiting with a big paper sign that I couldn't miss.

"Rodriguez." My mother's name. My name. The name that had journeyed from Spain to Colombia to the Bronx and then made its way half-way home again. I finally caught the eye of the woman holding the sign aloft only to see her drop it to the ground with a yell and begin crossing herself frantically.

"*Oye!*" I called out in my best Bronx Spanish. I ran up to her and put a hand on her small shoulder. "*Oye*, it's me. Paloma. Are you all right?"

"Ay, *Dios santo*, you gave me such a fright!" She took a moment to catch her breath and then looked at me with wide eyes. "It was Dolores coming back here like she never left! Dolores all over again!"

"Oh. Yeah. They say I look just like my mother."

She closed her eyes and heaved a few deep shuddering sighs. Then she picked up the sign, folded it up and put it carefully into the large woven bag that she was carrying. "Well, I'm Carolina. And I'm here to take you to Doña Isabel's house."

I followed her as she moved steadily forward through the crowd, still shaking her head. "I'm going to have to warn Doña Isabel," she kept muttering. "She'll faint if I don't warn her."

Carolina was heavy and short. Her hair was greying and trailed behind her in a long braid and she was wearing a faded blue-flowered dress, an off-white sweater and tan and red sneakers.

"This way, this way," she said, leading me briskly to the bus stop. "We take the number 47 bus into town and then we catch another bus to Santa Fe de Antioquia." She didn't offer to help me with my ungainly duffle bag nor did she glance back at any point to see how I was doing as I straggled along behind her. And when we sat side by side on that long two-part ride, she said not a word. I caught her stealing a look at my face from time to time when she thought my attention was fixed on the lushness of the passing scenery. But she offered me no information whatsoever about where we were going or what we were seeing.

A taciturn type, I concluded. Wastes nothing. Does no more than she needs to. I was right on the last two counts, as it turns out. And I could be forgiven for my mistake about the first, under the circumstances.

When we finally dismounted from the second bus in Santa Fe de Antioquia, Carolina put her head down and began running. "Go! Go! Go! Don't stop! Don't look around! Just go!" she said as she flew down the streets with me in tow. "Keep your head down! Don't let anyone see you! Keep going!"

Why didn't she want anyone to see me? And didn't she realize how hard it was to sprint down two-foot-wide sidewalks and cobblestone streets with a sloppily-packed twenty-five pound duffle bag?

Fortunately, it was early morning Sunday so there were very few people out. And those who were out moved aside quickly as they saw me and my peculiar guide, barreling on through.

We finally arrived at a whitewashed two-story house with a heavy dark red door. Carolina pulled a massive key ring out of her bag and fiddled with the locks till they gave. She then shoved me in and slammed the door shut. "Wait here!" she said and ran deeper inside.

I inspected the corridor in which she had left me. It revealed nothing. Long tan walls. A worn wooden floor. I waited a scant minute and then pushed the door back open again to examine the streetscape.

My grandmother's residence was the fourth in a row of twelve nearly-identical houses facing the twelve nearly-identical houses on the opposite side of the street. Every house was two stories tall, immaculately whitewashed and banded at the bottom with a thick coat of shiny paint. Some of those bottom bands were dark red, some were dark green, and one lone band was cobalt blue.

Every second house had a wooden balcony at the second-floor level, and every balcony except the one on my grandmother's house was covered in magenta, red, or orange blossoms. The house in which I had been sent to live was the only one bare of all flowers, of all color—of all beauty.

I peered down the street and saw that all the houses ended abruptly at the foot of the block. Beyond that point the street turned into a road bordered by long expanses of dry grass, unkempt trees and piles of garbage. In the far distance was a vista of purple-green mountains.

My grandmother, it seems, lived on the very edge of a very, very small town.

I stood and sniffed the air—so different than anything I'd ever smelled. I caught flowers and fresh bread and something else undefined but pungent. How on earth was I connected to this place?

My reverie was interrupted by Carolina's hand reaching out from behind the door to drag me back inside. "What do you think you are doing?" she hissed. "Get back in here! Close that door! Doña Isabel will see you now."

Once again I trailed behind her. Her sneakers made no sound but my standard-issue parochial school oxfords creaked loudly on the wooden planks. We walked the length of the corridor through a parlor filled with heavy, velvet-covered furniture and into a room dominated by a single long dining room table. There was a wall of windows covered in some kind of translucent paper with patterns of faded red, green, and blue fleur-de-lis. Traces of light sifted in through the colors. It had been deliciously breezy and bright outside, but in here the air was dark and still. Were those windows sealed shut? I made out a print of the Last Supper over the dining room table and on the left-hand wall a single framed portrait of a swarthy man with features so ferociously haughty and cruel that they cut right through the dimness of the room.

"I see you are admiring *El Español*," said a voice rising out of a chair to my right. "As well you might."

"Doña Isabel's husband," said Carolina, nodding.

My grandfather.

I spun around to see who had spoken and beheld a delicate figure in a dark brown dress discreetly decorated with thin black stripes. The sleeves reached to her wrists, the bodice to her chin, and the skirt to her elegant little ankles. Her hands were folded in her lap and she was seated as upright as a stick in a narrow chair. Her skin was the color of very pale café con leche, her hair was snow white, and her features as fine as those of my grandfather were harsh.

"I've been debating what you should call me," said the woman, using the formal Spanish term for "you." "And have decided that 'Doña Isabel' is best."

I stood still taking in those words. I also had given the matter some thought. I liked "Abuelita" but a couple of my classmates called their grandmothers "Mamita," and I figured it wouldn't be terrible if that's what my grandmother preferred.

"It's truly incredible how much you look like Dolores," my grandmother continued. "I can't imagine hearing 'Abuela' from someone who looks so much like my daughter. And, of course, 'Mama Isabel' is out of the question. You already have a Mama."

What could I say?

"You do speak Spanish, don't you, Paloma? Your mother said so in her letter."

"Of course I speak Spanish."

"Good. That should make some things easier."

9

The school year in Colombia divides up differently than it does in the Bronx. Winter break is from mid-June through mid-July. Since I'd arrived at the very end of May, it seemed pointless to start classes. So I had six long weeks ahead of me. I figured it would take me about two and a half days to scout out all the streets. I wondered what I would do when I was finished.

Carolina installed me in one of the small upstairs bedrooms. It contained a tightly-made single bed, a wardrobe, a crucifix, and a window that opened onto the street, letting in the sounds of roosters, motorbikes, and church bells.

"Breakfast is at six," Carolina informed me on that first day. "Lunch is at noon. Doña Isabel prepares her own *cafecito* at four o'clock—you can join her if you like—and I serve soup at seven."

Breakfast was coffee and a roll that Carolina picked up from the bakery on her way to Doña Isabel's house. Lunch was a poached egg or a half a can of sardines with some pickled hot peppers and a few Maria crackers on the side. *Cafecito* was just that: a cup of coffee with a few more Maria crackers. And dinner was a bowl of watery vegetable soup. No wonder my grandmother was thin as a rail and pale as a ghost.

And worst of all, I was forced to eat in silence. The first time I tried to make conversation Doña Isabel told me: "I'm not really used to chit-chat during meals."

"I'll die if I have to keep eating like this," I told Carolina after two days of that nonsense.

"It is how *El Español* ate," Carolina explained. "He couldn't stand Colombian food."

"But he's dead. And Doña Isabel isn't Spanish—she's Colombian. Why doesn't she like the food of her own country? And why doesn't she talk during meals?"

"She got used to liking what *El Español* liked. And when he insisted on being served and then left alone, she got used to eating by herself as well."

And where was my mother during all those childhood meals?

"Carolina, do *you* like to eat what my grandmother eats?"

"No, of course not," Carolina said, patting her ample stomach. "I serve Doña Isabel her food and then run home to make my own lunch."

"And did my mother like it?"

There was a long pause and then: "No. She didn't. I used to cook for her separately, and we'd eat it together in the kitchen while your grandmother ate in the dining room and your grandfather took his nap." She gave a brief sweet smile—the first I'd seen on that sour little face. "She did like her rice and beans, your mother."

The smile gave me an idea.

"Carolina, can't you and I do that too? Can't we make rice and beans together and eat it in the kitchen, like you used to do with my mother?"

Carolina looked startled. I forged ahead.

"I can even do some of the cooking. Save you the work. I'm a whiz in the kitchen, you know. Come on, Carolina. We can leave my grandmother to her sardines and have some fun—like you and my mother did."

Carolina's expression kept evolving. Scared, then mortified, then shrewd and pleased. She'd come to a decision that made sense to her. "No," she said. "Doña Isabel would never permit it. We have our routines, you know."

Meanwhile, the overall bleakness of daily life was even worse than the tedium of the meals. After breakfast, Carolina and my grandmother would settle into what they called their "business"—washing and pressing priests' vestments for the four main local churches. They would stand side by side at the stone double sink in the laundry room scrubbing away together. Once they were done, they would leave the scrubbed robes in one of the sinks and go collect the robes they'd hung outside to dry the day before. My grandmother would then iron all the dry robes while Carolina hung the newly washed ones in their place and carefully folded each newly ironed robe and placed it in her big straw bag.

After Carolina made and served lunch, she would deliver the clean robes back to the churches, pick up the robes to be washed, go home for her own meal and do the marketing for the following day. And while she was gone, my grandmother would take her nap and read the newspapers over her *cafecito*.

Finally, at six-thirty, Carolina would come back to bring the next day's washing and groceries, make and serve dinner, give the house a final once-over and bid us good night. And my grandmother would settle in to an hour of mending vestments or embroidering new ones till it was time for her to go to bed.

And through all those dreary procedures, I would pace the house. Parlor, dining room, kitchen, and laundry room on the first floor. Three bedrooms—one of them locked up tight—and a bathroom on the second. Not a single book in the whole house except a battered bible that I spied on my grandmother's night table when I was snooping around. No TV. No pictures on the wall save the one of Jesus looking sadly across his own dining room table and that terrifying portrait of my grandfather.

Neither Doña Isabel nor Carolina offered to take me out to show me around the town. Neither one asked me a thing about me or Manny or our life in New York. Not one single question. Didn't they care?

On the afternoon of the third day—nearly exploding out of my skin—I ran downstairs and begged my grandmother to let me go out to explore things.

"I'd rather you didn't," she said.

"How am I supposed to improve what you call my 'gutter Spanish' if I don't go out and talk to people?"

She colored. "Perhaps if you offered to help us with the vestments instead of just mooning around the house all day you'd pick up some new words from us."

I'd had no idea that she'd had that expectation.

"I'd be glad to cook for you," I said. "But I'm not washing out any old priests' robes. And, what new words do you think I'll learn at the laundry room sink? 'Oh, what a terrible stain!'? 'Pass me the soap, please'? I know all those words already."

My grandmother gave me a very severe glance.

"Oh, c'mon, Doña Isabel! Give me a break, here. Give me one good reason why I can't go out."

She stared at me for a long moment. "You'll go out," she said. "In the proper time."

"Doña Isabel, *this* is the proper time. And I'm perfectly capable of taking care of myself—I've been doing it all my life. Let me at least go run some errands for you. Save Carolina the trouble."

She glared at me again. "I'm getting very impatient with you, Dolores," she said.

For once I didn't know what to answer.

10

The following morning, as soon as Carolina and Doña Isabel were safely installed at the double sink with their scrub brushes ("no washing machine could get these robes as white as our hands," my grandmother had retorted when I'd asked why she didn't just buy a machine and be done with it), I put the front door on the latch and snuck out.

I inspected a park with a fountain in which water spurted out of the beak of an iron crane with outstretched wings. I strolled into a supermarket—La Muísca it was called—whose neat shelves held stacks of the canned sardines and Maria crackers that Doña Isabel liked so much. I peered into what must have been the original central market, smelly and bustling under a metal roof. Its stalls of fresh vegetables and fruits and *arepas* and cheeses and sausages made me faint with desire.

And I observed the chaos I was causing.

There was no mistaking it. Everywhere I went people looked up at me with startled expressions, whispered to their companions or just plain stared. It was really unnerving.

I was just about to head back—to admit that I should never have gone out—when I caught sight of something so wonderful that my every discouraged thought vanished. A shop with a window display of hand-tooled cowboy boots.

Cowboy boots are Manny's favorite thing. For years he lusted after the carved leather, pointy-tipped high-heeled footwear of the Wild West. As soon as he started earning money at Fernando's father's auto shop, the first thing he did was save up for this pair of silver-studded boots that he'd once spied in a catalog.

I have no idea why he developed that passion. Certainly no one else I knew shared it. This was the Bronx after all, epicenter of sneaker obsession. Young men literally killed one another over a pair of Nike Air Max 97s. The first time Fernando saw Manny standing in our kitchen with his showy new boots he cuffed my brother on the head and said: "What the fuck are you doing with those things? Trying to look like a goddam Mexican?"

But Manny was not to be deterred. "Hey, I'm allowed. Better than trying to look like some idiot black basketball player."

And here I was in my mother's little home town gazing at boots more ornate and beautiful than my brother could ever have dreamed of. I just had to send him a pair of those boots! I walked into the shop and up to the counter where a thin man with salt-and-pepper hair and a stained apron was holding an awl.

"How much do you charge for your boots?" I asked.

"Dolores, as I live and breathe," said the man.

"No. Not Dolores. Paloma. Her daughter. Doña Isabel's granddaughter."

"I could have sworn you were Dolores," he said, gazing at me with an appreciation that bordered on the lecherous. "She liked cowboy boots, too. Or men in cowboy boots, anyway. What size do you wear?"

"Well, I was actually thinking of them for my brother, Manny. Dolores's son. Back in the Bronx."

"I see. And what are you doing here in Santa Fe de Antioquia, Mamita? And why did no one tell me you were here?"

"I only arrived on Sunday. And Doña Isabel has basically kept me a prisoner ever since."

"Yes, I can just picture her doing that. Well, can you really blame her after what she went through with your mother? Here she thinks she's home free and who shows up at her door but Dolores reincarnate? Of course she doesn't know what to do with you. She's terrified."

I looked at him for a long moment. He looked reasonable, despite the hint of lecherousness. And he was actually quite handsome for an old guy. I'd take a chance.

"So…you knew my mother," I said. "What was she like when she was young?"

"Well," he said, leaning his head back. "For starters, she was the most beautiful girl in Santa Fe de Antioquia. Perhaps in the whole province. God, she was lovely." He put down the awl and rubbed his hands together. "And then, yes, she was wild," he added, putting his hands back down on the counter, palms down. "But no wonder. The poor kid practically raised herself. No supervision whatsoever. Doña Isabel stuck in bed with miscarriages and *jaquecas* half the time. They say it's why she had only the one daughter. And why she had her so late in life."

"*Jaquecas?*"

"Headaches so blinding she couldn't get out of bed. Headaches accompanied by stomach pain so fierce she couldn't sit up."

"Why? Why was she so sick?"

"For fear of the beatings, of course. Your grandfather—that sonofabitch—beat her up all the time. Or so the stories went. I do know for a fact that he was a drunkard. And a gambler. And the most macho man ever to walk this town. And that's saying a lot. People would cross to the other side of the street when they saw a certain expression on his face."

"*El Español?*"

"The same."

I stood on one leg and twirled my foot, contemplating how it might look in one of those boots. Thinking about what the boot-maker had said. Was he telling the truth? When my mother beat me, was she doing it with her father's hands? I briefly considered asking for more details and decided against it. I couldn't bear to hear anything more about it right then. So I steered us in a different direction.

"And what was my grandmother like before she met my grandfather?"

"Well, I was only a little boy at that point, so I can't really say. I do know she came from a very wealthy family. That they lived in a big house filled with beautiful things. But whatever she inherited, your grandfather gambled away. I also have a vague recollection that she was as exquisite as your mother, though in a very different way. What I remember best is that she was a fabulous horsewoman. I once saw her galloping through town on the biggest white stallion you ever saw. She rode sidesaddle, of course. But as well as any man. I guess she was pretty wild, herself, or else she wouldn't have fallen for *El Español*, would she? He was new in town and no one knew much about him. But he won her heart. Of course, she was just a young girl…."

He looked up as church bells suddenly interrupted him. A bunch of discordant peals and then twelve solid bongs.

"Oh my God," I said. "Lunch! I'd better get back."

"Come see me again soon, Mamita. My name is Miguel Grillo. I'll make you a pair of boots prettier than you ever saw. And a pair for your brother, too."

I ran all the way home and banged on the front door, panting. It opened after a moment to reveal Carolina's face transformed by fury.

"You ungrateful girl! How dare you? Your grandmother is having *El Ataque*, thanks to you! She hasn't had one in years!"

"What's *El Ataque*?" I asked. "You mean one of those headaches? Where is she? Let me see her?"

"God forbid! Why would she want to see you? You ungrateful, bad girl!"

I moved her aside, ran up the stairs and pushed open Doña Isabel's half-ajar bedroom door.

My grandmother was in bed, her eyes closed. She was moaning softly. She looked like a tiny peeled twig lying there in her long white nightgown. Had I done this to her? Was I the same kind of brute as my mother? As my grandfather?

Or was I more like my grandmother—the family member who gets brutalized?

Or was I something else altogether?

"Doña Isabel!" I walked up to her, stroked her head and began focusing on what she was feeling. I didn't dare touch her belly. She was far too dignified for that. Instead, I put my other hand lightly on her shoulder and pictured her poor stomach churning. Then I thought of the Virgin and said my little prayer to her under my breath.

Slowly, Doña Isabel's eyes opened and she looked up at me. "Blessed be the Lord," she said. "What have you done? All the torment has stopped. It's just stopped."

Relief radiated through my body. "Well," I said as I contemplated my hands, front and back, with a new degree of respect. "My brother's friend says I have 'healing hands.'"

I considered what to do next. I wasn't about to promise to be good from then on, was I? But I could at least give her head one last little stroke—reassure her that I was there for her. And so I did.

"Now don't you worry about anything else, Abuelita. Everything is under control. Just get yourself some rest."

And then I turned around, bumping right into Carolina, just half a step behind me.

"She'll be okay," I said. "Let her nap for a while, and she'll wake up feeling fine."

Carolina hustled me down the stairs.

"What did you just do? How did you cure her like that?"

"Oh, it's just something I'm good at."

She continued to look at me steadily, her face a mixture of begrudging admiration and irritable reproof. What more did she want from me? Oh, of course.

"And listen, Carolina," I said, poking her gently in the shoulder. "You also had a real fright, didn't you? So, I guess I owe you an apology, too."

She looked away. "It's been years—years and years and years—since Doña Isabel has had *El Ataque*, you know."

"Since *El Español* died, eh?"

"How do you know that?"

"Just another of my magic powers...I'm kidding, I'm kidding. But truly, I had no idea that I'd be causing such problems. I was prepared for you both to yell at me. But not for this."

"Humph."

"So, Carolina. Can you make me something unusual for lunch today to celebrate my healing powers? Scramble up my eggs with some tomatoes and onions and tabasco sauce instead of serving them in the tasteless puddle of water they've been poached in?"

Carolina gave me a look. But there was the very smallest trace of a smile under the look. "Well, there's a cantina down the street. I guess we could both go there and have a bite."

"After all I'm not a secret any more, right?"

"Right. But listen, Paloma, we can't have you running around like that.... Good girls don't. People will talk.... Your grandmother...."

"Yes, I know all about my grandmother and our family reputation. But you have nothing to worry about. Truly."

"What do you mean we have nothing to worry about? Look how disobedient you just were!"

"Disobedient maybe. But not a *putita*."

Carolina gasped. One thing to hint at that word, quite another to say it.

"Really, truly. I'm not into all that. I mean, men are fine and all, but...." It took some doing to say it. Still, what was I risking? I was already cooked. Might as well get it all out there with the rest of the spilled secrets of the day. "But they're not my thing. I'm an *arepera*."

Carolina crossed herself three times and then her hands flew up to her face. I couldn't tell whether she was crying or laughing. What had I done? What was she thinking? What would she tell my grandmother? What kind of lecture would I get now?

But she said no more. No lecture, no comment. Just a few more shakes of her head and a wipe of her eyes on the hem of her apron. Then she straightened up, patted me once on the shoulder, took her apron off and hung it on its hook and shooed us both out of the door.

11

The next day, right after breakfast my grandmother announced that she was taking me into town. We would stop by the school in which I would be enrolling and then go to church for the eleven o'clock mass.

"We'll be meeting Father Domingo," she informed me with a proud little nod. "He spent some time in America, you know. He was a priest in the Bronx for three years."

"At the Convent of Good Hope?"

Silence.

"Was it he who arranged for my mother to go there?"

Silence.

Still, she also said nothing about the events of the prior day, for which I was grateful. She merely asked me if I had a skirt and—when I said yes—told me to go and put it on.

Walking down the streets of Santa Fe de Antioquia with Doña Isabel was entirely different than galloping through them behind Carolina or exploring them on my own. Sure, there still were stares. But there were also deferential nods and soft murmurs of "Adios!" everywhere we went. People stepped off the sidewalks into the cobblestoned streets to allow us to pass. A few older men tipped their hats.

"You're quite the celebrity around here," I said.

"Well, I come from a very old family."

The school took up an entire block not far from the Parque Central. It was a two-story building made of the same thick white-washed adobe as the houses on Doña Isabel's street. There was a panel above the front door painted in bright colors with the school name—*Escuela Jorge Robledo*—and a big Colombian flag. We went inside and up a short flight of stairs to an office with wide-open windows and a large gently-turning ceiling fan. Beyond the windows I glimpsed an interior courtyard filled with palm-tree-lined paths and small concrete benches.

As we entered the office, the large woman behind the desk rose to her feet and greeted my grandmother warmly. My grandmother nodded back at her with a proprietary air. It occurred to me that my mother had probably gone to this school. Perhaps even Doña Isabel herself.

The woman then turned to me: "Well, Paloma. I'm very pleased to meet you. My name is Maria Velasquez Cruz. The students call me Niña Maria. You won't be starting classes for another few weeks but this might be a good time for you to meet your future classmates."

I hadn't considered that possibility. I thought we were just going to fill out some application forms. For all my bravado, the thought of entering a new classroom full of students made me very nervous. I had never really been a hit with my fellow students back home, after all. But clearly absolutely nothing was going to go the way that I wanted in this confounded country, and so I ducked my head in a nod and allowed her to rush me down the hall into a big classroom on the other side of the staircase.

I barely had enough time to register the fact that girls and boys were allowed to sit together and that girls were permitted to wear navy blue pants when Niña Maria announced, "Children, children! Your attention, please! I want to introduce the little American girl who will be joining us after the semester break. Her name is Paloma Rodriguez. Doña Isabel Teresa Gonzales de Rodriguez is her grandmother. She grew up in New York. In the Bronx. Isn't that right, dear?"

Those words were pure magic. The kids stood up from their desks and shoved each other out of the way to crowd tightly around me. In vain their teacher—a small man with a small mustache—tried to herd them back into their seats. Eventually he just sat down again while calling in a weak voice,, "Children, children! Please, show some courtesy to our guest!"

"What's it like in the Bronx?"

"It's exciting. It's big. Much bigger than here."

"Are there skyscrapers?"

"Everywhere!"

"Can you buy drugs on every street?"

"Yeah—and they all come from Medellín!"

"Have you met Snoop Dogg and Tupac?"

"No, but my brother knows them personally."

"And do you know Derek Jeter and Mariano Rivera?"

"I see them all the time. You can see Yankee games from our living room window."

"Is it true that everyone in the Bronx eats McDonald burgers every day?"

"Yes."

"Is it true that there are people lying out on the streets?" One of the boys demonstrated. "Like this? Dead? Shot?"

"Yes."

"How come you speak Spanish so well?"

"Everyone in the Bronx speaks Spanish. It's required."

"And are you...?" one of the girls pushed her way between her fellows to get closer to me than anyone else. Her face loomed barely inches away from mine. Her teeth were so big, her lips so red, and her eyes so glistening that I thought for a moment she was going to bite me. "And are you personally...are you *personally*...tough, tough, tough? Do you live for danger?"

I stared back at her as hard as she was staring at me. My heart started pounding.

"Yes," I said. "I'm personally tough, tough, tough. And I like danger quite a bit."

"Good," she said, grinning with that wide red mouth. "Then I know we're going to be really good friends."

"Okay, children," said Niña Maria at last, her tone decisive. She took my arm and led me toward the door. "That's enough for our little guest right now. She'll be back soon enough." I looked over my shoulder at my new friend as we left. "Lupita," she mouthed. "I'm Lupita. Don't forget." And then Niña Maria closed the door behind us.

My grandmother was waiting patiently in the hall. "Okay, Paloma," she said. "Thank Niña Maria and we'll be on our way."

Our next stop was the *Catedral Metropolitana de la Inmaculada Concepción.* It was a small white-fronted church—surprisingly dark inside, given the sharpness of the sunshine immediately without. Not exactly St. Nicholas of Tolentine, the Cathedral of the Bronx.

We were twenty minutes early for the mass, but my grandmother clearly had other things to do first. She walked briskly up front to a statue of the Virgin and contemplated it for a minute. Then she knelt down with impressive spryness, looked up at me, and said, "Hand me a taper."

I reached toward the cluster of votive lighters stuck head-down in their box of ashes, removed one and handed it to her.

"Light it first, *muchacha!*"

I did so and she held it over the nearest unlit votive candle, murmuring something too soft for me to hear. She then handed the taper back to me to extinguish and lifted one elbow in my direction so I could help her to her feet.

"What were you praying for?" I was Catholic enough to know that one doesn't waste a chance to petition the Virgin.

"For *El Español*'s soul. As I have every week for the past fifty-odd years." She turned away from me and headed toward a door on the right.

"And now," she said loftily, looking back at me over her shoulder, "we mustn't keep Father Domingo waiting any longer."

Father Domingo had a pale face, a tall baggy body, and large vague brown eyes behind thick glasses. He wore a vestment that had undoubtedly been lying wet and crumpled in our sink at some earlier point that week. His glance slid toward me and then quickly moved away.

"Ah, so this is the lovely Paloma," he said, clasping my hands in his moist grip. "Dear Dolores's youngest. Welcome home, my child, welcome home."

Damn it, what did he mean "welcome home"? I had not "come home." My home was the Bronx. I held my breath to prevent myself from saying something really rude, but it turned out to be unnecessary. There was no interrupting him.

"How wonderful to see you here in our beautiful Cathedral," he continued at top speed. "To see you standing with our wonderful Doña Isabel. What on earth would we do without her?"

I snuck a peek at my grandmother. She was standing very straight, her own eyes half-closed. Her face looked much bigger than usual, as if the priest's words were literally puffing her up. Seeing her like that made me totally lose track of his monologue. Finally, I tuned back.

"…must have seen the new *Jesus Crucified* statue to the left of the altar? Yes? No? Well then why don't we just walk right out here and gaze at it? That's real hair, you know. And real gold in the lettering of the 'INRI' over Jesus's head."

He took a breath.

"But of course—exquisite as it is—the *Jesus Crucified* simply dims in radiance beside the six statues that we bring out every year for our *Semana Santa* procession. The six statues that were carved in Spain and then transported to our Cathedral for its inaugural mass, so very long ago. Oh, I can hardly wait to watch your face next spring! Just picture this: The strongest young men of our city dressed up in purple-hooded splendor, hoisting those beautiful statues onto their firm straight shoulders and carrying them from the Cathedral to the edge of town and then back again. How the band plays! How the crowds stream out! What an extraordinary occasion!"

He leaned toward me and paused significantly. I backed up a bit.

"But then, of course," he continued, "once the procession is over, we don't just leave those statues out in public for the rest of the year. Oh no, no, no. They're too special for daily viewing—for daily familiarity. We sequester them safely away within the houses of the finest families of Santa Fe de Antioquia till they emerge once again for their sacred annual march."

My grandmother drew an audible breath.

"And most blessed of all, of course, are the families chosen to host the two most precious statues for the year in-between processions. The family chosen to host the statue of Our Savior, carved in Valencia in 1627. And the family chosen to host the statue of the Blessed Virgin Mary, carved in Segovia."

My grandmother cleared her throat. Her face was practically three times its normal size.

"Well, my child," the priest concluded, staring out into the great space at the back of the church. "I think that is enough strong emotion for one day. You and our dear Doña Isabel should take your places in the pews. It's time for the mass. And welcome home, dear child. Welcome home."

12

A couple of weeks after school started up again, I finally worked up the courage to take my first step with Lupita. I came home to find my grandmother sitting in her usual late-afternoon seat at the dining room table, paging through her beloved *El Nuevo Siglo*, and I walked close enough to feel the gentle heat rising off her body.

"Doña Isabel?" She greeted my presence with a nearly-imperceptible exhalation of annoyance. I'd been warned by Carolina that this was my grandmother's sacrosanct private time. But, really, there was never a good time for anything in that house. And I had to take action before I lost heart.

"Doña Isabel?"

Another sigh as she finally looked up. "Yes, Paloma?"

"Doña Isabel, this Wednesday I'm going to my new friend Lupita's house for dinner after school. So you won't have to worry about feeding me that evening. And I'll be sleeping over afterward. So you don't have to worry about my coming home by myself after dark."

"I don't see why you have to go home with one of your classmates," she sniffed, folding the newspaper into quarters and smoothing it with one hand. "You have a home of your own to come home to."

But she didn't say no. And I secretly rejoiced. Not just because she wasn't opposing me. But because I'd finally figured out how to handle her. Asking my grandmother for permission was always a big mistake. Her first response was invariably "no." And trying to sneak around her was a challenge. Unlike my mother—who let countless misdeeds slip by because she wasn't really interested—Doña Isabel had her radar trained on every detail of my behavior.

So that left me only one option: simply announcing my intentions. It seemed to work almost all of the time. It made me sad, actually, that ready acquiescence to any show of authority. Clearly, my grandmother was no longer the girl who galloped through town on the largest white stallion that Miguel Grillo had ever seen. Something inside her had been permanently broken.

But, hell, sometimes it was the only way for me to get anything done.

Managing Lupita, however, was a whole different story. I had no idea how to deal with her. From the moment that classes started up again, she clung to me, whining incessantly. When was I coming to her house? When was I going to sleep over? Wasn't I excited about all the things we were going to do?

She didn't have to tell me what those things were. It was clear enough from the way she kept wiggling her big soft breasts and lushly-padded hips at me. From the way she would take my hand in hers and make little circles in my palm with one finger while looking up at me with her big wicked smile.

It excited me more than I liked to admit.

Still, I found myself stalling. I had to make arrangements. My grandmother was difficult. I liked to take my time about things.

The last statement wasn't true, of course. I was just as impulsive as Lupita—and just as excited by the idea of finally exploring everything I'd ever dreamt about. But Lupita's begging made me dig in my heels. I don't take well to being nagged.

Eventually, however, her persistence and my relentless cravings won out. I announced that my grandmother had agreed to my visiting her that Wednesday, and she cackled and clapped her hands.

Our desks were arranged alphabetically and, as luck would have it, Lupita's last name was Romero, so she sat just to the right of me. On the first day I'd arrived in class, she figured out how to slide close enough to me to rest one sharp elbow permanently on my desk top. And on the day I announced I'd be going home with her, she managed to push her chair so close that I feared she'd end up sitting in my lap.

The hours flew right by and, I swear, the dismissal bell had never clanged so loudly. And no sooner than it had sounded than Lupita grabbed me by the wrist, pulled me out of my chair, and dragged me through the corridor, down the stairs, and out onto the street.

I would definitely have to do some fancy footwork to keep ahead of this one.

Lupita lived on the far western border of Santa Fe de Antioquia. The houses on her block were smaller than the ones on my grandmother's street. They were made of wood, not adobe. Their roofs were corrugated tin and the road in front of them was made of dirt. Each house was fronted by a small yard covered with that thick stubby growth that passes for grass in Colombia. Some of the houses had trees in front of them and almost all had objects—parts of old stoves, old bikes, cardboard boxes—strewn around on the ground.

Lupita's house had chunks of what seemed to be an old car lying near the enormous mango tree to the left of her door. Two tires and a twisted green metal fender leaned heavily against the white paint that covered the tree's gnarled lower trunk.

Lupita started rummaging around in her bra for a key till she noticed that the door was already ajar. She wasn't the most observant person. She pushed the door open with a flourish and we entered a living room filled with its own assortment of found objects—a stroller, a playpen with one side tied on with string, a box of diapers, a couple of rag dolls. And four skinny boys, wearing nothing but baggy blue shorts with bright red "DIM" (*Deportivo Independiente Medellín*) insignias, were running around madly, kicking two soccer balls across the mess.

I ducked out of the way as one of the balls went speeding

by my head and one of the boys charged after it, practically knocking me over.

"Let's get away from these monsters!" said Lupita, grabbing my hand.

She led me through a door on the left into a tiny enclosed space just wide enough for a single bed with a light green chenille bedspread and a small wardrobe with three drawers and two warped doors. There were no windows opening onto the street, but high up on one wall was a small interior window leading back to the living room. Lupita reached up and pulled at a string hanging from the ceiling and a light bulb went on. She then pulled a second string and a small ceiling fan began to turn. She tossed both of our book bags across the room, pulled off her shoes and socks, and began spreading her toes.

"C'mon," she said. "Take off your shoes, too. We have an hour till dinner. What shall we do? Shall we fool around? There's a bolt on the door."

I kept my shoes on. Her feet suddenly frightened me. So present. So naked. I balked. "Let's do our homework. Get it out of the way. Is there anywhere in this house that we can do homework?"

"You're a spoilsport, you know that?"

"No, I'm just…never mind. Let's just get it done, okay?"

I walked over to where my book bag lay on its side on the floor and picked it up. She then reluctantly retrieved hers as well. We walked back into the living room and parked ourselves at the long table that stood at its center.

We had history and math to do. I began reading the assigned history chapter while Lupita diligently bent over her own text. I closed the book when I was finished and she immediately closed hers as well. Then I pulled out my math workbook and flexed the spine back and forth a couple of times before laying it on the table—and she did exactly the same.

A soccer ball landed on the table in front of me and I tossed it back behind me without looking. Then I leaned back in my chair, sifted my fingers through my hair and wiggled my shoulders around a bit. And by the time I had straightened up again, the oldest of Lupita's brothers had materialized at my side.

He was two years ahead of us. I recognized him from the school corridors. He was a handsome boy—handsomer in his soccer shorts and rumpled hair than he was in his usual ironed shirt and slicked-back pompadour. His skin was the color of mahogany and lightly filmed with sweat. He was breathing hard. He smelled nice.

"Hi, I'm Mauricio. I've seen you around school. Is that your math homework? What are you doing these days? Blockhead over here can never tell me."

Lupita kicked violently in his direction, but he hopped backward gracefully before her foot could make contact.

"Quadratic equations," I said proudly, and showed him the page and my calculations.

"Let's see what I remember from Don Pepito's lessons," he said, grabbing my pencil. He was standing so close that I could see the whorls in his tight little brown nipples and the ribs moving under his skin as he breathed. He leaned forward and scribbled in the margins of the workbook.

"Hey—don't screw me up."

"I'm not screwing you up. Take a look. Is this how you do it?"

"Hmm. Well, actually no. I do it…I do it the way the nuns back home do it. Want to see?" I grabbed the pencil back from him and showed him the steps that Sister Bettina had taught me.

He grinned. "Hey, that's cool. The 'nuns back home'…are cool," he said.

"Yeah…in fact."

"The Bronx, huh?"

"The Bronx."

Lupita finally lost it entirely. "Okay, already. Out of the way, monster!" she said. She stood up, grabbed him by the waist and pulled him backward. "Get back to your football and leave us alone!"

I watched him shake her off and amble back to the game with calculated nonchalance. But when he reached one of the balls, I was pleased to see him kick it with barely concealed viciousness.

I still had the knack. Boys liked me. I didn't have to do a thing. They just did. Smiling to myself, I finished my assignment and then leaned over and finished up Lupita's for her as well.

"Okay, that's great," she said, slamming her workbook shut. "Good? Satisfied? Let's get supper ready. Mami and Papito will be here any minute. Go set the table, brats! Supper's on the way!"

Surprisingly, all four brothers snapped to attention. Lupita could be very persuasive when she wanted to be. Or maybe it was just the prospect of food that got them going. They slid past us into the kitchen, took out the place settings and began pitching them onto the table while we went to the refrigerator, hauled out three enormous pots, and put them on the stove.

"Pork stew, rice, and beans," said Lupita. "How does that sound?" We lit a low flame under each pot and after a few minutes I picked up the top of one of them and drew in a few long breaths. My stomach let out a rumble and Lupita poked me in the side.

"Hungry, eh?" she said putting one bare foot on my ankle and rubbing up and down. I jumped at the electric charge that it triggered. It was finally all going to happen. There was nothing I could do to stop it. I was both thrilled and scared out of my wits.

A moment later the front door opened and in walked Lupita's parents, each carrying a bag of groceries. I expected to feel guilty, thinking about why I was there—knowing what I was going to do with their daughter under their own roof. But, instead, as I watched them move toward us, all the day's tension seemed to leave me. They looked so normal, so calm, so comfortable. The mother was as dark as her children and as firmly round as Lupita. She had pinned her hair up in a messy bun and was wearing a polka-dot dress and lots of lipstick. She gave me a kindly look that I recognized from somewhere but couldn't quite place.

The father was the odd one out in the family—white-skinned, sloped, and shapeless, like one of the wontons at the Hom & Hom Restaurant back on Fordham Road. Nonetheless, when he caught sight of me and smiled, I saw a trace of Lupita's glittering wolfish grin under his thin black mustache. He wore a red checked shirt and had a baby draped casually over his left shoulder.

"I know your parents, Lupita. Where do I know them from?"

"You ever go to the Central Market?"

"Yes, all the time. I stop in at that little soda fountain near the back on the way home from school most days to have a *mora con leche.*"

"Well, so that's where you know them from. They have a stall in there, right near the front on the left-hand side. You must have seen it: "*Flor del Campo* Provisions: You Need It—We Got It"?

Of course. My mind retrieved a sudden vivid image of the stall's painted logo and of the small couple within, standing behind big barrels of dried grains and legumes. I walked by that stall nearly every day and sometimes got close enough to surreptitiously dip my hand into the barrels as I passed. I loved the pleasant cool feel of beans and rice and corn streaming between my fingers.

If Lupita's parents ever noticed me do it, they never said anything. And they said nothing now.

Lupita gave the stew one last stir, whacked the spoon across the edge of the pot a few times to shake off the last drops of sauce, and put it down on a dish at the side of the stove. Then she ran up to her father to take the baby off his shoulder and into her arms.

"*Nenita! Nenita mia! Josefina linda! Belleza!*" She buried her face in the baby's stomach and made flatulent noises with her lips. The baby giggled and kicked and Lupita giggled back. "This is my baby! All mine! Aren't you, Josefina? Aren't you? Here, want to hold her?"

She shoved the squirming bundle at me and I held it tentatively. I had never held a baby.

"Not like that, idiot! Here, give her back to me!" She clutched Josefina back to her breast with one clearly practiced arm and gestured for us to sit down with the other.

Supper was a quick and noisy affair. Lupita's parents spent most of the time shushing the boys—who kept yelling about some recent match between *Deportivo Independiente Medellín* and *Atlético Nacional*. But they also managed to throw me the occasional friendly glance. And they made sure that my plate stayed full.

Her mother was one fabulous cook. And, man, it was the first time I'd had enough to eat since landing in Colombia.

Lupita, meanwhile, was totally fixated on the kid on her lap. It was a relief to have her pay attention to someone besides me for a while. But it was also disconcerting. She cooed at it nonstop while spooning bits of red beans into its tiny mouth. Then she would lick the spoon and take a mouthful herself.

The meal ended as abruptly as it had started. Everyone stood up—Lupita still holding the kid tightly to her voluptuous chest. My fears of the unknown had been soothed by the wonderfully satisfying food and the noisy normalcy of the Romero family, and I found I was finally ready—more than ready—for the explorations that lay ahead.

So why the hell was Lupita still fussing over that stupid baby?

At long last she turned to me. "Josefina was a miracle child," she said, giving me a wink. "Mami and Papito thought the factory had shut down. But *surprise!* Well, what do you expect? Papito can't keep his hands off Mami, can you, Papi? So God finally said 'okay—you want another kid?' and sent us our little angel." Her mother swatted Lupita's bottom and her father raised his eyebrows, but everyone was grinning broadly. "Didn't He, *Nenita?* Didn't He, *Corazoncito Mio?*"

Lupita gave one last big wet kiss to Josefina and then handed her off to her mother.

And then she pulled me into her room.

13

Assumption Day—August 15th—was due to arrive on a Saturday that year, which meant that Monday would be a holiday for all the schools and banks, and the town would be immersed in celebrations for three whole days. Colombians just love their long weekends.

My grandmother and Carolina spent six full hours at the stone sink on that Thursday, scrubbing a host of priestly vestments till they were snowy white and then hanging them lovingly on the clotheslines out back to absorb the last magically bleaching touch of the tropical sun. They were then both back at their posts at five thirty the following morning, hauling all those robes inside and ironing and folding them with such intense concentration that neither one even bothered to look up as I walked into the kitchen to pour myself my cup of coffee and grab a roll from the paper bag that Carolina always left for me on the counter.

As I came closer, sipping my drink, I could hear Carolina asking whether she could go home right after lunch that day.

"Of course," said Doña Isabel, grandly. "We'll surely be done with all the robes by then and you can just drop them off at each of the churches. They are offering festive lunches at the Cathedral every day this weekend, and there's more than enough soup for our supper-time needs. So, there will be nothing more for you to do here and you should feel free to attend Masses to your heart's content."

Carolina grunted. I stepped further into the room. Still no one looked up.

"There is no holier Mass than that of the Assumption of the Virgin," Doña Isabel continued in a voice that let me know she was actually fully aware of my presence. "Some people say that the Easter Mass is the most beautiful and meaningful one of the year. Some say that it is the Christmas Mass. But for me, the holiest Mass is the one at which we celebrate our Blessed Mother's Assumption—body and soul—into heaven, to be crowned as the Queen of the Universe and sit for all eternity by the side of her beloved son and in the presence of our Heavenly Father."

I had no idea whether or how to respond to all the nonsense she was proclaiming for my benefit, but thankfully she began speaking again before the silence became awkward. "And this year, because of when the holiday falls, there will be no less than six full Masses in our Blessed Mother's honor. Two apiece on each of the three days: Saturday, Sunday, *and* Monday!"

"Six Masses!" Carolina echoed dutifully.

"And at each of those Masses," my grandmother continued, "Father Domingo will be wearing a very special Assumption Stole over his white robes. Covered with embroidered celestial blue flowers and gold and crimson crowns, and each crown emanating shining rays of light."

This time she paused definitively, and this time I knew exactly how to chime in. Why should I deprive her of what she so desperately wanted to hear, after all? Carolina had somehow managed to say what was necessary, and she obviously disliked all that church stuff as much as I did. It wasn't such a big deal for me to do the same.

"And did you embroider that 'special Assumption Stole' yourself, Doña Isabel?" I asked.

My grandmother looked up at me and then down again shyly at her ironing board.

"It took me a full year," she said. "A full year!"

"It must be very beautiful."

"Well, you'll be able to see it for yourself," she replied, snapping back to briskness. "When you accompany me to all those Masses."

I swallowed the last bit of my roll and took the last swig of my coffee. Could I force myself to say what she so clearly wanted me to say? And then could I actually do it? Yeah. Sure. Why not? What else did I have to do with my time?

"Yes, Doña Isabel," I said, walking up to her and placing my hand on my shoulder. "Yes, I guess I will."

Things, however, did not quite work out as either of us had planned.

Doña Isabel came into my room at six forty-five the next morning—flushed with irritation that I was still in bed—to find me battling cramps so excruciating that I could barely move. I had woken up with a bang of pain an hour before and had remained curled in a ball with one hand on my stomach murmuring my mantra about the BVM ever since. Not that it helped. For some reason, I've never been able to heal myself.

"Paloma! Why are you still under the covers? Why are you whimpering like that? What's the matter?"

"Cramps. The worst cramps I've ever had. Who knows why? I never get cramps. Never."

"Emotion. Emotion about the Virgin."

Jesus! "No doubt, Doña Isabel. No doubt. But I'm afraid you'll have to go to Mass by yourself this morning."

"Well, such are the burdens of womanhood," she asserted, nodding to herself. "But they, too, shall pass. Perhaps you'll feel better in time for this afternoon's service. And surely you'll be well enough for both the Masses tomorrow. And for the ones on Monday. It's a real blessing when the 15th falls on a Saturday, isn't it? So many chances to celebrate."

"So many chances," I gasped as a particularly horrendous cramp gripped my lower belly.

My grandmother started to leave the room, but stopped midway and turned back to me.

"And Paloma? The big mahogany breakfront in the dining room?"

"Yes?"

"The bottom left-hand cabinet…?"

"Yes?" Ouch.

"Where I keep my three fine crystal glasses…?"

"Mm hmm." What three fine crystal glasses? Where the heck was she going with this?

"Well, there's a bottle of sherry inside, tucked behind those glasses. It's a special day, after all. I don't think it would hurt you to have a little sherry and sugar in some nice hot *manzanilla* tea for your cramps. It often does the trick…."

And thus it was that I was seated in the little green Adirondack chair in the corner of my grandmother's kitchen, happily nursing my third or fourth cup of that tasty drink when Carolina marched in with her big straw grocery bag.

"Carolina, what are you doing here?" I asked pleasantly. "Aren't you supposed to be down on your knees in church?"

"Very funny," she said, putting her bag on the floor by the counter, taking out a small package and walking to the refrigerator. She opened the refrigerator door and stuck the package inside. "Remind me that this is here when I leave. It's sausages for my dinner. Not the sort of thing your grandmother would like to find in her house."

"And Carolina, what on earth were you doing shopping on Assumption Day? I didn't think the supermarket would even be open on a holy occasion such as this."

"Well, we're living in modern times. It stays open till noon," she said, briskly. "And it was having a sale. Sardines were going for half-price, so I thought we should stock up. And sausages were on sale, too."

And then she turned her back to me. Her long grey braid swung back and forth as she bent to pull the cans out of the bag and then spread them out on the counter for a final tally.

"And what about *you*, Paloma?" she asked, when they all had been accounted for. "What are *you* doing sitting in the kitchen getting into mischief when you promised your grandmother that you would go to Mass with her?"

"I have cramps," I said with whatever dignity I could muster. "The worst cramps I've ever had. Or, at least, that's what they were like when I woke up this morning. They seem to be better now."

"Alcohol will do that," she said. Carolina had a nose like a bloodhound.

She continued moving the cans around as I looked happily into my cup. "Doña Isabel told me to drink it," I said.

"Humph. Well, actually, I'm very glad I found you here," she said, her back still to me. "There is something I've been meaning to talk to you about, and I can't do it when Doña Isabel is around."

"Oh?"

"Yes. You have been making your grandmother very unhappy, you know. She would never say a word to you about it. She's far too much of a lady. But I've been watching her suffer and I can't let it go on any longer."

"What on earth have I done? I've practically been an angel!"

"It's…it's…it's all that time you spend with the Romeros," she said. "With…what is your friend's name? Luisa?"

"Lupita."

I put my cup down on the arm of the chair and sat up as straight as I could. My head was whirling. What, exactly, was Carolina driving at? Did she suspect that Lupita and I were more than just friends? Had I been so mistaken in thinking she was fine with my being an *arepera*? Had she and my grandmother been stewing about it ever since? And what did they want from me, anyway? Shouldn't they just be relieved that I wasn't gallivanting around town getting pregnant like my stupid mother?

I said nothing for a moment, dreading what might be coming next. It took a few seconds for Carolina to stick out her chin and begin to speak, but she finally did.

"You…you come from a very good family, Paloma," she said, practically spitting through the many gaps in her teeth. "One of the best in all of Santa Fe de Antioquia. And the Romeros…the Romeros…are *chuzma*! *Pura gentuza*! You shouldn't be hanging around with them like that. You are lowering yourself."

Vulgar. Low class. Lowering myself.

The last of my foggily blissful mood evaporated. I was wide awake and fighting mad. How dare she say that?

"The Romeros are very nice people," I fired back at her. "They treat me very well."

"That has nothing to do with it."

"Do you mean that they're *poor*? Well, aren't we poor, too? Don't you think I know why everything is so threadbare around here? Why you and Doña Isabel are so miserly about the food? Why she gives me five Maria crackers—five and no more—for my *cafecito* every afternoon? Why you would profane a holy day to go to the supermarket just because sardines are selling at a bargain price?"

"That's different," said Carolina. "That's very different."

The worst part was that I actually had a pretty good idea about what Carolina meant. I knew that it wasn't just a matter of poverty. It was something else—something much more complicated than that. I probably couldn't have put it into exact words at the time, but somewhere in my young gut I grasped the core concept that was fueling her words.

It didn't matter that my grandmother had only three cut crystal glasses left from a set that had probably once numbered in the dozens. She'd once *had* those dozens of glasses and was being very, very careful with the three that were left. The Romeros, on the other hand, had never had much of anything, they weren't very careful with what they did possess, and their tendency to keep wantonly creating new mouths to feed ensured that there would never be much of anything for any of them in the future, either.

Somehow, money and class and sexuality and self-control were deeply conflated in my grandmother's mind.

A lot of other things suddenly fell into place, and I found myself emboldened by the thrill of comprehension. Or maybe it was the sherry.

"And if you want to talk about vulgar," I said, very slowly. "Then let's talk about someone who really *is* vulgar. Let's talk about my mother. *Whom you never seem to want to talk about.* But who, you should know, spent my childhood working in a bar and sleeping with anyone she thought might do her a favor. If you want to talk about vulgar…if you want to talk about low class…."

Carolina spun around. "Don't you dare—don't you dare speak that way about your mother!"

"And why not? She's my mother! I have a right! It was I who had to live with her through all those years while she did all that—not you! Neither you nor my grandmother can even bear to hear about how she ended up. And yet *it's all your fault.* You threw her out of her home for 'acting like *chuzma*' and so that's what she became!"

Carolina was so red-faced that I was afraid she was going to have a heart attack right then and there. Or to hurl one of the sardine cans at me.

"It wasn't I who threw her out, young lady!" She was practically shouting. "That was your grandfather! And, well, yes, your grandmother, too, if you must know!" And then her voice got very quiet. "I would never have thrown her out. If it had been up to me, I would have taken her into my house and taken care of her—and her *nenito*, too. I had no one but her. And she had no one but me. I loved her. And she loved me. I miss her every day of my life."

She spun back to face the counter, leaving me to gaze at her heaving shoulders. She opened the cabinet and began putting the sardine cans on the shelf, one on top of the other with tightly wound precision. Click. Click. Click.

I picked up my cup again and took a sip. Funny how Mama had never so much as mentioned Carolina to me. So much for my mother's love.

"I have no one either," I finally said. "And..." and I don't know where it bubbled up from but out it popped: "And I miss my mother, too. I mean...." Damn those tears, where were they coming from? "I mean, I don't miss what she was.... But I miss what she...might have been...."

Click. Click. I swear: Carolina's broad back softened. Even her bone-straight grey braid seemed to loosen up a bit. Without looking at me, she walked over to the refrigerator, took out her greasy little package and walked back to place it carefully down on the counter. She then took two onions, a tomato, a red pepper, and a bunch of cilantro out of her straw bag and placed them down to the right of that package. Finally, she pulled a wooden chopping board and a cleaver out of the drawer and placed them down on the other side.

"Your grandmother won't be home for a few hours," she said. "Those church affairs go on forever. Aren't you always bragging about what a good cook you are? Why don't you show me what you can do? We can have some sausages and peppers for lunch."

14

"Why won't you ever talk to me about your time in Colombia, Paloma?"

One of the loveliest things that I discovered about Serach in those first months that we lived together was that she truly believed in personal privacy. Her favorite topics were all substantive. Math problems or art works or the quirks of the NYC subway system. Why some medieval scholar made some perplexing remark about some obscure passage in the Bible. Why my patient was receiving one treatment over another.

She never gossiped. She never went on and on about her own neuroses. She didn't ask pointed questions about my previous romantic relationships—in fact she made it clear that she'd rather not know anything about them. Nor did she grill me about the complicated morass of my family.

And, perhaps most importantly, she never wanted to sit for hours poring over the details of our own relationship. A couple of my past girlfriends liked to do that. They didn't last very long.

No. Serach—who could spend hours worrying at an equation or tracking down some minor inconsistency in one of her client's accounts—was generally and gratifyingly content to steer clear of all that emotional stuff. To let me feel my own feelings, think my own thoughts and wrestle with my past on my own.

Generally.

Once in a while, however, she would get some crazy bug in her head and I would become the conundrum that she needed to solve. The smallest, oddest things would set her off. She once spent more than an hour sulking and scowling—all the little knobs in her brain clearly whirling away—over the expression that I'd had on my face while we were watching an opera. It took all my efforts to tease out what was bothering her. And then to explain myself. And then to comfort her. Go figure.

And now she was clearly off on one of those jags again.

I'd had the afternoon off. I'd made some rice and beans and avocado salad and codfish stew, and then I'd decided that the perfect finishing touch for my little Colombian feast would be some *arepas*. And so I'd gone off to Jackson Heights (a neighborhood that contains more Colombians than the entire province of Antioquia) to the *Sueños de mi Tierra Panaderia*, the best South American bakery in the city.

I'd brought the *arepas* home, warmed them up perfectly, buttered them up just right and placed them on the dinner table in front of Serach with a flourish. But instead of just enjoying them, she'd begun scrutinizing my face with that intensely-focused look of hers and wondering out loud why I'd spent a full half-day "schlepping all the way from Prospect Park South to some bakery in Queens for these plain little corn cakes."

Yes, sure, it does take three trains to get from our house to Jackson Heights—and then three more to get back. But, really. This is New York. There are few direct routes between Brooklyn and Queens. So you do what you have to do.

But, no, when Serach is in one of her investigative moods, she has to get to the bottom of things. I must have done it because I was homesick. Because I was pining away for Santa Fe de Antioquia. Because there were things about my time there that I needed to talk about. And wouldn't I feel so much better if I just allowed myself to do that?

"The *arepas* were just a whim," I'd said. "I didn't buy them because of some deep Proustian desire to dive back into my childhood. Don't you ever get whims?"

"You didn't see the look on your face while you were eating them, Paloma. I've never seen you look so…I don't know…sad? Angry? Regretful? What were you thinking about?"

She wasn't looking so great to me either, at that moment. I usually love to watch her as she puzzles through a problem. Her expression is so fierce while she's agonizing over it and then so sweetly satisfied when all the factors and columns finally balance out. But I wasn't feeling particularly charmed right then, when the subject she was puzzling over was me. What did she mean that I looked angry and regretful? I was just eating my *arepa*. Colombia was over for me. It was in the past. I'd dealt with it, put it all behind me. What did she want out of me, anyway?

I finally managed to get her off the subject by the time we got to dessert. Steered us into a conversation about a patient who had been worrying me. We'd cleaned up and I'd gone to write up my notes on that patient and calm down a bit. And when I'd unwound enough, I'd invited her to bed and had romanced her thoroughly. That usually wipes out any last bits of irritation simmering between us, so I figured that we were finally in the clear. And yet here she was starting in all over again.

She was taking a different tack, but it was just as exasperating. "Paloma, I thought you liked being my teacher. My *Rebbe*. Here I am, a person who knows nothing about Colombia. And here you are with all that first-hand knowledge. Talk to me. Tell me about it."

"I've told you already. There's nothing to say. And I'm falling asleep, here. That's what you do after having good sex, Baby. You roll over and drift off. So please just leave me be."

"Oh, Paloma, you disappoint me. I thought only men acted like that. I thought that for women…the best part of sex is the cuddling and talking that goes on afterward. And… sometimes you like to do it.…"

She threw one slim arm over my shoulder and began tracing two fingers gently up and down my spine. I'd taught her that trick myself. I didn't think I could feel the rush of desire rise up again so quickly—especially since I was beginning to really lose patience with her. But there it was.

My voice was thick. "That's not the way to get me to talk. That's the way to get me to…."

"Yes, yes, of course." She raised her fingertips obediently.

Her silence, however, remained accusatory. She'd clearly seen something in me that bothered her deeply. And there was nothing I could do except either get really angry with her (which I didn't want to do) or come up with something with which to pacify her. She's like a tank, once she gets going. Unstoppable. Thorough. It's why her clients love her.

"All right, Serach. I tell you what. I'll give you three words that describe how I felt during my two long years in South America. And then you'll pipe down and we'll go to sleep. Okay?"

"Uh-huh." Her fingers began making contact again, caressing my shoulders so softly that I could barely detect it. It was as if she couldn't help herself.

I brushed them away gently but definitively.

"Serach, cut it out! I'm on board with this. Leave it be. I need to concentrate if I'm going to come up with the right words." Oh, God. What would work? What would get her off my back without getting me any more upset? Ah. I know. "Hungry," I said. "The first word is…'hungry.' I was half-starved almost all the time."

"All that delicious Colombian food all around you and you were starving?"

"Well, my grandmother didn't really believe in cooking. Or in eating. Or in feeding people. I had to be terribly devious to get what I needed."

"My poor Paloma. So how did you manage?"

"Well, sometimes I just went out to the market and bought myself something to eat. And sometimes I went to a friend's house—the mother of one my friends was a fabulous cook. And sometimes I successfully badgered my grandmother's maid, Carolina, to prepare a good meal for me. It seems she'd always cooked and eaten with my mother, so I figured she'd be willing to do the same for me."

"But she wasn't? Didn't she love you as much as she'd loved your mother?"

Clever Serach. She'd zoomed right in on the point within the point.

"Hardly. She put up with me. Said I 'grew on her like a fungus.' Occasionally did something nice for me. But I was a very poor substitute for my mother, I'm afraid."

"That must have hurt. So, did she talk about your mother all the time?"

I waited a second to collect myself. "No. And that was the other thing she wouldn't do for me. Talk to me about my family. I'd ask her what my mother had been like as a girl. Silence. I'd ask her what my grandfather was like—he was supposedly a real sonofabitch. Silence. *I'd ask her who Manny's father was.* Double silence."

I suddenly realized that I'd never told Serach anything about how or why my mother had originally landed in the Bronx. That she'd been pregnant. That she'd been disgraced. That she'd been exiled. Oh, well. Another time.

"You know," I continued (might as well forge ahead), "in certain parts of the Bronx, if a girl sleeps around a lot—if she gets pregnant without being married—it's no big deal. It happens all the time. Hell, I don't even really know who my own father was."

Serach winced hard enough that I could see it in the dark. Oh, God. Had I really never told her that either? Guess not.

"But in 1981, in my grandmother's ultra-Catholic house, something like that still carried a real stigma. So I was very curious about what had gone on with my mother. Had she run around like crazy, or was it just one single irresistible man who'd made her pregnant? Someone so attractive that she'd been willing to risk everything just to get into his bed? I was dying to know.

And Carolina, who had been my mother's closest confidante—
who had to have known all that—stayed closed tight as a box on
that subject. She'd actually press her lips together and shake her
head at me whenever I brought it up. She let me know that she
loved my mother, all right. But she absolutely refused to help me
understand *who my mother was.*"

Leave it to Serach. I thought I was being so careful.
Keeping it all about the food thing. What could be emotionally
complicated about that? And yet she'd managed to steer me right
into talking about the true hunger I'd felt all the time I was in my
grandmother's house.

"Well, I guess she didn't want to betray your mother."

"But my mother was gone! She'd abandoned us both. And I
was right there! She could have helped me."

Serach nodded. Paused. Smoothed my hair. Smoothed my
cheek.

"And the second word?"

"What second word?"

"The second word describing your two years in Colombia?"

What word could I come up with that was safer than
"hungry"? Less likely to get me all worked up again.

"I was bored. Bored out of my wits the whole time."

"No great art galleries in Santa Fe de Antioquia, eh? No
wonderful little off-off-Broadway theaters?"

"No, Serach. Nothing like that. Absolutely nothing of any
interest in that entire town. Nothing but a school that taught
me English that I already knew, math that I'd already mastered,
and hundreds of useless facts about Colombian history and
geography. Nothing but streets that shut down at eight o'clock
every single night."

Well, she'd achieved what she wanted with me, my Serach. I
was finally wide awake and plunged deep into the memories of
those far-away times. How had she done it? I propped myself up
on one elbow and began remembering out loud.

"For the first few months I was there, I would wait till my grandmother began snoring and then sneak downstairs and out the front door to pace those dark little streets. I stayed in the shadows. No one ever saw me. Of course, who could have? No one else was out. I would prowl around once or twice a week at first, hoping that maybe—just maybe—there might be something to see."

"And?"

"And all those dull historic monuments were as just dull in the moonlight as they were in the daytime. The one time that I was bold enough to walk all the way to the *cantina* that stayed open late, all I saw inside was a bunch of drunkards slumped in their seats or clutching at the prostitutes who hung out there with them. I took one look at them, bolted right back home again, and didn't go out so much alone after that."

Jesus! Now I was caught up in those even older childhood memories of bars and drunks and the women that they clutched. Well, I certainly wasn't going to go into all *that* with Serach. Nor was I going to talk to her about my other regular evening forays—the ones I made to Lupita's house. The ones that weren't nearly as unpleasant as my solo strolls into town. Some things were just none of Serach's business.

No, what I had to do was guide us back into less dangerous territory. Tell her something that would satisfy her curiosity and yet not rile me up again. Ah. Something religious. Serach was always curious about religious matters.

"Of course," I finally volunteered, "returning to my bedroom after those late-night expeditions wasn't the most pleasant thing in the world, either. Not after I realized that I was sleeping right next door to a locked room containing an eight-foot-tall statue of Jesus Christ with meticulously rendered wounds and real human hair."

"Paloma! How frightful! What on earth was that thing doing in your grandmother's house?"

"My grandmother was storing it between Holy Week pageants. Don't ask. It's much too complicated. But you can't imagine how unsettling it was to know I was just one thin wall away from that thing."

"Of course I can. You poor dear! So is 'unsettled' the third word?"

"No," I replied—so quickly that it surprised me. "The third word is 'angry.'" All right. There it was. I hadn't wanted to get into all that, but what could I do? The third word was definitely "angry."

"I mean…most of the time I managed to plod along, thinking: 'well, maybe this isn't so bad, after all.'" I said, sighing. "But then all of a sudden and for no apparent reason, I'd find myself shaking with rage."

"Rage against your grandmother?"

"No," I said, surprising myself once again. "No…. She drove me crazy, of course. She had so many idiotic rules. But in the end…in the end, I came to really love her. She hadn't had it so easy herself, you know. And she was just as stuck with me as I was with her, when you come right down to it."

Those last few sentences felt very strange in my mouth. I had certainly never put any of that into words before. But they were, perhaps, the truest words that I'd said all night.

For how else could I explain all the things I'd begun doing for Doña Isabel? How I'd begun going to church with her not just on that crazy Assumption Day weekend but on every Sunday. I never went as far as to take Holy Communion. The thought of entering a confessional with Father Domingo—or of him placing a wafer on my tongue with those pale, damp fingers—made me absolutely queasy. My grandmother would give me this rueful look whenever I stayed stubbornly on the pew as she made her way to the front of the church, but I would shake my head firmly and she never actually protested out loud. After all, there I was dutifully walking with her to the Cathedral and back home again and sitting through that entire Mass and preparing the taper for her to light the candle and make her petition to the Virgin. And, oddly enough, I found that I really wanted to do all that. How could I not? She'd looked so small going off all by herself every week in her best striped dress with her best black bag.

And how could I not help her out when she let it slip that my mother had stopped sending her *ayuditas*? I'd run to my room as soon as she'd said it, grabbed whatever remained of the three hundred dollars that Manny had first given me and pressed the bills into her bony hand.

"I couldn't possibly accept this," she'd said.

"You must," I'd answered.

And how could I not stay home from school to help her launder all those damned priestly vestments on the days when Carolina didn't show up? She'd accepted without protest my assurances that cutting a few classes wouldn't make any difference in my learning. It was clear that it was a struggle for her to do it alone, and that she knew it.

"There are three types of people in this world, Paloma," she had told me one Friday when we found ourselves moving our scrub brushes back and forth in tandem. "Those who cause suffering. Those who endure suffering. And those who rescue others from suffering. Have you considered that perhaps that's where you fit into God's scheme of things? As one of the people who rescue and heal?"

At first, I'd cringed at those sanctimonious words. Not long afterward, however, I found myself fantasizing about how I would go about rescuing a string of beautiful maidens from their suffering. And liking the idea very much. Who understands these things?

Serach had remained perfectly still while I went through that whole long internal monologue. But at a certain point I realized that she'd begun speaking.

"So, why *were* you so angry, Paloma?"

"What?"

"If you weren't mad at your grandmother, what *were* you so mad at?"

"I was mad because I thought—*hell, I knew*—that I deserved better."

"Ah," said Serach with more of an edge to her voice than usual. "Well, you did. You did deserve better. No one deserves to be stuck in a box like that, with no way to get out." Then she sighed and her tone came down a notch. "But did you actually know what you *did* want? What you knew you deserved?"

"No, it was all pretty vague. Broader vistas, maybe? A bigger stage to perform on? I don't know. All I knew was that I'd never get what I wanted in Santa Fe de Antioquia. That I'd only get it if I somehow found my way back to New York."

"And so how did you finally arrange it? You've never really told me."

"Oh. Well, as soon as my brother Manny got on his feet and got a place of his own, he sent me my airfare and said I could come live with him. And I grabbed that lifeline with both hands—just like he'd always said I should—and was out of there in a flash."

"So he never forgot about you, your brother."

"Manny forget about me? Hell, no. How could he forget about me? He's my brother! Brothers and sisters don't forget about one another. That's the closest bond there is."

I suddenly realized that Serach had stopped stroking my hand. That she'd gone very quiet again. Oh, Jesus, I'd forgotten all about that peculiar little brother of hers and how much she missed him. So now it was my turn to be the comforter. The soother. The strong one. Well that was okay. That's how I prefer it. Still, I was damned if I was going to do my soothing with words. I was done with words for the night.

I turned over and began to kiss her. I started with those pale, silk-smooth temples of hers and moved slowly to those supple lips and on to that lovely neck. I kept going southward till I heard the swift intake of breath that confirmed that I was on the right track. And then I lifted my head for a second and grinned at her in the dark.

"So, Serach…. Any more questions about Colombia?"

"No!"

"Are you sure?"

"Yes!"

"Good."

15

In 2002, when not everyone on Fordham Road—or in Colombia, for that matter—had a computer on hand, it wasn't so odd that I was still receiving snail mail. Not that Manny wrote very often or very much. He would, however, occasionally send me silly post cards of New York landmarks with "Wish you were here!" printed on the back. And in the last week of September of 2001, he sent that very welcome postcard of Yankee Stadium stamped with the words: "Not even terrorists mess with the Bronx Bombers!"

But this time what he sent was a real letter in a real envelope with a real check inside.

Querida Hermanita,

Mama disapered with a New Man. Joe retired to PR. He sends you Hugs.

AND I GOT MARRIED. I have 2 sons reddy-made and One of my Own on the way. So Come Home, Hermanita. I have a real Home now. Here is your AIRfair.

Your Loving brother, EMMANUEL ALBERTO

Lord, I'd never realized how illiterate my brother was. Thank God for the nuns who had saved me from a similar fate. On the other hand, how well he was doing! Married! And a father! Barely twenty years old and already a grown man! I suddenly couldn't stand my life in exile for a single moment longer. I ran to Doña Isabel and told her I was going home.

She said nothing for a long moment. And then she said, softly, "So, I'm losing you again."

"No, you aren't. Never! I'll send you letters every month and as soon as I start working I'll put *ayuditas* inside them. And I'll never forget your kindness—yours and Carolina's. You'll always be in my prayers. I promise."

I suspected that saying good bye to Lupita would produce volcanic results. It was one of the reasons I'd never had the guts to dump her despite her regular bouts of block-headedness. Well, that and the fact that I loved spending time with her family. And that a lesbian school girl didn't have a whole lot of other options in Santa Fe de Antioquia, Colombia.

But, just as I'd feared, my statement produced this violent eruption of yelling and crying and beating on that splendid chest of hers.

Eventually, however, she rubbed her eyes with her palms and wiped her nose on her sleeve.

"I knew it wouldn't last," she said. "You've always been headed for the big time. But here's a kiss to remember me by. Don't ever forget what we had."

Oddly enough, it was Carolina who took things the hardest. Who would have thought it? She wept on and off for hours, crossing herself and asking whatever she and Doña Isabel would do once I'd abandoned them. My grandmother finally stepped in. "Carolina, hush!" she said with that calm that never failed her. "It's the will of God."

The night before I left, Doña Isabel knocked on my door. I opened it to find her standing in her nightgown clutching a clumsy bundle wrapped in deep blue velvet.

"Doña Isabel! What is it? It's so late for you to be up."

"I've given the matter a great deal of thought," she said. "And I've decided to give you something."

"Come in, come in." I hesitated to ask her to sit on my bed. It seemed so intimate. But what else could I do? I sat down and patted the mattress next to me.

"Last year, after we'd finished our year of hosting the statue of our Lord Jesus Christ, Father Domingo—may God always smile down on him—realized how bereft I felt." She took the seat I'd offered. "And so he had these made for me."

She put the bundle down and unwrapped it carefully. "Look! A pair of exact replicas of the original statues. He commissioned them from a master woodworker in Medellín."

And indeed, that's just what they were. A miniature Jesus with painted blood running down his face and chest and a head covered with something that probably wasn't real hair but that (on the other hand) might well have been. Likewise, a miniature Virgin Mary. Unlike Jesus, however, the Blessed Mother's hair was only painted on. And she was actually quite lovely in her carved pale blue robes covered with silvery stars.

"Father Domingo must truly think a great deal of you."

"Well, yes, I do think he does. I come from a very old family, after all. But then, so do you. So I want you to have them."

"I couldn't possibly!" It was the first time she'd ever included me in her ancient lineage, so I couldn't help but be moved. But there was no chance on earth that I was going to take that Jesus statue home with me. It scared the living daylights out of me. The Bronx Irish, bless their souls, had never been so morbidly explicit about Our Lord's corporeal attributes.

"But yes, you must. They'll remind you of your stay here. And they'll protect you when you get back home. New York is a dangerous place these days, you know." She crossed herself.

"I am overwhelmed by your generosity, Doña Isabel," I stammered. "But you absolutely must not give up both of your beautiful statues. I'll tell you what. You keep the statue of our Savior and I'll take the one of the Blessed Mother. And we'll each think of the other whenever we see the one that we have. It will be a bond between us."

My grandmother actually looked pleased. "That's a very nice idea."

"Yes, I think so too."

"All right, then. I'll leave you the Blessed Virgin and the velvet cloth in which to wrap her up. And I'll go buy another length of it for my Jesus later this week."

"Good. And now, you go get some sleep. We both have to get up very early."

"Yes, Hijita." Yes, *my daughter*. And I received the first and last hug my grandmother ever bestowed on me.

16

What struck me most when I first spied Manny at the Newark air terminal was how substantial he'd become. His dimples were now cozily imbedded in ample cheek rolls and his sturdy body squarer than ever. He swiped the duffle bag right out of my hands, threw it on the ground, picked me up by the waist and spun me around.

"Hermanita! You've become a woman!"

"And you, Manny, have become a man!"

"Have I ever! Ay-yay-yay. Three times over. Wife, children, house. The full catastrophe!"

For a while, we drove off in happy silence. Finally, he smiled a private smile.

"So, Hermanita. What is she like, our abuelita?"

"Well, for starters, she doesn't like that term. She prefers 'Doña Isabel.' She's very serious. Very Catholic. Wears long, long dresses that cover her up from chin to ankles to wrists. It took a while, but in the end I think she finally accepted me. And you, too. There are some gorgeous cowboy boots for you in that duffle bag. They're from her."

"Hey, Hermanita! Thank you!" He grabbed my shoulder and squeezed.

"But never mind our grandmother, Manny. I'll tell you all about her later. What I really want to hear about is you and your new family! Tell me everything!"

"Well, first of all, I'm fully on track to becoming a partner in the *Los Milagros* Auto Shop. Fernando's father admits that he can't do without me."

"That's fabulous, Manny! And Fernando?"

"Gone. No interest at all. He's enrolled in the Marines and will be deploying out to Afghanistan any day now."

I heaved a sigh. I'd been looking forward to spending some time with him again.

"And your wife?"

"Ah, my Beatriz."

"What is she like? Is she Colombian like us?"

"No, she's Dominican—and as beautiful as they come. And she's older than I am so she's also very wise."

"Just how much older?"

"Five years."

"And she has two sons?"

"Two sons. But they're *my sons too*, now. The adoption papers just went through. And *coño*, how they love me! And then, in just over three months, Ramon Rodriguez will arrive. And look out, world!"

There was nothing to reply to that so I just leaned over and rubbed his upper arm a few times with my knuckles as he skillfully stick-shifted down the highway.

"And does Beatriz work outside the house, too?"

"She does. She takes care of this old Jewish lady in Brooklyn. Cooks for her, cleans for her, does everything she needs. Takes her for...what's it called? Dialysis? She can manage anything, my Beatriz."

He shook his head side to side a few times. I could hear the vertebrae popping in his formidable neck. "The lady is missing a leg," he said, after a moment. "Which means that Beatriz has to bathe her, too. And she has to be very, very careful when she does that. The lady is gay. Who knows what she might try to do with my beautiful wife?"

I hit him.

"No offense, no offense. But really, Paloma, maybe you can give Beatriz some hints? Tell her what to avoid doing if she wants to protect herself?"

"¡*Pendejo*!"

Manny laughed. "It's good to have you home, Hermanita."

I had to laugh, too. "Manny, your life sounds wonderful. But it also sounds as if…you and Beatriz have your hands full. Answer me honestly. How can I possibly stay with you with everything else that's going on? I'll try to be helpful of course, but I'm bound to be a burden."

"Hermanita—you're family. There's always room for family. I couldn't do anything for you while I was still living at Fernando's. But now that I have a home of my own, my house is your house—*mi casa es su casa*."

My totally thick-headed, unperceptive, ridiculously generous *pendejo* of a brother.

17

Here's what I was expected to do: Shop and cook. Get the two boys—Negrito and Gordito—up, dressed, breakfasted, and safely delivered to day care, five days a week. Pick them up at the end of the day and serve them the dinner I'd made. And then serve a second round of that dinner to Beatriz when she came back from work and a third one to my brother once he'd washed the grease from his hands and changed from his coveralls into the clean jeans and T-shirt that I'd laundered earlier that day.

And—oh yes—pitch in at the register at the *Los Milagros* Auto Shop on Saturdays, whenever the woman who was supposed to be there decided she didn't have to show up. Which was most of the time. ("If Fernando's father weren't screwing that idiot's brains out, he'd never put up with her behavior," Manny explained. "But it sure works out for you, since it gives you the chance to earn some spending money.")

The first night I arrived, Beatriz informed me that I would be sleeping on the couch in the living room and that I should keep all my things in my duffle bag and keep the duffle bag shoved deep under the couch at all times. She also told me to be sure to dismantle all the bedclothes, fold them neatly and put them away in the hall closet as soon as I woke up. And that as soon as I had finished serving the last dinner shift I should wash every dish and pot I'd used and put everything away.

And did I mind all those bossy orders and all those tiresome chores? No, oddly enough, I didn't. I was never unaware that—family or no family—my position in Beatriz's house was conditional on my good behavior. And, perhaps even more to the point, I recognized and respected the fact that it wasn't just me laboring like an ox. That *everyone* in that household did far more than their share.

My sister-in-law was an incredible worker, whatever else she was. She was a flawless housekeeper. I suspect the only reason that cleaning duties were omitted from my own assignments was that she knew that I'd never be as thorough as she was. She vacuumed and dusted all morning every Saturday and—pregnant out to there and slaving all day for "that annoying old woman"—she would come home every weeknight to whisk toys away, clean spills, and (I swear) get down on her knees on the bathroom floor to give the tiles a final once-over before she went to bed.

And Manny—Jesus! He was at his post in the auto shop six days a week before dawn and he didn't leave till he was sure that everything was back in its place and ready to roll for the following day. And the moment he returned home, both Beatriz and I basically ceased to exist for the boys. It was all about their father. And he gladly did whatever they demanded of him.

"Papi, Papi, pick me up!" they would yell as soon as he walked in. And no matter how deep the slump of his shoulders when he'd first appeared in the doorway, the sight of those boys would light up his face. He would lift them up and toss them around till they shrieked with joy. He would sit them on his lap while he ate, nuzzling them and talking to them and giving them bits of food from off his plate. And as he carted them off to bed, he would hug them to his chest with a ferociousness of love that brought tears to my eyes, every single time I saw it.

So what could I do? I kept my mouth shut (some of the time) kept to the rules (most of the time) and did my work (all of the time). It was a fair deal. I was back in New York. Nobody gave a damn where I was or what I did, just as long as my chores were taken care of. And I had one entire day off every single week to spend any way that I pleased.

Sundays were a true Sabbath day of rest in that household. No one went to church or expected me to do so. Beatriz slept in and then read the papers all day. Manny got the boys up and then sprawled with them on the couch in front of the television to watch cartoons and ball games and eat Cheetos and drink orange soda till it was time to order in Chinese food for dinner.

And I took to the streets.

The neighborhood was a whole lot dirtier, a whole lot noisier, and a whole lot tougher than I remembered. ("Hermana, you turned into a snob living with our grandmother in the 'town that time forgot,'" Manny told me the first time that I remarked on the litter constantly blowing down the sidewalks. "It's always been like this. And what do you expect, when the Sanitation Department has never even heard of this part of the Bronx?" And when I yelped as my hand unexpectedly knocked into that gun that Manny kept so casually stored between a pile of unpaid bills and a box of paper clips in the top drawer of the desk at *Los Milagros,* he had only laughed and shrugged. "Well, Hermanita, like I told you. This isn't Disneyland. This is the Bronx.")

But what did any of that matter to me? Fordham Road was still the best place on earth. I could run up and down its full length eating mango slices with salt and hot sauce to my heart's content. I could take the Bx12 bus out to Orchard Beach to watch the waves of Long Island Sound slip in and out, in and out, just like I used to do. I could even take the D train to the Q and go all the way out to Coney Island to see the real ocean, if I liked.

And I could buy myself presents at the 99 Cent Store on the corner of Davidson Avenue. Man, that place was a paradise of treats. The first time I went in with my auto shop earnings, I took a good hour poring over all the possibilities before finally and triumphantly placing a bright red lipstick, some mascara, a frilly bra, a low-cut shirt, and a pair of high-heeled shoes on the counter in front of the cashier.

I'd developed a taste for all those things at the Romero house. Lupita and I used to sneak into the bathroom whenever we could to try on her mother's make-up and lingerie and spiky heels by the dim glow of the lightbulb hanging from the ceiling. Outside of having sex, it was our favorite thing to do.

We knew that we'd be in serious trouble if we were ever caught, so we were very careful to take everything off and put it tidily away well before her parents got home from work. But for the few delicious moments that I could stare at myself in that cloudy little mirror over that constantly dripping sink, I was totally entranced. I loved the sight of the glamorous young woman who smiled back at me. And I vowed that I would find a way to turn into that woman on a permanent basis as soon as I could.

And so it was that I rushed back to Manny's house with the purchases I'd made with my first precious paycheck and locked myself in the bathroom to try everything on. I primped in front of the mirror till I was satisfied that I'd created exactly the effect that I'd wanted and then I opened the door and sauntered out to receive the accolades that awaited me.

Beatriz looked up from the chair where she had been paging through the *Sunday Daily News* and burst out laughing.

"Jesus, Paloma," she said. "You look like *La Cucarachita Mandinga!*"

"Like who?"

"Like *La Cucarachita Mandinga*. Don't tell me you don't know who she is? Every Latina girl hears that story at least a thousand times before she reaches puberty. Every Latina mother likes nothing better than to tell it."

"Well…our mother wasn't much of a storyteller."

Beatriz closed her eyes and began to recite. "*La Cucarachita Mandinga* was a very vain cockroach who took very good care of her house," she began, clearly savoring the chance to tell me something I didn't know. "And one day when she was sweeping the front porch she found a nickel. 'Oh, what should I do with this nickel?' she asked herself. 'I know—I'll buy some lipstick and rouge and paint my face so I can attract a husband.' So she dolled herself up and soon there was a long line of animals at the door, asking for her hand. First a rooster. Then a tree-frog. Then a dog. But none of them pleased her. Until finally *El Ratoncito Perez*—the mouse—won her heart with his squeaky voice. They got married in a big wedding where everyone danced and ate and drank too much. And then—just a few weeks later—*El Ratoncito Perez* fell into a pot of rice pudding that was bubbling on the stove and was cooked to death."

I had never before heard my sister-in-law speak at such length. She was generally a one-or-two-sentence-at-a-time woman. I was so startled that I could find nothing to retort.

It might well have all ended right there and then with me wiping off my lipstick and stewing in private till dinner time. But it seems that Negrito—the older, sharper, and handsomer of Beatriz's two sons—had also been intrigued by his mother's tale. Maybe she should have told him stories more often, since he seemed to like it so much. Or maybe it was just this particular story. Whatever the case, he wriggled out of his father's arms as soon as she had finished, galloped up to me and began running around me in circles, yelling: "Paloma looks like a cockroach! Paloma looks like a cockroach! Nya, nya, nya, *nya,* nya! Paloma looks like a cockroach!"

I swiped at him. I didn't make contact—he was one speedy five year-old—but he knew I meant business and it shut him up.

And in the meantime, Manny rose heavily to his feet and began approaching us with that deliberate step of his. He bent down, picked Negrito up by the ankles and held him upside down. It wasn't angry and it wasn't playful. It just sure as hell communicated who was who and what was what.

And then he looked at me carefully and slowly, top to bottom and back again.

"You're wrong," he finally said—ostensibly to his son, but looking straight at Beatriz. He spoke very quietly, but everyone could hear it. "Tía Paloma doesn't look like a cockroach. She looks like our mother."

He lowered Negrito gently back down to the ground and helped him to stand up. He then began walking slowly back to the couch. On the way, he stopped at my side. He rested his hand briefly on my shoulder and said even more quietly, "But don't wear all that stuff when you come to the auto shop, Hermanita. You'll start a riot."

18

Who knows how long I would have stayed at my brother's, if Beatriz hadn't given birth and her employer—Judith—hadn't taken a sudden turn for the worse? I'd made a workable place for myself in that crowded apartment. Established a pattern of begrudging tolerance with my sister-in-law. Bludgeoned my two nephews into submission through a combination of fierceness, charm, and outright bribes. I was reveling in being able to eat my own marvelous home cooking and thrilled by the freedoms that I was enjoying when I wasn't doing housework or babysitting.

And I was really beginning to like my job at the *Los Milagros* Auto Shop.

Well, who could blame me? I was able to spend solid time with my brother, away from his tiresome wife and sons. I was able to share in the pride that he so clearly took in his work. There was no car on earth that Manny couldn't fix. He was trusted by his customers and respected by his three young macho assistants (though they did tend to loiter around my desk a lot when he wasn't watching). He was even clearly appreciated by Fernando's father—a man who lavished praise on no one.

I liked the smell and the noise and the action of the place. The calendar that hung over my desk with all those pictures of busty ladies in skimpy blue-jean shorts and midriff-revealing blouses, looking sexily over their shoulders.

I loved seeing the effect that I had on the shop's (almost exclusively male) customers—even with my make-up toned down to what my brother considered a reasonable level.

"I've never seen so many men so willing to settle their bills without any fuss," Manny told me, shaking his head in wonder on the first day we began making record sales. "I bet you could even add in a few dollars to the total from time to time and they wouldn't complain."

And I liked earning money through my own efforts. What other sixteen-and-a-half-year-old girl with an education as full of holes as mine could find a nearly-regular well-paid weekend gig in the tough New York City of 2002? I was convinced that Manny was paying me a higher daily rate than he'd been paying the chicken-brained receptionist I was filling in for. But I wasn't about to protest.

So how could I stop myself from occasionally daydreaming that I might someday replace her entirely? That I could work with my beloved brother six days a week, earn enough to move to my own apartment, find some foxy girlfriend, and live near Fordham Road forever.

Gone, for the moment, were any dreams of broader vistas or bigger stages. I was satisfied.

And then little Ramon arrived in the world, and my whole fantasy came crashing down.

How the hell could one baby wreck everything so quickly? Beatriz's neat little house was turned into a bedlam of strollers and diapers and cartons of formula and that damned machine that she used for heating up the bottles. How was I supposed to cook anything with that contraption taking up all the counter space?

My two finally-tamed nephews returned to their old habits of constantly yelling and demanding things. My brother was so overwhelmed with joy over Baby Ramon that he basically forgot that I existed.

And my sister-in-law was fussier and bossier than ever.

And she was in the house, right on top of me with that screaming kid, 24 hours a day.

Judith had evidently promised Beatriz a full three-month maternity leave with the guarantee that she would be rehired after that point—a practically unheard-of arrangement for a home health aide.

But Beatriz, far from being grateful, couldn't stop worrying and complaining.

"Judith's getting more demanding by the day," she'd announced shortly before Baby Ramon arrived. "She's truly getting on my nerves. I don't know if I'm going to even want to go back there after my three months off."

And after Ramon was born—when Judith called to say that it was becoming a struggle for her to get to the bathroom alone at night and would Beatriz consider staying overnight when she returned—my sister-in-law hit the ceiling.

"Is she out of her mind? Has she got some nerve? I have a husband and three sons waiting at home for me, and she wants me to spend five nights a week out in Brooklyn instead of being with them? Well, what can you expect? What would she know about family life? The hell with her! I'm never going back."

Manny lumbered off the couch and took his wife into his arms. "*Calmate*, Beatriz. It'll all be okay. You don't have to go back. You'll find a different job when it's time. We'll manage."

"And what will Judith do?" I ventured.

"What are you talking about?" shouted Beatriz. "Judith is rich, what does she have to worry about? She has no kids, no family—no one but her big fat self to look after. She'll hire someone else. Probably the woman who's subbing for me while I'm on maternity leave. Jesus, Paloma! 'What will Judith do?' Jesus!"

Suddenly the squalling baby, bitchy Beatriz, and those two other pain-in-the-butt sons of hers were too much for me to bear. I saw the chance for a new life, a full-time job—a place to live that couldn't possibly be as cramped and messy and irritating as my sister-in-law's house.

I stood up.

"I'll do it," I said. "I'll take over. I've managed difficult old ladies before. I'm good at it. Tell Judith that your sister-in-law will be there as soon as she likes. And that I'll be glad to sleep there, seven days a week."

19

In 2003, the trip from Manny's apartment on East 205th Street to Judith's mansion in Prospect Park South, Brooklyn, was no big deal. You got on the D train at the Grand Concourse and changed for the Q at 34th Street, just as if you were going to Coney Island. But instead of going all the way to the ocean, you got out at Church Avenue—a short three and a half blocks from Judith's home. It was a very fast trip when the trains came on time, and so I arrived at her house much sooner than I'd planned. I put my duffle bag down on the porch, pulled out the key that Beatriz had given me the previous evening and carefully opened the door.

Nothing that my sister-in-law had said could have prepared me for the grandeur of that house. She'd said that Judith was rich, but I'd had little conception of what that meant. And she wasn't about to enlighten me.

The room that I entered after passing through a small vestibule was as big as the sanctuary at *La Inmaculada Concepción*. It contained an enormous rolled-up-and-plastic-wrapped rug and a sea of white-draped furniture including one huge unidentified object looming like an iceberg at the dead center of the floor. What on earth could it be? A table that big? A desk? No, of course—a piano. Manny had mentioned that Judith was a singer.

A fireplace with a massive mantelpiece covered in plastic spanned one wall. Big windows—also covered in plastic— spanned the other. And leaning up against the third and fourth walls were dozens and dozens of plastic-wrapped paintings.

"HELLOOOOOOOOO!" A voice that made me stand up straight blasted out from the doorway behind me.

"I have all sorts of things wrong with me but my hearing is just fine. I heard the door. Didn't anyone teach you that you shouldn't just walk into a person's house without saying something?"

"Oh, I'm so sorry! I found the whole situation a little…."

"Overwhelming?"

"Yes."

"Yes, I suppose it is. Well, never mind the formalities, we're past that now. I'm Judith and I assume you're Paloma."

She wheeled right toward me. She was voluminous. And missing one leg from the knee down. Hence the wheelchair. Both Beatriz and Manny had warned me about that casualty of her diabetes. But it was still a shock to see the stump poking through the opening of her bathrobe like that. She had a great deal of dyed-red hair piled up on her head and dramatic facial features. She got very close to me and enveloped my hand in both of hers, much as Father Domingo had done so long ago. But unlike Father Domingo—whose hands were so cold and limp—Judith's hands were warm and strong.

"So. Beatriz says you cook very well."

"I do. Though it's mostly just Latin food."

"That's all right. I've done several tours of South America, you know. Performed in the *Teatro Colón* in Buenos Aires and the *Teatro René Moreno* in Bolivia. And in your own native Colombia, I sang in the *Teatro Metropolitano* in Medellín. I love your kind of cooking. Of course," she leaned her head back, closed her eyes and smiled, "I love almost any kind of food. French. Italian. Mid-Eastern. Good old American. Eating…is something I'm supposed to be very careful about these days. But when almost everything else is gone in life, what is left besides eating? So. There are all sorts of cookbooks in the kitchen. No one's used them for a while—they've been just waiting for someone like you to come along. You'll experiment. You'll grow. They say that once you're a good cook you can learn anything."

"Yes, I'm sure I can. But listen. Let's clear something up. I'm not Colombian. That's my mother. I'm American. I was raised in the Bronx."

"No matter. You've lived overseas, haven't you? Beatriz said so. I like an adventurer! Someone who's traveled. Someone who's up for something new."

"Well, that I am."

She was silent for a moment, narrowing her eyes and giving the smallest, slightest smile.

"And then...as far as the rest of my routine...."

"Yes?"

"You aren't afraid of the human body, are you?"

"No, of course not."

"Mine is quite extensive. And very odd in several places. You'll bathe me, of course. There's a whole gizmo rigged up in the bathroom for that. I'll show you how to use it. And you'll sleep downstairs on a cot in the den so I can yell for you in the middle of the night if I need to. I'm set up right next door in the dining room—hospital bed and everything. Can't manage stairs any more, you know. And you'll take me to Downstate Medical Center for dialysis once a week. There's a car service that I use. They have these marvelous drivers—they'll help you haul me up and down to the street from the porch. At some point I'll have to go more often. And ultimately, I'll have to bring all the dialysis equipment right into the house. But we'll worry about all that when it happens. And meanwhile we'll enjoy ourselves. You don't sing, do you? I could give you voice lessons...."

"No, I'm not a singer. In fact, my brother always told me that I was tone deaf."

"Well, you can't have everything. But perhaps there are other things I could teach you."

"I'm sure there are."

"And last but not least, Frank is arriving tomorrow, thank God. He's going to supervise the painting of the living room. I don't normally live in such chaos, you know. Frank is my accompanist. He's a world-famous pianist and travels constantly. But when he's in New York, this is where he stays. So later today you should go upstairs and make sure that his room—it's the first one on the left—is aired and clean. Maybe you can get some fresh flowers for it? There are stores for that sort of thing on Church Avenue. In fact, you should probably explore the whole neighborhood a bit after you've washed me up and made me some breakfast. It's a fascinating area, in its own way."

"Okay."

"And listen, Paloma. I've put up with a lot of very bad aides, but I can tell you have promise. I'm sure we're going to get along very well."

20

By the second day I had adjusted to my new routine. Judith was bathed and fed. The shopping was done and the larder stocked with her favorite foods. I was cleaning up the kitchen when the doorbell rang three times. A key turned in the lock and in marched a tall thin man with greying light brown hair and oversized tortoise-shell glasses. He was carrying two enormous leather suitcases and was followed by three short, stout Mexican men lugging paint cans and ladders.

"JUDITH DARLING—I'M HERE!"

I disappeared into the dining room, thinking to help wheel Judith in to him but she was already way ahead of me, barreling toward us.

"Frank! Not a moment too soon! I have been living with those ghastly drop cloths for nearly three months now. You naughty man! Setting everything up and then blowing away like that. How was Berlin?"

"Very German, dear. But I wowed them all, despite their snooty ways. They thought I was simply fabulous." He turned to the Mexicans. "Okay, boys. You can put your things down. But don't even *think* about starting without me! Don't touch any of the drop cloths—it's all priceless antiques under there and Madame can't risk losing anything to your clumsy hands. And for *God's* sake don't get anywhere near the piano." He put down one of his bags and brushed the hair out of his eyes. "Judith, I'm going to put my things in my room and then I absolutely must eat something—I've had nothing but airplane food for twenty-four hours, God help me. I went straight from the airport to the paint store—see how much I love you, darling?—and then rode here in that awful paint truck crammed in with these boys' paraphernalia."

"You poor dear! Well, Paloma will fix you something nice."

"Thank God. I'll be right back. And remember—don't do a thing till I tell you, boys!"

"So, what would you like to eat?" I called as he zipped by me and began mounting the stairs.

He turned on his heel. "How about some softly scrambled eggs with sliced mushrooms sautéed lightly in unsalted butter and some fresh orange juice? And two slices of whole wheat toast with marmalade? And some coffee? Oh, God, yes, some coffee. Strong. Black. No need for milk or sugar. I'm not picky that way."

"It's exactly what *you* wanted," I said to Judith

"Well he knows it's what I like to eat, so we were bound to have it all on hand. He behaves like a princess on steroids most of the time, but he can be reasonable about certain things."

I served Frank and then poured myself my own cup of coffee and sat down on the other side of the table where I could get a good look at him. Clearly the only way to avoid being treated like a servant by this man was to establish my equality immediately and firmly.

"So you're Paloma—come to rescue our diva in distress."

"Looks that way."

"Do you love her very much yet?"

"Well, I…."

"Well, you absolutely *must* love her. That's what she needs more than anything else. She's my best friend in the whole world, and I'd be here myself full time catering to her every whim but an artist has to do what he has to do. I swear, Paloma, these are the most delicious eggs I've ever eaten. What luck! And now to work!"

The painters stayed for three days, scraping, plastering, priming, and finally painting the walls a shade of buttery yellow that seemed more appropriate to Santa Fe de Antioquia than to a house on a Brooklyn street. But what did I know? Frank—after a thousand complaints and requests to remix this batch or put an extra coat on that section—finally seemed perfectly satisfied. And Judith seemed pleased, too. She tipped the men extravagantly well from what I could see and they began collecting their brushes, rollers, empty paint cans, and ladders.

"Leave one of those ladders here—I'll need it to rehang all the pictures," Frank called out to them. "I'll phone you to pick it up when I'm done, along with the drop cloths."

The men continued cleaning up silently. Perhaps the tip they'd received helped. Or perhaps they were just used to being spoken to in that way. Is this then what Joe had always complained about? And Juana, too? I ran to the door as they were leaving and called out to them in Spanish. "Bye! Thanks for everything!"

They mumbled something over their shoulders as they descended down the stairs from the porch. Couldn't quite make it out. Clearly, I had no idea how to deal with all the nuances of this strange new world of mine. Or with the peculiarly ambiguous position that I'd assumed within it. Well, I'd have to learn.

Back in the living room, Frank was carefully pulling drop cloths off the furniture, unrolling the rug and placing each piece where it belonged while Judith surveyed his actions with approval. I dared not suggest helping him. Clumsy hands, indeed!

He finished unwrapping and rearranging everything except the piano and then stood absolutely still for a long moment, gazing at it. Eventually, he advanced on it like a large cat. He reached out with one long arm to grab the drop cloth and whipped it off in a single movement, throwing it forcefully to the ground behind him. Stronger than he looked, skinny Frank.

He then drew in a noisy and reverent breath.

It was, in fact, an extraordinary object. I had no idea that pianos could look like that. Its body was carved with bounteous flowers and leaves and its legs were garlanded by vines. Its color was somewhere between maple syrup and pure gold and it gleamed as if someone had spent hours polishing it to mirror-like brilliance. Was that my sister-in-law Beatriz's handiwork?

Frank walked up to it and began stroking it. He moved his fingers in slow circles along the top and then paced slowly all the way around it letting his hands drift across its full circumference. Finally, he squatted down and ran his palms slowly up and down each of the three legs in turn. It was so sensual that I flushed.

And then once he had finished worshipping every square inch of the piano's outer shell he uncovered the keyboard, propped open the top, pulled out the bench and sat down to play.

I thought the ceiling would fly off to reveal the heavens with that first piece. And as soon as he had finished, he moved on to play something that was as fine as glass. And then he paused, looked at Judith sitting beside me and hit a single cluster of notes. And with that, the voice of an angel began pouring right out of that fat, noisy lady in a wheelchair with a leg stump sticking straight out in front of her.

"*Pie Jesu Domine...dona eis requiem*," she sang. "Lord Jesus in thy mercy...grant them rest." Over and over again. It started out softly and tranquilly. It swelled to a level that made my heart vibrate. And then—slowly, slowly—it all faded back into silence.

If I hadn't loved Judith before, surely I loved her then. And I also found myself willing to forgive Frank for everything. I would have followed him to the ends of the earth if only he would play for me again.

"Beethoven. Then Bach. And then the fourth movement of the Fauré *Requiem*," he said, giving me his smuggest smile. "It's one of our favorites. You should have heard her perform it at the *Saint Chapelle*. The crowds wept. Just like you."

"Okay, *mes enfants*," said Judith. "Show's over. Get to work. Let's get that art back on the walls."

21

The next two days were spent in interminable bickering, reminiscences, cajoling, and compromise over where to hang each of the carefully unwrapped art works. I heard names of artists that were not entirely foreign to me. Picasso and Leonardo Da Vinci came up, for example. But there were also dozens of names that I'd never heard of before and a few that I never heard mentioned again. "Lesser artists," Frank explained.

Frank showed more patience than I ever would have expected. He climbed up and down the ladder for hours. He held up each work, asking Judith's opinion and letting her know his own. When he and Judith were finally in agreement as to locations and groupings he made markings on the wall with his little pencil.

Some of the works were actual paintings and some were prints carefully mounted under glass. Some were just black and white drawings. But whatever the medium, the subject matter fell into only one of two categories. Either naked ladies or the Virgin Mary.

I had never seen so many women displayed in so many poses. There were coy ladies and languidly uninhibited ones and positively obscene ones. In a few instances the figures were so distorted that I could barely make them out.

And I'd never seen so many Virgins. In several pictures she was standing stark still with a sad and startled face while she heard the announcement of just Who was in her womb. In others she was holding the Baby Jesus in various positions— standing on her knees, curled up at her breast, lying in her lap. There were at least three separate versions of her weeping at the Crucifixion. And finally, there were the two that became my personal favorites: the print of the 1655 Guercino *Assumption*, in which a dreamy but fully upright Mary is escorted by three lovely cherubs through rosy clouds to claim her rightful place in heaven and the similarly-stunning Bergognone *Assumption of the Holy Virgin.*

Frank fretted noisily over every work. But the piece that triggered his greatest agitation was the one he kept calling "The Modi." It was a full-fledged painting, not a drawing or a print. The woman depicted in it was attractive, no doubt about it, sprawled as she was on a divan with slitted black eyes, a come-hither expression, and a scrupulously rendered pubis. He kept sighing about it being "an original" and "a work of genius." But I really couldn't see what all the fuss was about.

For the two full days of the hanging process, I did little beyond listen to the bantering while carefully holding Frank's ladder in place. Nonetheless, I definitely felt less at sea than I had during the impromptu music recital.

I knew next to nothing about Beethoven, Bach, or Fauré. Music had never been a focal point of study either at St. Gertrude's or at *Escuela Jorge Robledo*, and all that Manny had ever played for me was salsa and rap. But I knew a whole lot about naked ladies.

Not to mention the BVM.

And so after we were all done—when we were sitting and drinking tall glasses of ice tea with lots of sugar and a mint sprig (Frank's favorite)—I felt emboldened enough to venture a comment.

"You know, I have a little wooden Virgin of my own. It's not an original, it's just a copy. But it's based on this really old Spanish statue. Would you like to see it? Perhaps…perhaps you'd even like to put on the mantel? I'd let you put it there, if you wanted."

"Sure, Paloma," said Judith after a pause.

I ran to my makeshift room and rummaged through my duffle bag. I retrieved Doña Isabel's velvet-covered bundle and ran back to place it in Judith's lap.

"Here—let me help you unwrap it," I said and bent over to do so. I carefully moved aside the folds of velvet, pulled the Virgin out and stood her upright to face my employer.

Judith just sat there silently for a minute. Finally, Frank strolled over, took it from her and began turning it this way and that in his long fingers.

"Well," he said. "It's not *absolutely* hideous. It does have a certain…primitive charm."

I walked up to him and took it back from his hands. I gathered the velvet cloth off of Judith's lap where it still lay and went quickly back to my room, rewrapping my little Virgin as I went.

For a long moment I just sat on my bed, cradling her in my arms. Finally, I took her out of her velvet swaddling and set her on the table next to me so I could look into her face.

I felt my shame and rage ebb under the calmness of her gaze. She was still as beautiful to me as ever. She still contained all the love that my grandmother had placed in her. Frank and Judith could never take that away from me.

But at the same time, what was stopping me from learning more about all that art that they went on and on about? About all the art that had, in fact, lifted me up so thrillingly on the day that Judith first sang and Frank had played that piece of Beethoven? Why couldn't I learn to feel comfortable with all that stuff as well?

Why couldn't I be bilingual?

Hell, I already was.

22

The next morning as I bathed Judith, she remained unusually quiet. But as soon as she was dressed and I'd pulled her wheelchair up to the breakfast table, she reached over and took my hand.

"Paloma."

"Yes, Judith."

"Paloma, please forgive Frank. He was unconscionably gauche last night."

"It's okay. Don't even think about it."

"No, Paloma, I can't help but think about it. It's the unbearable snobbery of our clan."

"Frank's not part of your clan, Judith! He's not Jewish. He's a lapsed Catholic. He told me so himself."

"I'm not talking about him being Jewish. And in any event, we Jews call ourselves a 'tribe' not a 'clan.' No—I mean the Clan of the Educated. It's the tightest clan in the world."

I took this in.

"We impose no religious qualifications on our membership but we have these very well-demarcated boundaries dividing those who are in from those who are out."

"Judith," I said slowly. "It's okay. Really. Let's just forget about it."

"No, Paloma. It is not okay. I was very embarrassed for you."

I went back to scrambling eggs, sautéing mushrooms, brewing coffee and making toast. It took a while for me to sort out what I wanted to say so I was glad that she respected my silence.

"The hardest part," I finally said as I poured out her coffee, "is that Frank is right. I mean, it's not good manners to look down on anyone. But the truth is I wouldn't know a good piece of art from a bad one. Or how to explain the difference."

She waited.

"And the thing of it is that…I mean I never really thought about it before but…I think I would like to be able to do that. I know it sounds crazy. But I wish that I could…."

"Join the Clan?"

"Yes, join the Clan. But I don't see how that could be possible."

"Don't be ridiculous! Anything is possible. Why, I'll induct you into it myself. Be your personal guide. I've traveled the world and studied at the greatest institutions, you know. My father was a scholar and a collector so we have quite a library to draw on right in the next room. You're bound to have seen it."

"Well, yes. I've been sniffing around. But do you really think…?"

"That I can give you a proper introduction to the world of art and literature and history? Paloma, you cut me to the quick. I'm old and halt but I can still teach. We'll begin with Berenson. His two-volume set on Italian Renaissance art is the best of the best. It's on the third bookcase to the left, right near the top. The whole bookcase is art history, alphabetically arranged, so you should be able to find it in a minute. Well, what are you waiting for, my girl? Hurry up and serve me my eggs! We have no time to lose!"

23

And so began the next phase of my education. It was definitely not what I would have gotten in any school that I might have attended. It was entirely based on what was available in Dr. Skollar's library and on what most appealed to Judith's tastes—and its methodology was highly unusual. Basically, she just had me read aloud to her from the works she selected while she corrected my enunciation and projection and asked me a slew of questions to make sure I'd understood what I had read.

"It's the only way we can attend to your elocution, your vocabulary, and your substantive knowledge at one fell swoop," she proclaimed.

We got through the Berenson and then zoomed through a few books on twentieth-century art. "We can forget all that in-between nonsense," she said. "The Impressionists are nothing but fluff."

We read several histories of the Jews. "Just as you can't understand Western art till you understand the way that Giotto painted the Virgin, you can't understand Western theology and law till you know something about us," Judith asserted. "We invented everything, you know."

When we got to Josef Eisen's account of the history of the Spanish Inquisition, I found myself sweating. Suddenly the pointy purple hoods of Antioquia's *Semana Santa*—and the prideful way that Father Domingo had spoken about them—made new sense to me. But Judith, with admirable tact, said nothing at all during those particular readings.

We spent a little time on the diplomatic history of World War II ("Isn't it marvelous how Roosevelt keeps calling Stalin 'Uncle Joe?'" Judith crowed. "Absolutely nothing on earth scared that man!")

And finally, we plunged into what Judith termed "the masters of the English language." We read *The Tempest, Hamlet,* and *Romeo and Juliet.* And then the King James Version of the Book of Genesis, the Gospel According to St. Matthew and Corinthians I. And then all of Lincoln's speeches.

When I first told her that I had already read the New Testament, she scoffed. "Not the way that I'm going to teach it," she said. "Do you sprinkle phrases from that glorious book into your speech? Do you let those incredible words pour off your tongue at the appropriate moment? You must learn to do so. If you memorize everything that I open your eyes and ears and soul to—if, for example, you memorize Christ's Sermon on the Mount as well as Prospero's last speech and Lincoln's Second Inaugural Address —you'll have the most beautiful words ever written at your disposal whenever the occasion calls for them. So go to it! Learn them!"

The one thing we didn't touch upon was music. When I asked Judith about it, she said that I had admitted to being tone deaf, so what would be the point? I wondered, however, whether it had just become too painful for her to think about the most important thing she'd lost in life. As far as I could tell, she'd never sung again after making me the gift of that one heavenly movement from the Fauré *Requiem.*

We skipped our lessons on Sundays, so I could go visit Manny and his family. And on Mondays, so we could go to the hospital for Judith's dialysis treatments. And on every other Wednesday, so she could go to the beauty parlor to have her "red touched up." Other than that, however, we studied together four or five hours a day for eight glorious months.

At some point during the ninth month, however, things began to change. I'd look up in the middle of my reading to find her dozing. Or she would ask the same question several times over. The dialysis appointments became a twice-a-week and then a three-times-a-week affair. She stopped wanting to be taken to the beauty parlor for her color touch-ups.

And then finally one day she said the words that I'd hoped I'd never hear.

"I haven't enjoyed anything as much as this education project since I last sang at La Scala," she announced. "But I think this is it."

I was aghast. "This is it? I'm all educated? No way!"

"You're educated enough to continue on your own. Just look how you've blossomed! Your speech patterns have changed radically. Your vocabulary has expanded exponentially. And your dramatic readings are glorious, thanks to my coaching. But my knowledge base is finally exhausted. And…and I am exhausted as well."

I was silent, so she continued without me.

"So now comes the hard part. I've been thinking about it. You need to bone up on what's on the GED exam and go take it. And then it's off to college with you to begin the journey toward a degree. You'll never get anywhere in life without that piece of paper, you know. So you're going to do whatever it takes to get through all that, and I'm going to pay. What would you like to major in? Hmm? What's the matter? Cat got your tongue?"

Going to pay?

"Paloma! I didn't educate you just to sit and chat with me about Hamlet's dilemmas. I'm not going to be here forever. You need to move forward. What are you going to do with your life when I'm gone? Be a home health aide to some other old lady?"

"I…don't know. Maybe. Or maybe I'll work in an auto shop."

"An auto shop! Paloma, be serious."

Snobbier than my grandmother, old Judith. Well, how on earth would she understand how wonderful it had been for me to work there with Manny? She had never had to live in the real world. But I held my tongue. She was offering me a choice, after all. She was asking what I wanted to do with my life. Who had ever done that before? Go for it, Paloma. Think big.

"Well, maybe a chef? I'm good at cooking…."

"It's a cut-throat world being a chef. Harder than being an opera singer, as far as I've heard. How about nursing? You have, in your own immortal phrase: 'healer's hands.' Couldn't stop my failing kidneys—no one could. But I can't tell you how many times you've soothed my pain just by stroking my head or clasping my hand."

"A nurse?" Suddenly all those old visions of rescuing—of healing—scores of maidens in distress popped back into my head. Hadn't thought about that idea for a while. But hadn't it appealed to me mightily? And hadn't Doña Isabel said that it was my destiny?

"Yes, Paloma. A nurse. If you're going to empty bed pans for a living, you might as well have some status and make a decent salary. So get yourself to the library and find out what you have to do and where you have to do it and how much it costs. And then we'll take it from there."

"But how can I do all that and still take care of you?"

"I'm going to hire a real nurse, Paloma. I've played Violetta enough times to know when I'm dying. You can still do the cooking for me, if you like. And I'll continue to pay you so you can keep sending your grandmother those '*ayuditas*' of yours. The house will be yours to use. We'll move you upstairs and get you a computer. And when I'm gone, you'll take it all over. The mortgage is paid up and the roof and boiler are sound, so you needn't worry. And there is enough cash to cover grad school, if you want to keep honing your skills. No—not a word of protest! You are not allowed to deny me this pleasure. It's decided and done. The Modigliani will be Frank's and you'll have to let him stay upstairs and play the Bösendorfer whenever he's in town. But the rest of what I have will be yours…."

I turned my head away from her so she wouldn't see my tears. I couldn't look her in the face. Not only had no one ever asked me what I wanted to do before, no one had ever offered me the tools I needed to do it. Manny was as dear and as generous as they come, but in so many ways he hadn't ever had a clue as to who I really was or what I could possibly be. We hadn't been raised to think in terms of possibilities.

"I don't know what to say," I said. "And whatever I say, I'm going to start bawling."

"At times like that, it's generally best not to say anything."

Years later, when I asked Frank why he thought Judith had done so much for someone who was no more than her home health aide, he threw up his hands.

"Paloma, you are so dense. You weren't 'just her home health aide.' You were the angel who swooned at her singing at the point when she thought she'd never have that effect again. The daughter she never thought she'd have. Plus, even at the height of her powers she never dared dream that she'd get a daily bath from someone who looks like a cross between Queen Latifah and Ava Gardner."

"Between Queen Latifah and who?"

"Oh my God! Never mind."

24

First thing in the morning at Maimonides Hospital, my colleague Shaneequa and I would go over the day's list of transfusion patients so we could prepare our seating strategy and line up the appropriate bags of blood.

Maimonides serves a population that is primarily Haredi, though we also see blacks, Latinos, Russians, and Asians from time to time. I'd known many blacks and Latinos before arriving there, of course, and I'd gotten to know people from the other two groups as well while attending Kingsborough and Downstate. But I'd never before had any real contact with Haredi—'Penguins,' Shaneequa called them—since they kept almost entirely to themselves.

And I must say they took some getting used to.

First of all, they insisted on maintaining their own little blood bank in a special refrigerator on the third floor. They said it was for fear of contracting HIV/AIDS. None of our assurances that we thoroughly screened every drop of blood seemed to make a difference to them. Ultimately, I suspect they simply abhorred the idea of receiving blood from anyone outside their community.

And then there was the fact that the men—while permitted by their laws to be touched by a woman who is not a close relative if it is done within a strictly medical context—flinched viscerally and obviously whenever I asked them to take off their jackets, roll up their sleeves and proffer their arms for the needle. And when things got really bad for them—when their veins were so shot that we had to put ports in their chests for their transfusions— they looked utterly disgusted every time my gloved hands made contact with the skin of their upper torsos. They never spoke a single word to me. And God forbid they should ever look me directly in the eye.

The women were easier to deal with, in some respects. At least they didn't squirm when I touched them and they spoke to me when necessary. However, the tone they took when they did address me made Frank's treatment of the Mexican painters seem positively couth.

Still, it was a job. A job that I needed. And, as the nuns at St. Gertrude's would have been quick to point out, the forbearance I was forced to cultivate was a virtue.

"So," I said to Shaneequa on that momentous Thursday morning in early 2009. "Who's on the slate for today?"

"Judging from their names, one male Penguin, Type A-positive, at ten o'clock. And then a male Penguin and a Penguin lady—we'll have to set up the curtain—at eleven thirty. But they're both Type O-positive, so that's a good thing. And then we have Gloria Johnson—that old black lady who likes to sing to herself? We'll have to keep the curtain up if the male Penguin is still here and hope that Gloria keeps her voice down. She's Type A-positive again. Then we get a break from whenever Gloria's done until four thirty when it looks like there's just one more Penguin who seems to be…um, Type A-negative. Could you possibly handle him alone? Dr. Rosenfeld has asked me to help on the fourth floor this afternoon."

The early shifts went by quickly. Shaneequa and I cleaned up easily after each person left. And when we were done and Shaneequa went off to help Dr. Rosenfeld, I took a small break to grab a sandwich in the basement cafeteria before running back to retrieve the A-negative blood bag from the Haredi refrigerator for the last Penguin on our list.

I returned to my post in what I had thought was plenty of time. But clearly I hadn't been swift enough. My afternoon patient, Serach Gottesman, had already arrived. And instead of being the old black-hatted, black-coated bearded figure that I'd been expecting, Serach turned out to be a very young Haredi woman.

Young women are rare in my procedure room. Most of the blood diseases that we treat affect older people. Only leukemia tends to strike the very young. It always tears at my heart to see a younger person struggling with that cancer—though, in fact, the chances of recovery can often be good for that group.

As I approached, I saw that this particular woman wasn't wearing one of those weird wigs of theirs. She still had her own hair—long, curly blond, braided, and fastened behind with a thick rubber band. She was definitely wearing one of those dreadful, baggy dark skirts however, and her legs were incased in thick stockings with seams down the back.

Jesus, God—do they actively *try* to look so homely?

She was all alone. She had found a stool, sat down and was bent over and hugging herself tightly. How long had she been there? I felt terrible. I rushed to her side and put my hand on her shoulder.

"Hi, I'm Paloma," I said. "And I'm going to help you get through all this."

And then she looked up at me.

Her face was a perfect oval, framed by a few wispy curls that had escaped the bonds of her braid. Her eyes were grey and held more intelligence and sadness than I'd ever seen in another human being. Fra Lippo Lippi would have painted her with utter tenderness. Crivelli and Bellini would have captured her despair. And Leonardo would have taken one look at her face and created a portrait as enigmatic and attractive as ever he had painted.

And yet beyond the sadness and sweetness I also glimpsed a steel-strong determination and—yes—a spark of feisty rebellion that positively thrilled my soul. Not to mention a slender, graceful body under all those dowdy clothes.

She held my gaze. She gave me a shy smile. And I was hers forever.

25

"Oh my God, Paloma, why didn't you tell me about that delicious boyish 'roommate' of yours? And why didn't you warn her that I show up from time to time? You should have heard the shrieks this morning when we ran into one another in the kitchen. We both jumped out of our skins. I spilled my orange juice *all* over the floor."

"Oh dear. My bad. But Frank, really, when was I supposed to tell you? You haven't been here for months. You don't write or call. You come and go as you please. And Serach and I…well, it's been a total whirlwind since she moved in last March. I'm sure I mentioned you to her—explained our arrangement. But you certainly didn't let me know in advance that you were going to arrive last night, so how could I warn her? And then you just slipped into the house and traipsed up to your room, quiet as a ghost."

"I was all set to tell you last week, and then there was this sudden change in plans and I had to come back sooner than I'd thought. And when I arrived you were sound asleep, all cozily tucked in with—who knew?—your new little buddy. So what could I do besides enter on tiptoe? I thought I was being very considerate."

"Well, no permanent harm done. You clearly survived the fright. And I assume that Serach is all right, too. I haven't actually seen her yet today—Wednesdays I leave for work super-early and she doesn't come home till late. But if she were really put out, she would have called."

"No, it's all fine. We became best of friends in about ten minutes. My word, she's cute. So graceful and trim and curly-haired and grey-eyed. Way better than the cast of tattooed characters that you used to drag home from the clubs. Or that tedious classmate who complained non-stop about her landlord.

Or the idiot who kept reapplying her lipstick while I was telling her about my debut at the Aspen Music Festival."

Frank had appointed himself chief arbiter of my romantic choices early on in our friendship. I would bring someone home for his approval and he would stand there like a fussy uncle, peering over his glasses and tapping his long foot in its handmade Italian shoe. And as soon as the person was out the front door again, he would turn to me and say, "Not suitable, darling." It annoyed the hell out of me, but he always turned out to be right.

"She's definitely in a class by herself, your new love. Who knew you had a taste for sylphs?"

"I had no idea myself."

"So, does she have a brother, dear? I might be interested…. Paloma, what's the matter with you? You're going to explode if you go on laughing like that."

"Yes, Frank, she has a brother. But he can't be more than ten years old. So just totally eliminate him from your dirty-old-man thoughts. And what is more, he's ultra-Orthodox—hook, line, and sinker. I swear, he's the strangest thing you ever saw. I only met him once. He came to the hospital and read Biblical texts with Serach while she was having her transfusion. That's evidently their 'thing'. He's skinny as a worm, wears a hat like a satellite and a coat that makes him look like a giant bat. And he has these long curls hanging down the sides of his face. Actually, poor Serach hasn't seen him herself since she came to live with me. Her family has written her off. Held a wake for her. Or whatever it is they do. She puts up a brave front, but I can tell she is devastated."

"I can't believe what you're saying. Is Serach ultra-Orthodox too? That lovely thing?"

"*Formerly* Ultra-Orthodox. Yes. And I take full credit for putting her into her blue jeans, ridding her of her superstitions, and basically bringing her into the twenty-first century."

"And she gave up all her tribal affiliations just for little you? You're quite the seductress, aren't you?"

"Well, she had a few good reasons for doing it. But I was definitely one of them."

"And how did you seduce her? Do tell!"

"I was very clever, if I do say so myself. You don't push Serach, you know. She's very cautious—very deliberate. A mathematician who likes to approach things just so. So at first I simply offered her a refuge from her suffocating family. And then I just waited patiently till she came around."

"And the details, Paloma? The juicy details?"

"Ah yes, the details. Well, you know that three-room suite on the third floor—Judith's childhood bedroom, bathroom, and study? I fixed them up meticulously for Serach. And then I very gently invited her in to take up residence here while she figured out what she wanted. No pressure. No expectations. But who can resist me, after all? Eventually, she melted under my charms and came tripping into my bedroom and my arms."

"And that's all you're going to tell me?"

"She's a very private person, Frank. I have to respect that."

"Oh, Lord, Paloma. You are a total pain in the rear end. But tell me. How has she dealt with all your Latina-ness? Your Catholicism? Must have been quite a culture shock for the poor creature."

"Well, I don't go constantly harping on all that stuff, you know. But yes. She puts up with all the pictures of the Madonna in the living room, for example."

"And the Picasso nudes? And the Kahlos with all those bloody umbilical cords? And those ghastly heads on the mantel?"

"Oh, she's especially partial to those heads, Frank. You have no idea. And—no thanks to you—she's also fine with my grandmother's little wooden statue of the BVM being right there on the mantel along with them. She thinks that it's sweet. Listen, she even managed Christmas dinner at my brother Manny's house last month. One of my little nephews fell totally in love with her. She sat down on the couch, pulled a book out of her bag to read to him, and within moments he was snuggled up against her side like he'd known her forever. She has a real way with little boys. I think they sense she's one of them at heart."

"And there's been no slippage back into the Jewish Dark Ages?"

"Well…."

"Hmm?"

"Well, I will admit that I caught her sneaking out of the house in a long black skirt and big hat, headed in the general direction of Boro Park, just last week…. She told me she still has this one friend there—some eccentric older woman named Frayda. That she occasionally goes to meet up with her. To find out what's happening back home."

"I love it! She dresses in drag to go back to her community?"

"Well, I guess you could put it that way. But you of all people should understand the ferocious hold that religion can exert on a person. You call yourself a lapsed Catholic but you still get all gooey over Christmas carols not to mention every Requiem Mass ever written. And you've never given up your 'thing' for the Virgin, have you? Anyway, poor Serach! You have to feel bad for her. It's hard to lose everything."

Frank ultimately turned out to be as good a friend to Serach as to me. But he never lost that malicious twinkle in his eye when it came to Shmuely. I knew he was dying to meet him and when Shmuely finally resurfaced in Serach's life, I briefly contemplated whether I should try to arrange a sighting, at the very least.

In the end, however, my respect for Serach prevailed and I erased the idea out of my mind.

Nonetheless, I couldn't resist taking Frank into my confidence regarding Shmuely's crisis and the steps I'd taken to solve it. With whom besides Frank could I share all that? Of course, I also told him that I would blow up the Bösendorfer if he ever breathed a word of what I'd done to anyone else.

"I swear, I swear. Not a single peep out of me."

"Well, it seems Shmuely had this medical problem." I paused for a moment while I decided how to frame it.

"Paloma, don't leave me dying of suspense."

"His penis was bleeding."

"Ooooh! Ouch! Genital warts?"

"Frank, he is just a little boy! Still in *yeshiva*."

"Who knows what happens in those religious places, dear? Just look at all those Catholic priests."

"Frank, put your filthy thoughts aside for one moment. No, it wasn't genital warts. It was like a discharge—a leak—that would go on for a few days at a time. It seemed to stop on its own, and then it would come back again. Supposedly at the same time of month."

"Terrifying. Like a woman's curse."

"Exactly what he thought. Which is why he finally violated his two-year boycott of poor devoted Serach to come seek out her help."

"But, darling, it *can't* have been the curse, now can it? So what was it?"

"I figured it was a urinary tract infection. A bad one. UTIs are pretty common, you know. And tend to recur if you aren't careful. Serach once told me that Shmuely's hygiene wasn't the best. That he was always the last one in the house to bathe. And that when he did, he'd basically just hang out in the mucky water that the last sister left behind in the tub, reading those tedious texts of his and not washing. That can do it."

"Studying the Lord's words in a veritable Petri dish of bacteria?"

"In fact."

"So what did Serach do for the poor boy once she heard what was happening?"

"Well, that's the point. She couldn't do much of anything. He absolutely refused to see a doctor. Didn't want anyone to know he was 'bleeding like a girl.' She begged and pleaded with him, but it was no use. Seems he's as hard-headed as she is. Eventually, I realized I'd have to take things into my own hands."

I paused.

"Paloma! Go on!"

"So the third time that Shmuely came over was on this Sunday morning in late spring. The first two times he'd arrived around ten o'clock, but this time he showed up considerably earlier. I had just stepped out of the bath when the bell rang and Serach was still in the midst of cleaning her teeth. I grabbed my robe—that gorgeous, clingy jade-green number that you brought me back from Paris?—and dashed downstairs before Serach could finish her flossing. I tightened the sash and strolled into the living room, nonchalantly towel-drying my hair and saying: 'Serach will be down in a minute, dearie. You caught us off guard. We were just getting up.' And then I sashayed around a bit more, straightening out this and that and crooning: 'Oh, let men have their showers…soaking in the bath is the most female of pleasures, wouldn't you say, Shmuely?' Serach arrived just then and gave me a look to kill. She's a total a mother-hen with that boy. But what did I care? I'd had a job to do and I'd done it. I'll put money on the fact that he never stepped into a tub again. God forbid that our boy Shmuely should indulge in something labeled 'a female pleasure.'"

"I like baths."

"Yes, I'm sure you do. But I suspect that you're a perfect little housewife about keeping the tub immaculate. And that you scrub every part of your own precious self within an inch of its life."

Frank sniffed.

"Well, anyway, that was the 'preventive' part of my strategy. But there was still the matter of a cure. Even if Shmuely never lolled in dirty water again, God knows what damage he'd already done to his system. Kidneys are tricky. Blood in your urine is no joke. And since he clearly wasn't going to see a doctor, I was forced to do some 'laying on of hands.'"

"Paloma, for God's sake! *Laying on of hands!*"

"Don't scoff, Frank. Healing is a complicated business. Do you want to hear this, or not? So hush. I went back upstairs to get dressed and when Shmuely and Serach had finished their little visit, I dashed downstairs again, opened the front door and bolted after him. As you may know, Haredi men don't let any women except their closest relatives touch them. And Shmuely's condition made him particularly skittish about inter-gender contacts. So I had to be very sneaky about it. Basically, I ran up behind him and clamped my hands on his shoulders so hard that he couldn't escape."

"Jesus, Paloma! How did he react?"

"He squirmed mightily, I can tell you. But I told him that I was a nurse—not to mention practically his sister-in-law— and so touching was fine. And then I spun him around, put my hands firmly back on his shoulders and said something to the effect that I knew he had some kind of medical problem and he should go to a doctor for whatever it was that was bothering him. And while I was saying all that out loud, in my head I was saying a little prayer for healing to the Blessed Virgin Mary."

"Paloma you are wicked beyond belief."

"Well, I had no choice. What else could I do? Serach was worried sick about him."

"And so? Did all your evil machinations work?"

"They most certainly did. Serach told me that the bleeding never came back. But Frank, remember your promise! Not one word. To Serach or to anyone else."

"Cross my heart and hope to die."

26

What I told Frank about my whole baths-are-for-women and laying-on-of-hands strategies was, in fact, the unvarnished truth. When it came to Serach's seduction (or to her first Christmas experience, for that matter) perhaps not quite so much. Well, Frank is ruthless. He would never have let me live it down if he'd suspected that careful little Serach had actually been three steps ahead of me when it came to jumping into bed for the first time. Or that the Christmas dinner that I'd planned so carefully had turned into a total fiasco.

I was still smarting over having been so stupid. Over having thought that dragging Serach into my crazy family for their Christmas festivities could ever have been easy. But, hell, I'd been so thrilled that Manny had liked her—so thrilled that he'd wanted her and me to be part of his celebrations—that I'd accepted his invitation without question.

"Serach, my brother Manny wants us to go to his house for Christmas. Would you even consider it? You know, Christmas isn't even really a religious thing any more. It's more of...an *American* holiday. A *commercial* holiday. You know. Gifts. Department stores. Ice skating in Rockefeller Center."

"Oh please, Paloma! For Jews, Christmas can never be anything but the holiday that confirms that we're outsiders. Even the *name* is a problem, since we're not supposed to as much as whisper the word 'Christ.' Do you know what we call it among ourselves? '*Gratzmas*.' Yes. Truly! And when we give those obligatory holiday gifts to the mailman or the superintendent or the cleaning lady, we're supposed to just hand them over with a grunt. Some people are willing to go so far as to say: 'Happy New Year!' But most won't even do *that*, because—for us—the New Year is Rosh Hashanah, and the whole January First thing is strictly pagan."

Serach watched me blanch at her words and smiled that private little smile of hers. She contends that the teasing in our house only goes in one direction. I know better.

"So…you won't go with me?"

"Of course I'll go, Paloma. When have I ever turned down one of your invitations to go on an adventure?"

Once Serach agreed, all I could think about was how to make it perfect.

We weren't due at my brother's house till six o'clock, so before heading off to the Grand Concourse, we took a detour to the Gerabadian house on Pelham Parkway.

Pelham Parkway is spectacular at Christmas time. It's a mostly Italian-American neighborhood and Italian-Americans know a thing or two about spectacle. Some of the homes flash a galaxy of multicolored stars while others are elegantly decked in thousands of pure white lights. Some have Santas and sleighs on their roofs while others have large inflatable snowmen slowly rising and collapsing on their lawns.

But the Gerabadian's house is in a class all its own. And they're not even Italian, judging from their name.

First of all, it's painted bright pink—flamingo pink—so that it stands out from all its neighbors even in the summer-time. But at Christmas, the base color isn't the main point. In fact you can barely see it, since every single square inch of the outer walls is covered with strings of lights and cubic zirconia, all sparkling at top voltage.

The main point is the show.

There are mega-lit statues of the Virgin Mary, St. Theresa, assorted cherubim, and the Savior himself on the roof—along with a huge camel whose harness twinkles with big Swarovski crystals. There are glittering life-sized manikins of movie stars and other celebrities, all exquisitely dressed in designer gowns. And they all twirl around from dusk till dawn—a cross between

Madame Tussauds and the Vatican—providing fantasy visions that can be seen for blocks and that attract visitors from miles around.

As Serach and I got off the 5 train at Pelham Parkway and began walking toward all that magnificence, my eyes were more fixed on her face than on any of the lights. What would she think?

And I couldn't have asked for a more gratifying reaction—she laughed and clapped her hands and exclaimed at it all, just like a little girl.

And how lovely she looked, herself! She was wearing this little white wool cap that I'd bought her and her little white down parka and her eyelashes kept glinting as they trapped the falling snow. She looked like an angel, I swear to God, and I was totally overcome with gratitude that I had her by my side.

"I bet you've never seen anything like this, before—eh, my dear? I bet you have no holiday like this in your neck of the woods."

"Well, we have *Succoth*."

"And what is that?"

"It's the harvest holiday. Every family builds a big wooden *succah*—like a shed—with a slatted roof and one open side. Some people build it in their back yard and some on their fire escape or porch. The holiday lasts for a full eight days, and we eat our every meal inside those little sheds—and sleep there, too, if we can—to commemorate the forty years that the Israelites lived in sheds in the desert."

"And so Boro Park at '*Succoth*' time ends up looking like this? Like Pelham Parkway?"

"Well, it's very nice. All the *succahs* are decorated beautifully, and everyone goes around and admires what their neighbors have done."

"And they're decorated with….?"

"With leaves and fruit."

"With leaves and fruit?" I made a sweeping gesture to the lights and movie stars and prancing reindeer and Swarovski crystals. "Leaves and fruit? Now that's *really* impressive!"

Serach, to her credit, laughed along with me.

Finally, we got on the Bx 26 bus heading back toward the Grand Concourse and my brother's house. I was happy, excited, and nervous all at once, but I kept my mind fixed on how warmly my brother had spoken about Serach after meeting her just once and took heart.

Inside Manny's apartment it was steamy hot, and the smells coming out of the kitchen were so good that I felt faint. We took off our coats and I put them in the boys' room. And when my brother appeared and gave us both big hugs, I felt a huge welling of pride in my chest.

"Bring out Beatriz, so she can meet Serach," I told him.

"Beatriz is pretty busy in the kitchen. She'll come out soon. We're just about ready to sit down—you two are late even by 'Hora Latina' standards. So, go get yourself some *ponche*—and some for Serach, too. And go find Negrito and Gordito and Anteojitos. They'd love to see you."

And then he disappeared into the kitchen.

There was definitely something going on with him—I could sense it—and it was beginning to make my nerves pop. I left Serach looking around the room by herself for a moment and headed into the kitchen after him but Manny caught me by the shoulders before I could enter, turned me around and pushed me back out into the crowd of people taking their seats at the table.

Serach and I sat down near the foot of the table, and once we were settled, I turned to the woman on my right—some neighbor, evidently—and introduced myself.

"Hi, I'm Paloma, Manny's sister."

"Ah, the famous nurse!"

"Well, not so famous yet. But someday, maybe. When I discover a cure for something."

"Where do you work?"

"Right now I'm at Maimonides Hospital, in Brooklyn. But eventually I hope to work at Memorial Sloan Kettering. I want to make cancer care my specialty."

"Well, I'm Rafaela. I'm a hairdresser. And I wish you good luck."

"Thank you," I said. And then I remembered my manners. "And this is my friend Serach Gottesman," I said, putting one hand gently on Serach's shoulder.

They nodded to one another briefly and then Rafaela turned back exclusively to me.

"And what does *Sara* do?" she asked.

"It's 'Serach.' She's studying to be an accountant."

Rafaela took a second, harder look at us. A look of frank curiosity.

"Jewish?" she asked, suddenly switching into Spanish.

"Yes."

"Makes sense," she said.

"What makes sense?"

"That she'd be studying to be an accountant. Isn't cooking the books a Jewish specialty?"

"No. It is not."

That's all I could manage to say. It was Christmas at my brother's house and I wasn't prepared to start a fight. At least not yet.

The main question was whether Serach had understood what Rafaela said. She didn't speak Spanish of course, but tone is everything. She might have caught the nasty gist of those words.

I scanned Serach's face. She seemed okay. The noise level in the room was such that it was hard to hear anything at all, let alone find meaning in a language that you don't speak. And in any event, her attention seems to have wandered away from Rafaela altogether.

I decided to focus more intently on protecting her wellbeing and began diligently explaining all the dishes that Beatriz's sisters had prepared.

My brother finally exited the kitchen and placed himself at the table, a few seats down from me. His face was this very uncomfortable shade of pink. And then Beatriz emerged as well, carrying the central dish of the Christmas meal—the platter with the suckling pig.

She looked sweaty and exhausted—well, she always looks exhausted—but there was a smile of triumph on her face that I hadn't seen since she'd recited the *Cucarachita Mandinga* story to me. She walked straight to Serach and put the platter with the pig directly in front of her.

Everyone was exclaiming so loudly that I couldn't make out what she said to Serach as she set her masterpiece down. But Serach flushed deeply, so it couldn't have been good.

I put my hand on Serach's shoulder protectively. And then, as Beatriz passed by me she said something that I *did* manage to hear.

"Let's see what '*La Pervertida*' does now," she announced and then marched back into the kitchen.

I spent about two seconds wondering what to do. Should I pry Serach out of her seat and rush us out of there? Should I ignore what I'd been seeing and hearing? Should I risk leaving Serach alone at the table for a moment and take my brother to task for allowing this to happen?

Laying into my brother seemed the most appropriate path. And since the crowd's attention was firmly fixed on the pig, I figured Serach would be safe for a while.

I yanked Manny out of his seat and pulled him into the boys' bedroom.

"What the hell is going on, Hermano? What the hell does Beatriz think she's doing?"

"Well, Paloma, she's clearly a little upset that Serach is here."

"Didn't you know that ahead of time? Couldn't you have warned me? Or did you not tell her that I would be accompanied by my *Jewish girlfriend*."

"No, no, no. She knew. I told her Serach would be coming."

"When?"

"What?"

"*When* did you tell her?"

"Well, about three o'clock today."

"Idiot!"

"¡Paloma, *calmate*!"

"Idiot! If you'd told her earlier and let me know her reaction, I'd *never* have subjected Serach to this—this crap!"

"Paloma!"

"So what bugs your dear wife the most? The fact that Serach is Jewish—or the fact that she's gay?"

Silence.

"Hmm?"

Silence.

"Does she think Serach and her people killed Christ?"

"No, she doesn't think that...."

"Or does she think that Serach will burn eternally in hell because she hasn't accepted our Savior?"

"No, I don't think that she thinks that, either, Hermana...."

"Or does she just think that Jews are stingy bastards who control the world?"

"Well...."

"Well?"

Manny's expression began shifting from guilt toward righteous anger.

"Well, Hermanita, she *works* for Jews. She *cleans house* for Jews. And they treat her...." His voice was definitely getting its edge back. "And they treat her like *shit*. Look down on her. Refuse to give her sick days or vacation time. Make her stay late to do some idiot extra thing and don't give a damn that she's got three boys at home with no one to look after them during all those extra hours."

I couldn't argue with any of that. I could believe it. I'd seen how my Haredi patients treated me and Shaneequa.

"Beatriz says," he concluded, staring hard at me with those glowering black eyes, "that if you want a taste of hell ahead of time, go clean toilets for a rich Jewish woman."

I looked down.

"Judith wasn't like that," I finally said.

"No, not exactly. But the old bitch left everything to you, not to Beatriz, didn't she?"

I suddenly pictured what it might have been like for Manny's boys if they'd grown up running around in my big glorious house instead of being crammed into my brother's overcrowded apartment. I felt bad. For about seven seconds. And then I regained my balance.

"Judith was no bitch, Manny. She was the most generous, the most open-hearted—the smartest—the most.... Anyway, Beatriz *quit* on Judith. And I bet that she wasn't all that great to her all along. That she looked down on her because she was Jewish... and helpless...and gay."

Manny didn't answer.

"And that's the other part of it, isn't it? Beatriz hates gay people! She thinks we're perverted!"

"Well...." the shamefaced tone had returned to his voice. I was definitely back on a roll.

"Well?"

Silence.

"Well? I'd never realized what she thought about lesbians because she's never said anything about us in my presence. And she must have known that I'm gay. You must have told her. So why did she never say anything about it before tonight?"

"Well, Hermanita, you're my sister. She wouldn't dare. And... you're tough. No one messes with you. And…."

"And?"

"And…well, you at least *look* like a *woman!*"

That was it. I was done. I was fried.

"I'm out of here. I'm getting Serach and we're going home."

I grabbed our coats off Gordito's bed and marched back into the living room with Manny following close behind me.

Serach had left the table. She was sitting on the couch with Anteojitos and reading one of his new books to him. We rushed toward them, but Serach held up one hand.

"I'm not done," she said. "Stand back. You're making us nervous. It's okay, Ramon. We're going to read it one more time."

"Hop on Pop!" said Anteojitos, happily. "Hop on Pop!"

Anteojitos was talking. My mute nephew was talking! Manny grabbed my hand. He had an expression on his face that I'd never seen. I was afraid he was going to start bawling.

I'm not sure how we got through the next couple of minutes. It's all kind of a blur. But somehow Serach managed to finish reading the book to Anteojitos and turn it over to Manny. Manny managed to hug each of us good bye. And Serach and I found ourselves back on the sidewalk in our coats and in the snow, heading for the D train.

"Serach, Serach, I'm so sorry!" I was finally able to say. "I'm so sorry about Beatriz! I'm so sorry about that pig. I am so sorry about this whole evening."

But Serach seemed to be in her own little world. She may even have been humming a little. "What? Oh, don't worry about it," she said. "I know that sort of stuff happens."

"How can I not worry?" I was actually stumbling over my words. "Beatriz should be going down on her knees to you, not behaving like a total bitch. You—you worked a miracle in there with Anteojitos."

"What do you mean a 'miracle'?"

"Anteojitos was talking, Serach! My nephew was talking! It was a miracle! Don't you see how miraculous it was? How on earth did you do it?"

"Oh," said Serach, her mind clearly somewhere else. "Well… it's Christmas, isn't it? Season of miracles?"

27

"Paloma, I've been thinking. It's been ten years since you last saw your grandmother. I know you write to her every month, but that's really not good enough. Don't you think she'd like to see you? Don't you miss her?"

"I do. But my life is so complicated. It's a long trip. It's…."

"She'll die like Carolina did, and you won't have seen her, and you'll never forgive yourself. And besides, you've been working like an ox as you like to say. As I have. We deserve a vacation."

"You'll go with me?"

"Of course I will. I've never been out of this country, you know. Goodness, I've hardly been out of New York. It will be refreshing. And your grandmother sounds like someone I would really like. Old fashioned. Upright. Religious. Pick some dates and we'll make it happen."

Serach is wonderful about getting things done. She helped me find a week in which I could reasonably escape my duties at Sloan Kettering. She notified her own clients that she would be away. She made our air reservations and booked us into a little hotel not far from the old age home into which my grandmother had moved once Carolina died. And then she helped me draft the letter saying that we were coming.

"Short, sweet, and firm," she instructed me. "Don't leave her any wiggle room to protest." How on earth did she know how to handle my grandmother?

The air was as magically warm and enveloping as I remembered it as we descended from the plane onto the tarmac at Medellín. The scenery on the two-bus ride into town hadn't changed a bit. And the streetscapes of Santa Fe de Antioquia were achingly familiar. The town is a designated national treasure. Nothing can be altered without going through a long, tedious bureaucratic process. And even then, approval is generally denied.

After we checked into the hotel, we went to visit my old friend Miguel Grillo—the owner of the boot store—and then dropped in on Niña Maria, still going strong as the head of the Escuela Jorge Robledo. Everywhere we walked people flocked to greet us and told me how glad they were to see me and how proud they were that I was now a hot-shot nurse at the largest cancer facility in New York City.

We spent that first day just wandering around saying hello to everyone. Serach was enchanted by everything we did and everyone she met. "Isn't it wonderful how beloved you are here?" she kept saying.

We spent the evening eating a quiet meal and taking a dip in the pool in the hotel's interior courtyard.

And I passed the night in a welcome reprise of past tropical encounters. The salsa throbbing through the walls. The slowly undulating ceiling fan wafting warm air across every part of my body. There's really nothing like it.

Only this time, rather than thrashing around in the clutches of an overeager teenager, I was in the arms of the love of my life.

Lupita may have been hot. But Serach knows all my secrets.

I wanted it never to end. But dawn inevitably arrived. And with it, the abrupt departure of all of Serach's nocturnal sensuality. Back to her normal practical self, she shook me briskly out of my slumbers.

"Okay, Paloma. Rise and shine. You told your grandmother you'd be there first thing this morning. So off we go."

Why was it so difficult for me? Was it that I felt I'd abandoned Doña Isabel when I returned to New York? That I couldn't bear to see her so old and alone? Hard to say.

All I know is that it cost me dear to take that twenty-minute walk to my grandmother's new living quarters. It's a good thing that Latin American women are so physically affectionate with one another. No one seemed to think twice about the fact that

Serach's arm was entwined around my waist as we walked. She was literally holding me up half the time.

We got to the big yellow building to which I now sent my letters and *ayuditas*. Over the door was a sign that said: '*Asilo de los Ancianos*'—Asylum of the Aged. None of that PC stuff that was taking over America. No pretty euphemisms obscuring the fact that it was the place that people went to die.

"Gird your loins," said Serach.

"I'm a goddam nurse. I deal with disease and death all the time. Why is this so hard for me?"

"It's different when it's your own person approaching death," said Serach. "But you aren't alone, my darling. I'm right beside you."

It took me a minute to find my grandmother in the interior courtyard to which we were directed. But then I spied her waiting for us in a small chair under a mango tree, as upright as ever and impeccably clad in one of her pretty long dresses. I ran up to her and took her hands in mine.

"Abuelita!"

"Hijita!"

My eyes filled with tears so fast that it took a moment to register the fact that an eerie layer of film was marring the blackness of my grandmother's pupils. She reached out to touch my face. "This is how I see, now," she said. "Let me look at you."

When she was finished tracing my every feature I said: "I want you to meet my companion, Serach. Serach, come here and let my grandmother see your face."

Serach came close, stood very still and allowed Doña Isabel to make a second inspection.

"She's very pretty, your companion," my grandmother said at last.

We chatted for a while about my work and about Manny and his wife and children. She refused to say a word about her own health or about the sale of her beloved house. She did however seem to want to talk about Carolina's death from a heart attack, some two years before.

"I stayed with her night and day during her last week on earth," my grandmother said with quiet pride. "The poor dear only wanted to be with me. And I was only too glad to help her. But after a while, she began acting so strangely. Angry. Agitated. Her last comments, her last wishes…I'll never understand them."

"Yes?"

"She absolutely refused to receive last rites. Father Domingo had retired by then, but I knew he would have come if I'd called him. But she got totally perturbed when I suggested it. Started talking about his robes, of all things. 'All that scrubbing,' she kept saying. 'All to no purpose. Still stained. Never cleansed.' She said she didn't want to hear any of his 'babble.' Can you imagine that? She said that all she wanted was *my* forgiveness. That she hadn't spoken up when she should have. That she had just been trying to protect me. That I'd suffered enough. What on earth do you think she meant? Spoken up about what? Protected me from what?"

We were all very quiet for a moment.

"She died in my arms."

"You must really miss her," I finally ventured.

"Carolina's mother worked for my mother till my mother died, you know. And Carolina was with me from the first day that I was married. I never needed anyone else."

And then my grandmother said that she was really tired and wanted to go back to her room to lie down.

"But before I go, I must tell you one more thing. There's something you have to do for me."

"Of course. Whatever you want."

"Have you been to the Cathedral yet?"

I gave a sheepish smile that she couldn't see. "No. Not yet."

"Okay. Well, now you have to go. And you have to light a candle to the Virgin."

"For *El Español*'s soul? Of course! I'd be glad to."

"No, Hijita. Not for *El Español*'s soul. For your mother's."

"For my *mother's* soul?"

"Yes. And for your own. I didn't only light those candles for *El Español*, you know. I also did it for myself. I prayed to be able to forgive. And now you have to do the same."

"Abuela! That's ridiculous."

"Is it? Well. Listen, Paloma, I really have to go to my room now. So please wave to the nurse to come help me."

And then she turned to face the place where she figured Serach was still standing, pointed to where she thought I was, and said to Serach: "Make sure that she does it!"

She spoke in Spanish, of course—which Serach doesn't understand. And when Serach gave my grandmother one of those sage little nods of hers, my grandmother—of course—didn't see it. But I swear a flash of real understanding passed between them, despite all the impediments.

And then the nurse arrived with a wheelchair to take my grandmother back to her room.

"I'll come back tomorrow!" I said as she glided away.

"Come back when you've done it," she answered.

And so it was that I led Serach toward the *Catedral Metropolitana de la Inmaculada Concepción* while recounting everything that my grandmother had told me—and asked of me.

"Serach, can you make heads or tails of what Carolina was talking about?" I asked when I had finished my retelling.

Serach looked at me with deep concern.

"I have some ideas."

"Yes?"

"Well, I don't think Carolina was saying that Father Domingo's robes were stained with food…I think she meant that they were stained with sin."

"With sin?"

"Yes, with sin. Isn't sin a big topic in Catholicism? Don't you talk about it a lot? Think about it a lot?"

"Yes, sure. I guess. But I still don't know what you're driving at."

"Well, tell me a bit about Father Domingo. What was he like?"

"He was a pompous old fart."

"And?"

"He was the revered religious leader of the best Catholic families of Santa Fe de Antioquia. Particularly of my grandmother."

"He was your grandmother's priest till he retired?"

"Well, except for a couple of years when he served in a parish in the Bronx."

"Really? What parish?"

"Well, no one ever actually said as much, but I always assumed it was the parish…where my mother was sent as a postulant. The parish where she stayed till they found out she'd arrived pregnant and kicked her out. I mean, how else would my grandmother have known to send her there?"

"Well then," said Serach, very carefully. She was typically scrupulous about making conjectures. She liked careful, step-by-step proofs. But in this case, she seemed willing to make the leap. "Well, then, if I had to make a guess, I would guess that Father Domingo…might have taken liberties with your mother. That he…might have been…the one who seduced her. The one who made her pregnant. And then arranged for her to go to the convent in the Bronx."

"Seduced my mother? That old bag? She could never have been seduced by him. She could never have had sex with him willingly. Or even half-willingly."

"Well, raped her then."

I had always pictured my mother's exploits as being totally voluntary. I remembered how sex-crazed I'd been myself at the age of fifteen. And how alluring to everyone, male and female alike. I'd pictured the young Dolores beckoning irresistibly to young men who looked like Fernando. Or Mauricio. Or even Miguel Grillo—whose latter-day wrinkles and greying hair were not enough to obscure the underlying attractiveness of his features.

I'd imagined her, in short, as being in full control of her own adventures. Well, in full control until the point that God took revenge and made her pregnant. I knew that the balance of power was rarely in a young woman's favor in any heterosexual relationship. But I had cherished the notion of her holding the upper hand with anyone she went to bed with.

This was my mother we were talking about, after all. *Conquistadora* of males, far and wide.

But if Serach was right—if it really was that ugly, tedious priest who had first wormed his way into my mother's body— then she was also right that it was rape. My mother would never have gotten involved with him without coercion. Joe was homely, sure, but he was—at least—a real man. A hard-working man. An honorable man. And all those men in the bar—well they came later. And they'd been her choice. And they'd done favors for her in return.

But Father Domingo would have offered my young mother nothing but shame. His act would have been a total abuse of his position. It would have been nothing less than assault.

And if it was he who had sired my beloved Manny, it was almost too horrible to bear.

"That disgusting beast! I'll kill him!"

Serach took me into her arms. She let me shake for a minute. She stroked my hair. Finally she said, very softly: "Will you tell Manny?"

"I don't know. God alone knows how he would react. And we can't be certain that Father Domingo really is his father." I sighed. "There could have been others after him. I actually hope so. My mother may have been initially violated…but at a certain point she was just wild."

"Yes, I suppose you could be right."

I managed to stay steady till we reached the top of the steps of the Cathedral. But when we got to that heavy carved door, I suddenly felt sick again.

"But Serach, even if Father Domingo isn't Manny's father—and even if my mother was a bit sex-crazed—he was still a monster." I stood stark still for a moment, remembering how his touch had made my skin crawl. "Serach, what if he's in there? I'll strangle him. I swear I will. I'll put my hands around that scrawny neck and squeeze till he collapses on the floor."

"He's not going to be there, Baby. You heard your grandmother. He's retired. And he's old. He's probably in another one of those 'asilos,' sitting in a wheelchair all gaga with his head lolling on the side."

"And, Serach, explain something else to me. How can my grandmother not have understood what Carolina was trying to tell her?"

"Well, did *you* get it right away? Or did I have to spell it out?"

"Christ!"

"Don't blame yourself, my love. If a person is programmed from birth to accept religious dogma, it's hard for them to see the truth."

"But did my grandmother really not have a clue?"

"She probably did, on some level. But she didn't have me there at her side—the objective outsider—to help enlighten her. And she certainly couldn't allow herself to figure it all out on her own. If she had, her whole world order would have collapsed. Asking you to forgive the daughter whom she'd sacrificed to that world order was as far as she could go." She paused. "So now you have to do it."

She pushed the door open and we entered. The muted interior light, the red and yellow tiles, the smell of incense were all exactly as I remembered them.

I steered Serach away from that gory *Jesus Crucified* and led her to stand directly in front of the Blessed Virgin. She contemplated the wood and plaster figure for a long moment, placing her weight first on one foot and then on the other and shifting her thin hips from side to side. And then she turned her intent little countenance back to me.

"Okay. So here we are. Go on."

I reached for a taper, knelt down, and bent my head. "I'm so confused. I don't know what to do."

"Of course you do. You reach over and light the taper. Then you light the candle. You pray for your mother's soul. And then you pray that you can forgive her."

But I couldn't move.

"So? Nu? Go on!"

"Serach, I'll do it…. I'll do it if you do it too," I finally said.

"What, light a candle for your mother?"

"No, Serach. Light a candle for *your* mother. And for your ability to forgive her."

"We Jews don't do that."

"Serach! Take a taper. You don't have to kneel. I know you guys don't kneel when you pray. But you do light candles for things all the time."

"Not for something like this."

"Serach! Help me out here. Do it with me. It will make it easier."

She took a taper. She bit her lip. And then she nodded.

We each lit our votive candles, one right next to the other. We each said our private prayers.

Then Serach reached down and lifted me up by the elbow. And arm in arm we walked out of the dimness of the church and into the brilliant sunshine of my motherland.

EPILOGUE: SHMUELY'S ACCIDENT

"Lust not after her beauty...nor let her captivate you with her eyelashes."

Proverbs, Chapter 6, Verse 25

Shmuely was frantic. How could his cousin Reuven ever have imagined that he was in a position to start thinking about marriage arrangements at this particular moment in time? Sure, his life had become a non-stop battle against those terrible carnal urges. Sure, it would be nice to know there was an appropriate outlet on hand—a viable strategy for satisfying his needs—so he could get back to the real business of learning.

But to expect him to take time off to meet this girl on the evening before his final examination with Rav Berson—the most terrifying *maggid shiur* in the whole of *Yeshiva Mir*? To expect him to even think about courtship rites when what he needed was to clear his mind entirely of everything but those complicated tractates of *Tohorot*?

"Please, Reuven, please I'm not ready for this right now. Reschedule it for another time. Maybe next month? Have a heart!"

But Reuven had been intractable.

"Next month will already be too late," he had announced. "Ruchel is solid gold. *Yichus* up to here. Not a single cause for concern in her entire family tree. And they are really interested in *you*, Shmuely. Willing to support your studies for as long as you like. Your mother, my aunt—that impossible woman—will *plotz* for joy if we can only make this match. Tomorrow night it is, Shmuely. That's when Ruchel can do it. Blow this opportunity and lose a once-in-a-lifetime chance for happiness."

And so Shmuely had allowed himself to be dragged into the lobby of the David Citadel Hotel to sit opposite that small intense girl with those prominent gums and listen to her talk on and on about the merits of different china sets. Her detailed analyses of what was important to look for in everyday *milchig* and *fleishig* china. Her vigorous opinions about the most important qualities to seek in any china set designated for *milchig* or *fleishig* meals at Passover time.

Throughout it all, Shmuely had sat there with his face fixed in what he thought was an expression of keen interest while his brain went over all the thorny scholarly arguments concerning the impurities associated with vessels and utensils, corpses and menstrual fluids. Actually, he thought the evening was going pretty well, all things considered. That before too long he could mutter a few last pleasantries and exit gracefully, having made a good showing and gotten all the preliminaries out of the way.

But then Ruchel had suddenly switched gears.

"So, Shmuely," she said, in that sing-song voice of hers. "So, tell me. Reuven says you're the only son. So…after *all* the attention that you must have received from *all* those women *all* your life, have you become one of those men who thinks he knows everything?"

"No, of course not."

"Really, Shmuely? After being the only man in the house for all those years? After having a mother who adored you and… how many sisters was it? How many sisters doting on you as well?"

"Five."

"Five? I thought it was four."

Shmuely's face colored and he looked down at his feet. There was Serach, once again entering his life and tying him in knots. When would he ever figure out how to think about her—how to talk about her? When would she leave him alone?

"If you already know the answer to something then why do you ask?" he managed to mumble.

"My goodness, I was just making conversation. Trying to open you up a little bit. If you said three words out loud tonight it would be a lot. I don't want to be the only one chattering away, here. So tell me about all those doting sisters. *How many of them are there?*"

"What difference does it make?"

"What difference does it make? What kind of question is that?"

"A silly question. A very silly question." Suddenly he knew he had to stand up. "Listen, Ruchel. It's been very nice meeting you and everything but I really do have to go home and study. *Right now.*"

And he'd fled.

And then, as if that weren't bad enough, just as he had arrived home—reprimanding himself soundly all the way—his roommate Menachem had looked up sleepily from his book and said: "Shmuely. We got an invitation to join my Argentinian relatives for *Shabbos* services and dinner tomorrow night."

Shmuely had been counting on just slinking home after his Talmudic grilling to a quiet *Shabbos* meal with a placid roommate who never said much and never asked any difficult questions. And now that roommate was telling him that he would have to go straight from Rav Berson's interrogations into a long night of the non-stop arguments (in Spanish, no less) that invariably dominated dinner conversation at the Porzecanskis?

No, that was not even a remote possibility.

"Thanks, Menachem, but I think I'll decline."

"You'll eat *Shabbos* dinner alone?"

"I'll eat alone."

"That's too bad. Well, listen, I'll do you a *mitzvah*. I get home earlier than you on Friday… and you're going to be a mess. I'll pick you up some Crispy Chik'n and potato salad. It will be here when you get here."

"Oh, Menachem! I'll owe you."

"Yes, you will, Shmuely. Yes, you will."

So it wouldn't be such a terrible thing. He would come home, drop off his stuff, take a shower, go to services, and then come back to eat quietly and in his own good company once services were over. And—even if he ended up spending the entire evening reliving every wrong answer he'd given to Rav Berson—it would be a hundred times more restful than sitting through a dinner with that unruly South American clan.

And yet when Shmuely had finally stumbled home after that grueling and far-from-brilliantly-executed examination, what had happened? Had he been sweetly enveloped in the peace and quiet and cleanliness of *Shabbos* at home? No, he had not. He had been confronted by an apartment in total chaos.

How could he have forgotten to do all the dishes and glasses and silverware that had accumulated in the *fleishig* sink? And how could Menachem have forgotten to do all the pre-*Shabbos* laundry?

The sink was brimming. Six days' worth of dirty socks and underwear and shirts were sitting in a mound on the living-room floor where the boys had tossed them all week.

And worst of all, no Crispy Chik'n. Menachem had forgotten!

Shmuely wasn't about to leave the whole mess right there in full view on the holiest day of the week. But he couldn't do much about it right there and then, either. He had to dash to the corner at top speed on the small chance that his favorite take-out place would not have completely closed up and he could wedge himself through the door and get his dinner.

He stuffed all the clothes into a king-size garbage bag and shoved it under Menachem's bed. He took all the dishes and glasses and silverware out of the sink and stuffed them—still encrusted with all that grease—back into the cabinet and closed the doors. He set out the candles. And then he flew out the door, down the four flights of stairs, across the sidewalk and into the street.

Right into the swerving, speeding path of that stupid bicycle.

There was one horrendous split second when both Shmuely and the cyclist realized that something terrible was going to happen. She'd braked with all her might. But it was too late. The bike turned over, catching on Shmuely's long coat. And then both young people had landed on the curb, with Shmuely underneath, the girl on top, the bicycle splayed beside them and both of them yelling.

The streets were already emptying out for *Shabbos*. There were no witnesses. No one to point out who had been right and who had been wrong. And no one to help.

The girl was the first to recover. Thoroughly shaken, she nonetheless had the strong intuition that she had sustained no major damage. Shmuely's warm body had broken her fall. She ran her fingers tentatively over her face, arms and legs. Both palms were bruised, droplets of blood slowly emerging from a slew of little cuts. But nothing was shattered. She could still flex her hands and move all her fingers.

Her forehead had scraped the ground a bit—she found blood there as well. But the helmet had staunched the full impact of the blow.

She pulled the helmet off carefully, shook her head out gently, repeated her name to herself a few times and concluded she had suffered no major concussion. Then she stood up, stuck the helmet in her backpack, and—pulling the hem of her T-shirt out of her jeans—used it to mop at her forehead, entirely oblivious to the shaft of tan midriff she was baring to the world.

Shmuely meanwhile still lay crumpled on the sidewalk. She bent down and peered at him. His yelling had been in English, so that's how she began. "Are you all right?" she asked.

"No, I am not all right. What's the matter with you, you don't look where you're going?"

"Me? I was looking out for everything just fine, thank you very much. It was you who were barreling into the street without looking." She reached down. "But never mind all that. Let's just get you up. You can't keep lying on the curb like a piece of lox."

She extended her hand to him but he didn't take it. Instead, he pushed himself gingerly into a sitting position using one arm while looking down at the other with an expression of horror.

"Something is really wrong with my left arm. It's numb and agonizing at the same time."

"Not good. Sounds like a break. Anything else hurt?"

"Everything hurts, but nothing as much as my arm."

"Well, let's get you up and see what's what. Can you stand? Are your legs okay? Here. Let me help you."

"I can do it myself." But he couldn't. His face twisted in pain.

"*Let me help you!* Give me your good hand!" She grabbed at it—it was warm and dry—and yanked. He stood.

"Legs okay? Ribs okay? You can breathe okay?"

"Yeah, that's all okay." He let go of her hand, wiped his palm on his coat, and cradled his bad arm. "But there's definitely something wrong here. OW! OW! And where's my hat?"

She spied it mid-sidewalk and ran off to get it.

"Here, let me put it on for you."

He finally stopped looking at his arm and stole a glance at her face as she placed it gently back on his head.

"You're not doing so well either—you're bleeding all over yourself!"

"I don't think it's anything serious, actually. My palms are scraped. My forehead is bruised. Is there a lot of blood? There is, isn't there? Well, the forehead bleeds really easily, you know." She mopped at it with her T-shirt again. "But basically I think I'm all right. I'm much more worried about you. We've got to get you to a clinic for some medical attention."

"I have to go prepare for *Shabbos*. It will be here any minute. Which, of course, means that no respectable clinic will still be open for business at this hour, either."

"Don't be silly. There's a *Leumit* Health Clinic in an office building twenty minutes' walk from here. It's open 24/7. I know it because I interned there last summer. All the University students use it. I'm not getting back on that bike—it's probably completely all off-kilter after that crash. And I'm also not about to leave you alone. So we'll walk together. It's not far. Really! Let's go."

He still hung back. "I shouldn't go anyplace that would be open on the *Shabbos*."

"It's okay to go to a *doctor* on the *Shabbos*. It's saving a life. Or in this case, a limb. Limbs are important. Aren't you in pain?"

Shmuely sighed. "Of course I'm in pain. I told you that."

"Then we'll go. The only question is," said the girl, stretching out her arms in front of her and rotating her wrists, "what am I going to do about my bike? I'm afraid I may just have to just leave it here, leaning against the wall of this building." She dragged it over, stood it up and pushed down the kick-stand as she spoke. "I didn't even bring a lock and chain to secure it to a lamp post. Well, I'll have to have faith that no one will take it. And truthfully, I can't imagine who would want to steal that beat-up old thing. And on *Shabbos* to boot!"

"No guarantees. There are *gonef*s everywhere."

She grinned. "Well, if I come back and find some *gonef* claiming that it is his—and I have no proof it's mine and he's willing to swear that he has a right to at least half of it—then I guess I'll be stuck dividing it in two. The *gonef* can take the front wheel while I take the back one, and then we'll have to find some way to divvy up the seat and the handlebars and the pedals and the basket and the bell. But of course, if I come back to find the *gonef* diligently *repairing* the bike, then it's a whole 'nother story. He'll have to give me an estimate for the cost of the repairs that he's made and I'll be obliged to pay him those costs before taking the bike back. And—last but not least—if I come back to find some Jerusalem City official standing over the bike and proclaiming that it belongs in the public domain because it wasn't left in a closed courtyard and couldn't fly away like a baby pigeon, then...Oy, I don't know what I will be able to do..."

Shmuely stared at her. What nonsense she was talking! Totally mangling all the Talmudic discussions of the laws of *shnayin ochazin*—of "two rival claims." Making a joke about them, even. How on earth had this T-shirted girl become learned enough in

Talmud to make such jokes? And why did her words give him such a fierce pang of mixed joy and sorrow?

But, of course. It was exactly the sort of thing that he and Serach used to love to do together. The sort of thing that he'd never been able to do with anyone else. The sort of thing he would certainly never be able to do with Ruchel, the china set expert. With Ruchel, his potential life companion.

What was with this girl? She even looked a bit like Serach. Well, like the new Serach. Like the Serach who also wore T-shirts and jeans with such casual ease. Except that the same clothes that made Serach look so disturbingly like a boy somehow only served to emphasize this girl's incredible femaleness. How did she do it?

Not that he'd allowed himself to look at any part of her body for more than a second or two. Still, how could he have helped but notice the sudden strip of midriff that she'd flashed at him so nonchalantly when she'd used her T-shirt to dab at her brow? Or keep his eyes entirely away from the T-shirt itself, now that it was all spotted in blood—so violently red on white—like the flag of some foreign country? Or avoid noticing the curve of the arm that she kept flexing so nonchalantly? Or the soft curve of her breast?

Maybe if he just looked at her face that would be safe? Or maybe not. He'd never seen eyelashes so long in all his life. Eyelashes like that should be forbidden.

Meanwhile, the girl stared right back at him with frank interest. She contemplated his pale cheeks, the piercing turquoise blue of his eyes, the arch of his eyebrows, the gold of his curls and the few scraggly hairs that comprised his beard. Would there be hair on his chest as well? What an intriguing-looking young man he was! Such a razor-sharp bone structure under all that pure white skin.

Well, no time for that kind of thinking right now. That kind of thinking could only lead to problems. And more to the point, she had to get them going. She poked him in the good shoulder.

"Come on, let's go! You don't want to mess with that broken arm. Follow me."

He started to walk. He couldn't help himself.

"I'm Alexandra, by the way. Who are you?"

"My name is Shmuely." No, that's all wrong. He hardly knew this girl. What on earth was he thinking? "I mean, my name is Shmuel. Shmuel Gottesman."

"And why were you running into the street like a crazy person?"

"I was going to pick up some dinner before *Shabbos* started. And now I won't even get my *Shabbos* dinner. Or get to go to services. Why did this have to happen to me?" He looked as if he were going to cry.

"Shmuel, buck up. We're in this together. At least you live around here. You can walk back easily when we're done. How am I ever going to get all the way back to Hebrew University on foot after dark by myself? Ach! Well, I'll figure something out. Maybe I can stay overnight with you?"

"*Chas v'shalom!*" What would Menachem say if he returned home from his aunt's house to find this brazen young woman camped out in the apartment that they rented from *Yeshiva Mir?*

Alexandra shook her head and grinned. "Guess not," she murmured. They walked for a little while in silence and then she said, "I bet you're wondering what I'm doing in Jerusalem—an American girl like me. And also, what I was doing biking around in your neighborhood."

"The questions had occurred to me."

"Well, I'll start from the beginning. I'm a student at the Hebrew University. Second year. Pre-med. And I'm hoping to go to med school here, too—probably in obstetrics and gynecology. Israel is way ahead of the curve in so many ways. The medical practices here are simply *awesome*. And why was I in your neighborhood? I was hoping to pick up a challah from that little bakery down the street from you. No one makes challah the way they do. Too late now, I'm afraid."

"And…and…how do you know so much about tractate *Bava Metzia*?"

"Oh, that's easy. Before I came to Israel, I went to *Prozdor* on the Upper West Side. You know—the Jewish Theological Seminary Sunday School? You've heard of it? No? Well, we didn't cover the whole Talmud, of course. But we covered *Bava Metzia* in pretty great depth in my last semester there. I'm not really observant or anything. But it's my heritage, after all. I owe it to myself to learn whatever I can. And then there is no better training for the brain than studying Talmud, is there?"

Shmuely said nothing.

"And now, tell me about you. I bet you're much more interesting than I am. One of those really smart silent types. I can tell. And you're an American too, aren't you? You don't speak English like an Israeli. What are you doing here in Jerusalem?"

"I'm attending *Yeshiva Mir*, in the American *chaburah*. I'm in my fourth year."

"And you came to Jerusalem to study because…?"

Shmuely had trained himself to give the same answer to anyone posing that potentially explosive question.

"Because *Yeshiva Mir* is world-renowned. It was a great honor to be accepted here."

"Hmm," she said. "Still…it's so far away from the States—and you had to have been very young when you came. Wasn't there any *yeshiva* good enough in your community?"

He looked away, kept walking, said nothing.

"Most people who choose to study abroad are adventurers," she remarked, almost as if she were thinking out loud. "Is that what you are, Shmuely? An adventurer?"

He didn't answer. She snuck another long hard look at him—carefully examined his slender, pale frame and guarded blue eyes. No—definitely not an adventurer.

"But some…" she continued, "travel far away because they are trying to escape something back home. Were you trying to escape something?"

Shmuely's face remained impassive while the rest of him shivered. Was this girl a sorceress? Had she somehow divined all the dreadful things that had propelled him like a rocket ship out of Brooklyn and into the air-tight, dependable all-male safety of *Yeshiva Mir*?

No—she couldn't possibly have divined them!

And—if she had—could she possibly imagine that he'd want to talk to her about all that? To discuss how suffocating the sheer femaleness of his home had become once he'd lost Serach's magical protection? Or describe the terror he'd endured when he thought that he himself was turning into a girl? Or put words to the utter mortification of experiencing that unbidden—unspeakably visible—sensation of pleasure when Rabbi Schneider had bent down to complete the sacred act of *metzitzah d'peh*?

Why, he'd never even told Serach about that final blow to his sense of manhood—that final catastrophe that had compelled him to seek out a place where no one could possibly know what had happened and where he wouldn't run the slightest risk of ever bumping into that *mohel* again.

"Shmuel? Shmuely? Are you with me? Hello?"

"I came to Jerusalem to study," he finally repeated, slowly and patiently—he'd always found that speaking deliberately helped ease his anxiety—"because *Yeshiva Mir* is known to be one of the best *yeshivas* in the world."

Alexandra heard the carefully controlled panic in his voice and decided not to press him any further. It could wait for another time.

"Okay, okay. Forget I asked. So…where exactly in America do you come from?"

"Brooklyn."

"Brooklyn! That's where I'm from too! Park Slope. And you? Boro Park?"

"Yes of course—where else? Boro Park."

"From a big family? Lots of sisters and brothers?"

"Just sisters."

"How many?"

Not again!

"Four. NO. Five. Five, definitely."

"You silly creature! Is it four or is it five?"

Shmuely looked sideways at the girl for a moment. And then suddenly—in a rush of emotion that he didn't quite comprehend—he found that this was something that he actually *did* want to share with her. Something that he was sure she would understand.

He didn't know exactly how he knew it, but it clear to him that this modern girl in her modern clothes was someone with whom he could finally talk freely about Serach. Someone with whom he could actually say her name out loud. Someone who would not condemn him for having kept his beloved Serach alive and part of his life all this time.

The only question was how to frame it.

Well, if she thought he was being silly, maybe being "silly" was the right way. Keep it light.

"Actually," he said. "Actually, the question of how many sisters I have could inspire a whole new Talmudic tractate." He gave one of his funny half-smiles and pulled at his beard wisps the way Rav Berson liked to do. "Where do I begin?"

Alexandra caught his smile and smiled back. And then she also took a risk.

"Let me guess. You have five sisters but your family disowned the fifth one because she married a *goy*."

She really was a sorceress, wasn't she?

"Well," he said, after a moment while he caught his breath. "Not exactly. Well, sort of. But only in a manner of speaking."

"Because she was *living in sin* with a *goy*?"

"Living in sin?"

What an innocent he was! He had no idea what she meant.

"It's just an expression, Shmuely. It means living with a man without being married to him. Which—by the way—I don't personally consider to be a sin at all."

They were walking down streets that were now almost entirely empty. No one could see them. No one could hear. It gave Shmuely the eeriest feeling of freedom.

"My sister isn't living with a man," he finally said. "She's living with a woman. As if...that woman were a man."

He had never said anything about that to anyone before.

"Oh! Well. Yes. I can see why that might not go down any too well in your community. Though...technically...there's nothing in the Scriptures that prohibits same-sex activities among women. In later texts, there's mention of a prohibition against women getting *married* to one another. And about certain sexual positions that we might take with one another.... But, it's not as if women would be spilling seed or anything. So there isn't as much to worry about. And if a married woman has an affair with another woman, I don't even think it's considered adultery. Of course, I could be wrong...."

No, she was right, as it turns out. Shmuely had done extensive research into all those laws himself, as soon as he'd realized what was going on with his sister.

"Yes, I know all that," he said, drily.

"And how did your family respond to Serach's choice?"

"My mother made us all sit shiva."

Alexandra didn't know what to say. They walked in silence again. Eventually, however, she decided it was all right to start in again—try to smooth things out, if that was possible.

"So," she said. "What's your sister's name? And what is she like, besides being gay? Tell me all about her."

"Her name is Serach," Shmuely answered. How good it felt just to say it! "And she's an accountant. And she's...special. She's...she was...she's always been good to me. And much more than a sister. More like a guardian—or a guide. I can't really explain it."

Shmuely couldn't believe what was happening. Here he was walking through the streets of Jerusalem as the late afternoon began drifting into *Shabbos* twilight with an American girl in a bloodstained white T-shirt, speaking about this forbidden topic.

His cousin Reuven knew that Serach existed, of course. But he knew better than to mention her. And Menachem and all the rest of Shmuely's *Yeshiva Mir* buddies knew nothing about her whatsoever.

"Sure, you can explain it. Try me. Good to you in what ways?"

"Well, she basically took care of me when I was little. Our mother…our mother was pretty busy, most of the time."

"Yes?"

"So it was Serach who brought me home from school every day. And read to me. And gave me treats. And once…once she saved me from…from a really terrible thing."

There it was again—that horrifying memory of the time that he'd bled like a girl! Why did his mind keep going there? Shmuely looked so stricken that Alexandra's hand flew out instinctively to reassure him. But then she remembered how scrupulously he'd wiped his palm when she'd simply tried to pull him up off the ground and slowly lowered it again.

"Saved you from what?" she finally ventured.

But he only shook his head vigorously. Looked away. Walked faster.

"So, what's Serach's girlfriend's name?" she said after another reasonable period of silence.

"Her name is 'Paloma.' She's…." Shmuely made a face. "She's Spanish."

"Spanish from Spain?"

"From Spain? No, not from Spain. From South America someplace."

"She's an immigrant?"

Shmuely shrugged. "I have no idea. Maybe. Maybe she was born here. I mean there. I mean in America. Or maybe not. They're all over the place now, those Spanish people."

Alexandra decided to let that one pass, too. "And what does Paloma do for a living?"

"She's a nurse. She met Serach at the hospital that Serach went to when she had…when she had cancer and nearly died."

Could things get any more complicated with that boy's family?

"Serach had cancer? What kind of cancer? Did she recover? Is she okay now?"

"She's fine."

They walked a while again without speaking.

"And do you like her?"

"Like who?

"Paloma. Do you like your sister's former-nurse-and-Latina-immigrant girlfriend, Paloma?"

"Like her? I don't know. I don't really know her. But…."

"But?"

"But one thing I know for sure."

"Yes? And that is? Nu?"

How to say it? Shmuely was suddenly whisked back into that living room full of all those dreadful pictures of naked ladies on that morning when Paloma had paraded around in front of him in that shiny green garment of hers. How it had clung to her every curve! The things that it had made him want to do! He shivered.

"She's…she's a wanton woman."

Alexandra burst out laughing. "Shmuely—you're adorable. You're actually blushing! How exactly is she wanton?"

"Well, she wanders around in…in her…in a garment that hardly covers anything. I came over to their house very early one morning and there she was, walking all over the place in that… in that thing. You're supposed to take precautions when you're around a man who isn't your husband. There is such a thing as modesty."

"Oh, Shmuely! You are too funny. She was in her own house and you probably got her right out of bed if it was so early in the morning. I'm sure she wasn't even thinking about what she looked like to you. After all, it's Serach she's interested in—not you."

"That isn't funny."

"Okay, okay. But the important thing…the important thing isn't whether you happened to see her walking around in some revealing garment one morning. The important thing is whether she makes Serach happy."

Shmuely winced. That was the hardest part of all, of course. Paloma *did* seem to make his sister happy. Happier than he'd ever known her to be.

"Well, does she? Does she make Serach happy?"

"I guess."

"And that makes you upset?"

"No. Of course not. I mean…."

How was this girl doing it? How was she teasing out all those feelings that he'd always been able to shoo away, like so many black flies? He wished she would just stop. And then—immediately—he desperately hoped she would go on. How incredible it was to talk about the matters that had plagued him for so long. It was frightening, sure, but it was also…wonderful.

"So if it doesn't make you upset, how does it make you feel?"

Silence.

"Judgmental, maybe? Hmm?"

He turned right around to face her directly for the first time. "No. Not judgmental."

"What then? Confused? It *is* a bit confusing, I'm sure."

"It certainly is! *HaShem* created us 'man and woman.' He told us to be fruitful and multiply. *HaShem* didn't intend for women to love women the way they're supposed to love men! So why does Serach…want to do that?"

"Shmuely, the only way to describe the way that *HaShem* created human beings is: 'complicated.' We don't always choose what we want or whom we love—or what stirs us sexually. I've felt things for girls, myself—and I'm basically *cis* and straight."

Cis? Straight? What was she talking about? Did what she was saying have anything to do with the terrible thing that had happened with the *mohel*? Was what he'd felt actually okay? Was it just a momentary sign of that "complicatedness"?

But there was no time to pursue that potentially reassuring train of thought, for Alexandra was continuing to barrel along without pause.

"So Shmuely, even all our 613 laws can't change what we feel. And what's more—as you yourself admit—what Serach is doing isn't even explicitly forbidden by those laws. And most importantly, Serach isn't hurting anyone by being gay. It's not as if she's wrecked someone's marriage…seduced some young girl…."

"*Chas v'cholileh!*"

"So? Nu? What is it that bothers you so much?"

He took a breath. "I don't understand…why she couldn't just be happy with a husband and children, like other women. Why she chose Paloma over all that. *Why she chose Paloma over me.*"

"Ah, so we finally get to the heart of the matter. Shmuely, Shmuely, a brother is one thing and a partner is quite another. Serach's entitled to her own life with a partner of her choice. It's no different than if she were married to a man."

"But…."

"And I'm sure it wasn't easy for her to do what she did. It sounds as if she loved you dearly—cared for you deeply. It must have broken her heart to leave you behind like that."

"But…."

"And when you come right down to it, it wasn't Serach 'choosing Paloma' over you. It was your family—your community—choosing religious rigidity over *her*. Declaring her dead. Forcing *you* to choose."

There was a great deal more that she could have said on that topic, but he looked so appalled that she held her tongue.

"I'm sorry, Shmuely," she said, after an appropriate pause. "I didn't mean to upset you. Forget it. All I was trying to say is that what your sister is doing is honoring the person that she is. And that you need to keep working at accepting that."

Shmuely nodded. Almost imperceptibly. But definitely a nod.

"Oh, I have accepted it," he finally said, sighing. "I've accepted that she and…and Paloma…are together. I mean, what choice have I had? They *are* together. And she's still my sister. It's just that…."

"It's just that you've missed her being a regular part of your life. Missed her so much that you managed to keep visiting her even after your mother declared her dead. That must have taken some real doing. And that says a lot."

They walked for another block in silence, but this time it was not a difficult silence. It was almost companionable.

"And have you managed to stay in touch with Serach, even now that you are in Jerusalem?"

"Yes," he confessed. "We have kept in touch through Skype. I tell the *maggid* in charge of the computer room that I'm calling 'one of my sisters' and don't say exactly which one. And Serach… manages to behave herself for the ten minutes that she's on the screen." He gave her that mischievous half-smile that so few people ever saw. "There are definitely some advantages to having lots of sisters. No one can ever keep track of them all."

"That's very cool." She waited a beat. "But doesn't it make you sad that you can't see her for real? Don't you miss actually *being* with her?"

"Of course I do," he said, suddenly serious again.

"So why don't you invite her to come visit you in Jerusalem?"

Shmuely sputtered. What a thought! It had been okay— barely okay, perhaps, but at least safe—for him to visit her in that *goyishe* neighborhood of hers. That neighborhood into which no member of his community would ever have cause to wander. And, while risky, it had been okay (necessary even) to bring her back to Boro Park that one time, cleverly disguised as their sister Mierle, to see the *mohel*. And with a little subterfuge, it had remained okay to keep in touch with her by Skype.

Because all those things were strictly contained. Carried out on his terms.

But to have her here in Jerusalem, running around on his turf doing whatever she pleased? Arriving in his apartment, unannounced? Or at the *Yeshiva*? Associating with him in public in those inappropriate clothes of hers?

"I can't do that!"

"But you *should* invite her! I bet she'd love it here."

"Impossible! What would she do while she was here? Where would she stay? Where would we meet?"

"Oh, I don't know…there are lots of hotels in Jerusalem. And there are certainly more than enough things for her to do while you're off studying. I know! She could stay with me! I could show her around. And you could come over and spend time with us whenever you liked. There are always lots of people in our apartment at any given time. Besides my two roommates there are always at least one or two guests. We have a pull-out couch and two sleeping bags. My best friend Ruthie stayed with us for an entire month last summer. Everyone wants to come to Jerusalem, you know."

Shmuely was certain that he was flushing from top to toe. His head was spinning. What was this girl suggesting now? Not only that he should re-connect—really re-connect—with Serach but that he should do it in such a way that he would have to stay connected with *her* as well?

The thought shook him to his core.

But suddenly there was no more time to dwell on all those deeply troubling—and enticing—possibilities. Alexandra had come to a complete halt in front of an office building and was motioning for him to stop as well.

"We're here," she said. "We've arrived."

She rang the bell and someone buzzed back. She stuck out her less-damaged hand and hauled the heavy door open. And then they walked toward the back of the lobby to the elevator.

"It's on the top floor. Six flights up. The elevator is over here."

"I'm not going anywhere on any elevator." That, at least, was absolutely inviolable. No elevators on the *Shabbos*.

"Okay, we'll walk."

When they reached the top of the stairs, Alexandra opened one more door and led Shmuely down a short corridor to the clinic entrance. She then rang the last bell of their journey and they were buzzed in once again.

Four people were already seated in the waiting room. A Muslim woman in head-scarf, black pants, and fancy gold sandals. A Palestinian man in a kaffiyeh. And two secular-looking Jewish teens in sweatshirts and jeans.

Shmuely eyed that little crowd, digested who was there, and fell completely to pieces. All the delicious ambiguity—the lovely lightness of spirit—that had buoyed him along throughout that whole magical walk to the clinic evaporated entirely.

Suddenly, it hit him completely and irrevocably—the fire with which he had been playing.

How clear it finally all was—the ease with which absolutely everything unraveled once you broke even the smallest Torah mandate. The ease with which a man could go from talking freely with a woman to stretching the tenets of the *Shabbos* to associating with goyim–to who knows what else?

Maybe it was okay for this modern girl to live with one foot in and one foot out of the Torah. That was her business. Her choice. And maybe it was okay for Serach to "honor herself" by living with a woman the way a woman lives with a man. Again, her choice. And maybe, in a case of life and death, it was permissible for an observant Jewish man to choose to see a doctor on the *Shabbos*.

But since when was a broken arm a matter of life and death? And so how could he, Shmuel Gottesman—the sole male, the pride and hope of his family—have felt that he had that choice?

What he'd allowed himself to do was just plain wrong. He should have just gone straight home after the accident. Dealt with the pain. Waited to seek help. Avoided this whole perilous, equivocal adventure.

He had been tempted and found wanting. He would have to make amends.

Meanwhile, Alexandra marched blithely up to the front desk and realized that the receptionist was the same young woman who had been working there when she'd interned at the clinic during the previous summer. They greeted one another warmly. Alexandra recounted the story of the bicycle crash in her flawless Hebrew and listened attentively to the receptionist's response.

And then she returned to Shmuely to find him still awkwardly standing with his arms gathered tightly to his chest.

"Shmuely, sit down already! Everything is good. The receptionist is my friend, Rivka. She knows you can't fill out paperwork on the Sabbath, but she says she'll work some magic and get you in. And she said it would be about twenty-five minutes, but she'll speed things up if she can. She knows you're in pain."

Shmuel finally sat down clutching at his arm, and Alexandra, taking stock of his growing discomfort, placed herself in a chair at a distance from him and tactfully immersed herself in a magazine.

The four people ahead of them were called in one by one. They each left the waiting room and then returned again in due course. Meanwhile, Shmuely's silence became denser and denser.

What was troubling him? Alexandra couldn't figure it out. They'd been doing so well! Well, perhaps his arm was really hurting him now. Sometimes in cases of a broken bone, after the initial numbness and shock wear off it can turn into real torment.

The last patient ahead of them reentered the waiting room, collected her things and departed. And a few moments later a white-coated doctor stuck her head in and motioned to Shmuely. It was not any of the doctors whom Alexandra had gotten to know that summer. It was some new woman with a clean young face and black hair pulled severely back from her brow.

Shmuely stood but he didn't move.

"It's all going to be okay, Shmuely," Alexandra leaned forward and stage-whispered to him. "They really know what they are doing here. And I'll be right here waiting for you when you come back. Go on! Go inside with her!"

He continued to stand stock still for one long moment. He almost walked out right there and then. But then he came to a decision. He was already there. His arm was truly killing him. Perhaps it was all right for him to seek medical help, after all. He followed the doctor out of the waiting room.

The examination proved seriously distressing on several fronts.

First of all, there was the fact that this doctor was a woman. Yes, of course, it is technically permitted to receive a medical examination from a female. But still. It was not something that Shmuely would have preferred.

And then there was the actual physical pain. The doctor was as gentle as she could be. She found a way to get him out of his coat and shirt sleeves with a minimum of movement and stress. But it was excruciating nonetheless.

And when she finally gave him a shot of something that took all the pain away so she could move his arm around freely for the X-rays, there was the matter of the X-rays themselves. There was no way that such a procedure could possibly be permitted on the *Shabbos*.

Eventually, that part of the ordeal was over. But then the doctor placed the developed films on a screen and lit them from behind to show Shmuely all the bones of his hand and arm. And try as he might to avert his eyes—uncomfortable as it made him feel to watch her flick yet another electrical switch on the *Shabbos*—he couldn't resist sneaking a peek.

"See the ulna? Right here? Broken clear through? But nothing else is wrong, thank God. Your elbow is intact. That's always the biggest danger. Even the radius is intact. And that's usually the first to go—it's by far the more fragile of the two bones of the forearm. So it could have been much worse. Still, no more bike-riding for you for a while, young man!"

"It wasn't me who was on the bike," was all he could manage to say. Why was she joking about any of this? Didn't she see how miserable he was? Was she so totally unaware of how hard it was for him to make sense of anything that had taken place that evening? Or to figure out what he was going to tell everyone about what had happened?

He would have to concoct a tale that had no specific timeline—a tale vague enough to allow everyone to assume that the whole thing had occurred well before *Shabbos* began. A tale about some cyclist and some person who had led him to the clinic but that included no mention of the particular girl who was behind it all.

A tale that would completely erase those eyelashes and that melodic voice and the way that she had been able to tease out his most private—most innermost—thoughts and tempt him with such dangerous ideas.

A tale that would re-erect the appropriate *mechitzah* against her, and all girls like her.

While Shmuely contemplated all these matters, the doctor expertly bound up his arm in a plaster cast that extended a few inches above his bent elbow and held it steady until it was dry. She then slipped his good arm back into its shirt sleeve, slid the other sleeve over the cast, draped a sling over his shoulder and eased the broken arm into it. Finally, she maneuvered his good arm into its coat sleeve, buttoned him up, and gave him an absent-minded pat on his back.

"I'm giving you a prescription for a pain killer. The discomfort will get pretty severe as soon as the local anesthetic wears off."

"I can't fill a prescription tonight. It's *Shabbos*."

"Have that nice girl you're with do it for you."

Was the fact that they were together so obvious? Shmuely looked so aghast that the doctor shook her head and reached into a drawer. "Okay. Wait. Good. I have some packs of samples that should last you through tomorrow. I'll open them up and empty the pills into a zip-lock bag, so you don't have to use a pair of scissors on the packages. That's forbidden too, isn't it? But you *are* permitted to open a zip-lock bag, right?"

"Yes. But I can't carry it home with me. It is not permissible to carry anything."

The doctor shook her head. Then she expertly slit open the packages, poured the pills into a zip-lock bag, sealed it up, leaned over and swiftly tucked it all into his coat pocket. He wasn't fast enough to stop her.

"Let me be very clear with you, young man," she said in a tone that he had never heard from any woman but his mother. "You're going to be in real pain in a couple of hours. Take the pills home with you. You'll be glad that you have them."

He flinched, but he didn't yank the bag out of his pocket and toss it on the examination table the way he wanted to. He knew he didn't deal very well with pain.

"I won't bother giving you the care instructions," the doctor continued, pressing her lips together briefly. "So I'll just tell you the main thing, which is to keep the cast dry. Bind it up in plastic when you shower. Watch out when you do dishes. And come back in a week, so I can see how you're progressing."

Not much chance of that, of course. As soon as *Shabbos* was over, Shmuely would go see a real doctor at the *Bikor Cholim* Hospital where everyone observes *Shabbos* and where the only other patients would be members of his community.

He nodded noncommittally to show he'd heard her and then left the room without thanking her and without looking back.

"Shmuely! Are you okay?" Alexandra ran to meet him. "Is it broken after all?"

"Yes, it's broken. But the doctor set it and I'm fine. I just…I just have to be very careful not to get it wet."

"You'll make a follow-up appointment?"

"Look, the doctor's motioning for you to go in. Go! Get your own wounds looked at. Don't worry about me anymore."

"Okay, but wait for me, Shmuely! My cuts are nothing—my session won't take but a minute, I'm sure. We can walk back to your neighborhood together and then I'll continue on to the University on foot by myself. You don't have to put me up for the night. I understand. And I'm tough. I've walked longer distances before."

As she'd predicted, Alexandra's contusions were nothing to worry about. The doctor swabbed her palms with alcohol, put two temporary sutures on the cuts on her forehead, asked her some questions to test whether there had been any cognitive damage and told her to wait a bit before going to sleep to make sure there were no late-emerging signs of concussion.

Alexandra thanked the doctor and rushed back into the reception room. No Shmuely.

"Rivka, where is he? In the bathroom?"

"Flew out of here like a big black crow as soon as you left the room. I yelled after him but he didn't even answer me. No big loss, if you ask me. Not your type."

"Of course he's not my type, but I thought we'd kind of made friends. And I certainly expected him to do the right thing and wait for me."

"Really? A Haredi boy? They live by their own rules, you know. Anyway, never mind him. How are you planning to get back to the University?"

"I'll walk."

"Nothing doing! All that distance? Stick around till my shift is over at eight o'clock and I'll drive you. I've figured out a route that avoids the main neighborhoods in which they stone those who dare to drive on the Sabbath."

"I left my bike near *Yeshiva Mir*. Can we possibly drive by and check on it?"

"No way! That's 'Stoning Central' over there. And anyway, I remember that bike of yours. Piece of junk. Do yourself a favor and get a new one."

Alexandra laughed. "Okay. I accept your kind offer and your wise advice. I just wish…I mean…Shmuel was an odd duck but I was…really kind of hoping we could be friends. He had this really interesting back story. It got to me. And he was…there was…I thought there was an opening for us to have…I don't know…something."

"Leave it, Ali. Just leave it alone."

While Alexandra was absorbing this advice, Shmuely slowly picked his way back home. It wasn't all that easy—he hadn't been paying much attention to the route on the way out. But he somehow managed to orient himself and eventually found himself back at his building.

He nudged the front door open—the *yeshiva bochers* who filled the building had all agreed to leave it ajar on Friday evenings so no one would have to carry keys on the *Shabbos*—and ran up the stairs to his apartment. He bent down and fumbled under the mat for his key, unlocked the door, slipped the key back, and walked inside as quietly as he could. He stood very still for a moment, catching his breath and peering around carefully by the muted glow of the single small light that they left on in the living room all *Shabbos* long.

His inspection brought him great relief. Menachem had clearly not yet returned. There was no coat tossed on the couch, no hat planted on the table, no shoes shoved underneath it.

Bless those chatty Argentinians and their long, late-night dinners! He would probably have enough time to do everything he needed to do. To relax a little, get undressed, and get into bed without having to interact with anyone while his emotions were so raw and his brain still churning. To work out an account of the evening that would satisfy a roommate who showed limited interest in anything that didn't concern him directly.

Suddenly aware that he was starving, Shmuely walked into the kitchen, opened the refrigerator door and took inventory of the contents, best as he could in the semi-darkness. There wasn't too much to choose from. A half-eaten *parve* chocolate cake, a bottle of seltzer, and an uncovered plate with a few slices of salami on it.

The slices were greyer than they probably should have been and their edges were beginning to curl upward unappetizingly. But what could he do? He was so hungry.

He pulled out the plate and put it on the table, leaving the refrigerator door open. Walked back to the refrigerator, grabbed the seltzer bottle and tried to uncap it with one hand. Gave up, shoved it back on its shelf and slammed the refrigerator door shut again with his knee. Walked back to the sink, took one of the dirty glasses out of the cupboard and filled it with tap water.

It was too late for him to light the *Shabbos* candles. There was no challah in the house, no wine over which to say *Kiddush*. Menachem had clearly not only neglected to pick up the Crispy Chik'n—he had forgotten to make those other crucial pre-*Shabbos* arrangements as well.

Shmuely sat down wearily at the kitchen table and contented himself with saying the blessing that was appropriate for salami. And then he picked up one of the slices and took a bite.

It was tougher than an old shoe.

"Never again," he said out loud, shaking his head heavily, as the day's events began to truly sink in. Never again would he leave *Shabbos* preparations to Menachem. Never again sit down to a *Shabbos* meal as desolate and bereft as this one.

He took a sip of the water—definitely lukewarm—and began slowly and deliberately ticking off all the other things he would need to do to ensure his future wellbeing.

He would need to bring an end to this lonely and temptation-ridden bachelor's existence. Finish courting Ruchel and marry her as soon as possible. Leave her to take care of all the things that a wife takes care of, so he would be free to fully focus on his studies.

His arm began to throb. He remembered the zip-lock bag, fished it out of his pocket, opened it with the help of his teeth and grimly spilled two pills into his mouth.

He would need to wrap himself ever-tighter in the protection of his community. Avoid ever again making himself vulnerable to the ideas of someone from the outside.

He took a second sip of water, swallowed the pills, made a face, and put the glass down again.

He would need to re-lock all his darkest secrets in a deep, private place in his heart. Stick to the Torah. Exclude everything else.

He lifted up the piece of salami again, found he couldn't manage a single additional bite and let it fall back onto the plate.

He would need to banish all further thoughts of bringing his sister more fully back into his life. Too much room for embarrassment. For temptation. For corruption. His children would never even know they had an aunt named Serach. They would never sneak chocolates out of her handbag or burst into helpless laughter from her tickling. Never marvel at all her silly stories or find comfort in the warmth of her lap.

He picked up the plate to bring it to the refrigerator. It took him a moment to realize that he would have to put it back down again, open the refrigerator door (and leave it open) and then go back for the plate. He closed his eyes briefly. "Patience!" he thought. He went through all the necessary steps, slammed the refrigerator door shut and trudged into his bedroom, awkwardly manipulating his coat buttons and wondering what else he would have to learn to do differently, now that he had only one functioning arm.

And in the meantime, Alexandra rode back with Rivka without saying another word. Rivka took her friend's silence for acquiescence that the whole Shmuely thing was over and done with and best left alone and Alexandra was not about to argue any further with her. Within her own mind, however, all the details of the evening kept flying around.

And how could it be any different? How could she not remain intrigued by the idea of someone like Serach blossoming within a Haredi family? Or by the memory of Shmuely—so sad, so mysterious, so unexpectedly funny—so full of untapped potential? When would she ever get another chance to become friends with someone like him?

She knew where he lived, more or less. And after a bit of Internet research, she figured out where the American *chaburah* of *Yeshiva Mir* met and what its daily schedule was. So bumping into Shmuely would just be a matter of timing it right.

She decided that the best time would be late on the following Tuesday, when the break in her classes would dovetail nicely with the break in his. She borrowed a bike from a friend and headed to the American *chaburah* building. And—yes—at precisely four forty-five there was Shmuely coming out of the door with a bunch of fellow students.

She planted herself in a place in which he couldn't possibly miss her. And exactly as she had intuited would happen, his gaze slowly rotated to meet hers. He just couldn't help himself.

They were truly turquoise, those eyes of his.

She saw a flash of recognition followed by a grimace of pain. And then that sweet face became a mask.

"Shmuely!" she called out. "Shmuely!"

But he didn't respond. He burrowed deeper into the mass of his fellow black-coated, black-hatted *yeshiva bochers* and fell into careful step with them.

For a few moments, Alexandra was able to track where he was by picking out that flapping empty left coat arm and the distinctive tilt of his head. Eventually however, the signature details of his silhouette were swallowed up and his figure became indistinguishable from all the others.

He was safe. For now.

GLOSSARY

Abuela .... grandmother
Abuelita .... little grandmother. A term of endearment
achiote .... a pungent orange seed used to spice and color Latino food
adios.................................. goodbye (also hello when used in passing)
aliyah ('making aliyah') .... moving to Israel. Literally: "going up"
anteojos, anteojitos ... glasses, little glasses. Literally: "little in front of the eyes"
apikoris .... heretic
arepa .... a Colombian corncake
arepera .... Colombian slang for lesbian. Literally: "an arepa maker"
arroz con gandules... rice with pigeon peas
ataque .... Latino slang for any unexplained medical crisis. Literally: "attack"
Atlética Nacionale .... one of Medellín's two top soccer teams
Avenida Central.. Central Avenue
ayudita .... a helpful gift—generally cash. Literally: "little help"
baruch HaShem .... Praised be God
belleza .... beauty
Bet Din .... Jewish court of law
Bösendorfer.. a make of grand piano
brikh-hu.................................... "Blessed be He"—a prayer refrain
bris.. ritual circumcision
bocher .... boy, bachelor
Bubbe.. Grandma
cafecito.............................. an afternoon coffee break. Literally: "a little coffee"
calmate.. calm down
Camp Romemu.. Camp "Exalt"
carniceria.. Spanish butcher shop
chaburah .... a learning group at Yeshiva Mir
challah...... the special—generally-braided—bread that is eaten on the Shabbos
chas v'cholileh, chas v'shalom .... God forbid
chicharron .... the crisp skin of a roast suckling pig
chossn .... groom
chuzma.. vulgar
cis................................... comfortable in the gender one is born into
cochinadas.............................. garbage. Literally: "pig refuse"
colón .... Columbus
coño .... damn
congojas .... messes
conquistador/a .... a conqueror (m. and f. forms)
corazoncito.. little heart
daven, daveners .... pray, those who pray

Deportivo Independiente Medellín .... one of Medellín's two most powerful soccer teams

Dios santo .... dear God

Don ....a title of courtesy for a Latino or Spanish man

Doña...........................a title of courtesy for a Latina or Spanish woman

El Español .... the Spaniard

El Nuevo Siglo .... the new century

El Ratoncito Perez......................................The Little Mouse Perez

Elijah Chair.................. the seat in which the person holding the baby being circumcised sits

Esav...Esau

Escuela Jorge Robledo .... School of Jorge Robledo, founder of Santa Fe de Antioquia

farmishte ....befuddled

fleishig* ....meat

Flor del Campo .... wildflower

GED ....a high school equivalency diploma

gonef.. thief

gordito ....little fatty

goy, goyishe .... a non-Jew, non-Jewish

halacha .... Jewish law

Haman.. the villain of the Purim story

Haredi....................................a fervently observant Orthodox Jew

HaShem ....God. Literally: "The name"

hatafat dam bris... a ritual drawing of blood from an already circumcised penis

Hatzolah ....the Orthodox ambulance service

Hermana, Hermanita ....Sister, Little Sister—a term of endearment

Hermano... Brother

Hijita ....Little daughter—a term of endearment

hob rachmanus... have mercy

hora Latina.. Latin time

jaqueca ....migraine headache

Josecito.. Little Joey

Josefina.. Josephine

Kaddish.. a central element of Jewish services

kashrut (laws of) ....the laws governing cooking and eating

kallah ....bride

keffiyeh, kaffiyot............................. traditional Mid-Eastern headgear

kenahora..keep away the evil eye

Kiddush...........the blessing said over wine or grape juice to sanctify the Shabbos

*By halachic law, it is forbidden to eat meat and dairy together or at the same meal.

kreplach .... a Jewish dumpling
kugel .... pudding
La Cucarachita Mandiga ....The Mandinga Cockroach
La pervertida .... the pervert
lashon hara..evil gossip
linda .... pretty
locura .... craziness
Los Milagros...The Miracles
ma-ariv... Jewish daily evening service
maggid(im), maggid shiur ....yeshiva teacher(s), master yeshiva teacher
Mameleh.............................. Little Mother—a term of endearment
Mamita .... Little Mother—a term of endearment
Manitas.. Handyman
Manzanilla ....chamomile tea
mechitzah........ the barrier separating the women from the men in synagogue
meshugge ....nutty
metzitzah b'peh .....suctioning the blood from a circumcision wound orally
Midrash, Midrashim....... Torah interpretations by rabbinic scholars after the
    Temple era
mikveh .... Jewish ritual bath
milchig* .... dairy
mincha.....................................Jewish daily afternoon service
mio, mia...............................my, mine (m. and f. forms)
mitzvah .... Literally: "a commandment" Informally: "a good deed"
mohel...........................the rabbi who performs a ritual circumcision
mora con leche.......................a blackberry milkshake
Mordechai... the hero of the Purim story
Moishe, Moshe...Moses
muchacha, muchachita...................... girl, little girl
Muísca ....the indigenous people of present-day Colombia's Eastern Range
nada ....nothing
Negrito..Little black one
nenito, nenita.................................. little baby (m. and f. forms)
Niña...................... a title of courtesy often used for teachers. Literally: "girl"
nu..so
oye..hey
parve.........neither dairy nor meat (and therefore able to accompany either one)
Papito.................................... Little Father—a term of endearment
pasteles..................................... traditional Dominican Christmas dish
patitas de chancho.......................................pigs' feet

*By halachic law, it is forbidden to eat meat and dairy together or at the same meal.

pendejo ....idiot—Literally: "pubic hair"
plotz..to faint from emotion
ponche ....Latino egg nog
postulant ....a probationary candidate in a religious order
PR...Puerto Rico
pura gentuza...really low class
Purim............a holiday celebrating the Jews' triumph against the Persians
putita ....little prostitute
querido/a...dear (m. and f. forms)
Rav..Hebrew term for rabbi
Rebbe...teacher
Rene Moreno .... a noted Bolivian historian
Rosh Hashanah...................Jewish New Year—the first of the High Holy Days
Ruchel...Rachel
sandek.......................the man who holds the baby during a bris
shlep...to lug oneself or something else
Semana Santa...Holy Week
seudis mitzvah...celebratory feast
Shabbos.............the Jewish Sabbath—a day of strictly-regulated rest and prayer
sheitl .... wig
sheyn meydl..pretty girl
shiva................................the seven-day mourning period for a close relative
Sh'ma...a central prayer of the Jewish people
shtieblech .... storefront synagogues
shul ....synagogue
shvach...weak, deflated
sofrito.........................a sauce of tomatoes, onions, peppers, garlic, and herbs
stuffed derma.....matzo meal, chicken fat and onions cooked in a cow intestine
succah.....................the wooden booth used in the harvest holiday Succoth
Succoth..............the harvest holiday that celebrates the Exodus from Egypt
Sueños de mi Tierra Panaderia...............Dreams of my Country Bake Shop
tallis ....prayer shawl
Talmud....................................a central text of Rabbinic Judaism
Tatteh...Father, Dad
Tía .... aunt
Tatteleh...................Little Father—a term of endearment
Tohorot..............the book of the Talmud covering the topic of ritual purity
Torah..................................the first five books of the Jewish Bible
tractate Bava Metzia......the section of the Talmud that deals with property law
tsuris..heartache, problems
Yakov ....Jacob

yarmulke .... Jewish skullcap
yeshiva..Jewish school
Yeshiva Mir.................major Jerusalem yeshiva serving international students
yichus...family reputation
Yitzchak...Isaac
Yosef..Joseph
Zayde...Grandfather

About the Author

Photo by Joyce Ravid

S.W. Leicher grew up in the Bronx in a bi-cultural (Latina and Jewish) home. She moved to Manhattan after graduate school and raised her family on the Upper West Side, where she still lives with her husband and two black cats. She spends most of her time writing about social justice issues. *Acts of Assumption* is her first novel.

www.swleicher.com

Acknowledgments

I am grateful to all the many friends, relatives and colleagues who sat through my endless chattering about this book, patiently read through early versions and offered me encouragement. Particular thanks go to a few good souls whose astute critiques helped shape the work: Linda Corman, Karen Fisher, George Goodman, Madeline Holder, Paula Koz, Margarita Leicher, Chris Matthews, Sandra Matthews, Martha Millard, Emily Mirra, Nell Pierce, Lucy Robins, Nina Robins, Hiie Saumaa, Ron Spainhour, Lori Ubell and Lewis Warshauer.

My extraordinary publisher, Joan Leggitt, offered impeccably on-target recommendations regarding plot, style and design. I felt completely confident the moment I entrusted myself to her steady hand.

The work of The New York Women's Foundation provided the grounding and inspiration for the book. A portion of the royalties made on every copy will be channeled toward supporting its mission.

In the past, I would smile indulgently when reading lavish acknowledgments of the spouse or partner who endured months (years) of obsessive behavior. Could living with an author really be that arduous? Indeed, it can. Tony you have been my truest and best supporter. Thank you!